RAISING the DEAD

susanne DOBBIN

RAISING THE DEAD
Copyright ©2025 Susanne Dobbin

978-1-998815-42-5 Soft Cover
978-1-998815-43-2 E-book

Published by:
Castle Quay Books
Little Britain, Ontario, Canada
Jupiter, Florida, USA
Tel: (416) 573-3249
E-mail: info@castlequaybooks.com | www.castlequaybooks.com

Edited by Marina Hofman Willard PhD
Cover design and book interior by Burst Impressions

Library and Archives Canada Cataloguing in Publication
Title: Rasing the dead / by Susanne Dobbin.
Names: Dobbin, Susanne, author.
Identifiers: Canadiana (print) 20250238349 | Canadiana (ebook) 20250238357 | ISBN 9781998815425
  (softcover) | ISBN 9781998815432 (EPUB)
Subjects: LCGFT: Christian fiction. | LCGFT: Science fiction.
Classification: LCC PS8607.O226 R35 2025 | DDC C813/.6—dc23

NOTE TO THE READER

LET ME START by introducing myself. I've been a Christian since 1986. Jesus knocked on the door, and I opened it a crack; he stuck his foot in. He took me by surprise and changed my entire life. Because of his leading, I worked as a child protection worker for over twenty years, until I retired. Although it's not my area of study at university, I've always had an interest in writing and have been writing as a hobby since I was a teenager. I've written several unpublished books, poetry, and short stories. The stories that roll around my brain are endless, and I think I'm a better storyteller than writer, but I'm learning. In fact, studying is another one of my hobbies. For this book, I researched biomedical nanotechnology, Jewish marriage ceremonies, specific locations, and other topics that helped me flesh out the details.

My interest in this field started in 2021 when I had a dream about a man who wanted world power and intended to use nanobots in food and medicine to kill his enemies and control the masses. That dream was a jumping-off point for what became *Raising the Dead*. While this is a fictitious story, much of the science in the book is closer to fact than fiction and is becoming more plausible every day.

Raising the Dead is set in the not-too-distant future, using the world of nanotechnology as an integral framework. It is the classic story of good versus evil. Christians fight against a man bent on misusing the technology to obtain money and power on the world stage. If the reader is unfamiliar with nanotechnology, the following is a brief synopsis with reference to specific issues that arise in the book.

The rate of scientific advances since the Information Age, which started in the twentieth century, is staggering. It is difficult for the average person to fathom, and computers are often at the core of these breakthroughs. Processing capacity has increased exponentially, while computer size has decreased at the same rate. Currently, the smallest processors are at the microscopic level. These are called nanorobots after the unit of measurement, nano.

Nanotechnology is expected to have the ability to enhance our lives now and in the future. For example, in the biomedical field, it is suggested that not only could diseases be cured, they could be prevented in the first place. For the first time in human history, artificial intelligence (AI) and nanorobots (nanobots) hold the promise of extending lifespans and enhancing human capabilities. Some people would gladly allow their bodies to be flooded with tiny computers if they thought the outcome would be living with vitality, strength, and endurance beyond what is currently possible. There are a few individuals who have opted for cryonics, to have their bodies cryogenically frozen at death, in the hopes of being revived and cured in the future. Could nanobots be used to revive the dead? While there are still problems with the technology, those individuals with chronic or deadly illnesses believe the benefits outweigh any risks.

The use of nanoparticles is relatively new, but several negative consequences have already been discovered. Nanotoxicity is the term used to describe the harm caused to humans and the environment. For people, nanos interact with the human body at the cellular level. The nanos can penetrate blood-cell barriers and have the potential to kill the cells throughout the body and in the brain. Nanos can be inhaled, injected, ingested, and absorbed through the skin. Currently, they are found in many products, such as sunscreen, adhesives, clothing, car paint, and other objects we use daily. It has been shown to cause problems with respiration, neurological impairments, and environmental issues in soil and water. More research is needed in all areas, including the biomedical field and the use of nanorobots, to find solutions to any potential harmful impact.

In addition to the unintended detrimental effects, these inventions have the potential for abuse. Computers can be hacked. The original objective of the software in the nanobots could be subverted to destructive or deadly ones. No matter how many regulations and safeguards are put in place, if someone has the will to use the processors for anything other than the originally planned purpose, they will find a way.

Whether there is a risk of abuse or not, many individuals would be hesitant about allowing AI and nano chips to be implanted in their bodies, distrusting the new technology, worrying about the risks medically and from ill intent—and for many Christians, because of their fear of "the mark of the beast" referenced in the Bible.

This brings me back to this book. Woven throughout *Raising the Dead* are elements from the book of Revelation. The villain is a type of antichrist. The heroes are Christians. They are the world's security guards, the watchers, the resistance fighters attempting to thwart the abuse of nanotechnology. The story advocates for Christians to pray always and act when necessary. Sometimes, Christians need to be Davids and fight back.

Is it ethical to use AI and nanotechnology to enhance a healthy person? In this book, I propose that it is not the technology but how it is used that determines what is morally right. As for raising the dead, there are instances in the Bible where that miracle occurred, such as Lazarus and Jairus's daughter, along with a handful of others. It is not unusual today to hear of individuals revived after being declared clinically dead. These are God-directed occurrences. However, I wonder about cryogenically frozen people. A question raised in the book is, once their spirit has left their body for good, what spirit would inhabit the raised person?

The story is fictional. If there are any similarities between real life and my characters or situations in the book, it is completely by chance. Like many other authors, I fell in love with my heroes. Through them, I hope to capture the Christian experience of continual prayer in the face of adversity, even when God does not seem to be listening. It is about trusting him in the dark times because it is often in hindsight that his handiwork is revealed. I hope that when reading this book, you will enjoy the story, like the heroes, and strengthen your faith in Jesus.

Happy Reading,
Susanne Dobbin

PROLOGUE

"HE WAS DEAD! Bullet in the head. Dead!" Michael Graham's voice was raised, and his arms waved, hitting imaginary attackers in the air. He couldn't believe he was looking at the man who had kidnapped him and threatened to torture him to exercise control over his friend, Breanna.

His wife, Isabella, nicknamed Itsy, moved from the sofa to sit on the floor beside his chair. She laid her head down on his leg, tears escaping from the corner of her eyes. Michael stopped his rant and gently caressed her head to comfort her. The last thing he wanted was for his bride to be worried or frightened.

Michael and Itsy had flown from Toronto, Canada, to Tel Aviv, Israel, to visit their best friends, Breanna and her husband, Joshua Abrams. Itsy took a cab to the Abramses' home while Michael finished up work at the hotel. When he arrived, Michael found the three of them sitting in front of the television, looking like they had seen a ghost. Twisting to face the screen, he was in disbelief, and he dropped into the chair. It felt like a sucker punched to the gut.

"This nanotechnology can heal many diseases and illnesses. As you can see in my case, it can build body mass, bone and muscle, as well as regenerate injured body tissues. It's exciting to think that it's only a matter of time before I can release it to the public." It was the same Irish accent, but the voice was deeper with a hint of controlled rage beneath the surface.

The newswoman leaned closer to the muscular man sitting in front of her. "Are you saying people could access this technology to become like you?"

He followed her lead and closed some of the distance between them. Staring into her eyes, he smiled widely. "Bigger, stronger, and with a body that can heal itself of injury. It would be available to everyone."

The young woman let out a nervous giggle, and her chest visibly rose and fell several times as she fought to catch her breath. The raven-haired beauty was clearly taken with the interviewee. She didn't take her eyes off his. After an embarrassing silence, she cleared her throat. "Um, ah! Could you tell us your plans for the future?"

He nodded and leaned back in his chair. This time, he faced the camera. "I intend to rebuild where I left off. In my absence, the trade deal I drafted was signed by four countries. My company went public, but I retain controlling shares through subsidiary firms. That deal is now being expanded to include many other nations, so I will take over the helm of that company again and work with world leaders."

The interviewer licked her red-painted lips and bobbed her head excitedly. "That is wonderful. My understanding is that the first countries to sign the agreement are extremely happy with the outcomes so far."

"Yes, it was beneficial to all of them." He glanced at her, and she grinned, looking pleased at the breadcrumb he offered her. Switching his focus to the camera, he continued, "But as I said, my other passion is to work on nanotechnology. I will gather the leading technicians, programmers, and scientists again to get back to work." He emphasized the word *scientists* and narrowed his eyes as if he was looking through the lens right at Breanna. Michael quickly glanced at his friend, who sat squeezing Joshua's hand.

The Irish man on television said, "The main factory was sabotaged, but I have other factories around the world producing nanobots. We will work to reinvent the programming that was destroyed." He moved closer to the camera. "Inside me are the nanobots for these programs. We will remove some of them from my body and use them to copy more." He gave a half smile, and his eyes gleamed. "I believe these programs and nanos can do for others what they did for me. Think of it: we will heal the sick, prevent death, and maybe even raise the dead."

Michael couldn't wrap his head around what he was seeing and hearing. The man they believed was out of their lives forever had survived a bullet wound to the head and a plane crash, and now here he was on television, blowing their sense of security out of the water.

1

BREANNA'S STOMACH WAS in knots as she watched Edward Connor on television. She had to fight the wave of nausea that threatened to have her lose her lunch. When Michael raised his voice, she cringed. It wasn't his nature since he had married Itsy, but this wasn't something any of them could have imagined in their wildest dreams.

Joshua put his arm around his redheaded wife and drew her close. She closed her eyes, wishing that this was only one of her bad dreams. Ever since she heard Edward had died, the man no longer haunted her. It had been eight months since the plane crash, and she had felt safe again.

Now here he was, very much alive. Edward, who murdered her professor and tried to kidnap her and Michael. Edward, who tried to force Breanna to marry him. Edward, who created a nanocomputer project called the God Factor and programmed nanorobots to kill his opponents undetected. Edward, who said he was the God Factor and, like God, he'd have power over life and death. Edward, who Breanna dreamed was the prophesied antichrist.

Edward was discussing how his sister used nanotechnology on him to save his life after he was shot in the head and his plane crashed. Breanna had helped write the program for this technology, so she knew better than anyone the effects it would have on the man. She also knew that Edward would want her to continue her work with him, willingly or not. The man was ruthless and would stop at nothing to accomplish his goal.

As Breanna shook in her husband's arms, tears pricked her eyes. *I've cried too many tears over Edward and the people he killed.* She felt anger rising in her chest, and she puffed air out of her lungs.

Straightening herself, she gazed at her husband. Joshua, the black-haired, brown-eyed, olive-skinned Jewish man Breanna fell in love with, helped her sabotage Edward's killer nanobot technology. He rescued her and Michael when Edward kidnapped them, and he was her imagined angel who caught her when she was shot and fell from the crashing plane. He was her rock. "Edward will not have control over my life … our life. We've built a wonderful home here in Israel. I love your family. I love my job as a professor. You love your job as a professor too. He won't ruin it."

Joshua was impressed with Breanna's resolve; he always knew she was brave. Still, he ground his teeth in frustration. Once again, he was worried for her well-being with this madman on the loose.

Itsy rose from the floor and stood with her hands on her hips. "Well, if ever we need to pray together, I think the time is now." Itsy had become a Christian after Breanna. She had told Michael about Jesus, and after seeing the changes in his two women friends, he also accepted Jesus as his saviour. Joshua had been the first in the group to become a Messianic Jew, thanks to Breanna's professor and surrogate father, Dr. John Steinberg.

The four of them moved closer together and joined hands. Joshua began, "Lord Jesus, we come to you to ask for help in standing up to this man. Let your Holy Spirit empower us again. Protect Breanna from him." The other three followed with prayers of thanksgiving and praise to God.

When they finished and released each other, Itsy asked, "What's our plan of attack?"

Michael laughed. "There's my spunky little wife." He wasn't joking about the *little* comment. He was six feet two inches, and Itsy was five feet one, so their height difference was notable.

Joshua smiled warmly at his wife's best friend. "That was my impression right from the start. Breanna's bodyguard has a pretty good kick if I remember correctly."

The blonde lady chuckled at the description of her. "Mess with Bree and you'll have me to answer to, as you can attest."

Breanna was looking at the group of people who were so dear to her. *Thank you, Lord. I am so lucky to have them. But don't let anything happen to them because of Edward.*

She leaned forward. "I propose that Joshua and I back up all our work at the university and be ready to shut down anything Edward might use. Let's think of ideas to deal with this, and we can discuss them later at dinner. Should we meet at the hotel at about six?"

Michael said, "Sounds good. I've got something I need to do right away, also."

"Are you going to mess with Edward's trade deal?" Joshua said.

Michael nodded. "Absolutely."

2

BREANNA WAS IN a Montreal hospital recovering from the gunshot wound to the stomach she had taken prior to Edward Connor's plane crash. Joshua arrived for a visit bearing a gift. He pulled out a glass goblet and a small one-person bottle of red wine. He poured the wine and offered it to Breanna, asking, "Will you be my wife, Breanna Welsh? If you take a sip, you will be consenting to be my betrothed. It's one of several steps in a traditional Galilean Jewish wedding. It represents a covenant between you and me and God."

She had consented to marry him before the kidnapping, but this ritual touched her heart. Breanna accepted the glass and drank. She said, "I agree to be your betrothed." After she handed it to her fiancé, he took a sip as his part. She asked, "Is it normal for the groom to make all the arrangements for the wedding since I'm stuck here?"

"In Jesus's time, the husband's family did most of the work. The bride's duty was to be ready when the time came. The groom would go to his father's house and build an addition for him and his bride to live in after they marry."

Her face dropped. "We're not going to live with your parents, are we?"

He repressed a smirk. "Would that be so bad?"

"I don't know them. They don't know me." She was shaking her head. "No, I can't do it unless I have to … we don't have to, do we?"

Joshua laughed so hard he had to gasp for air. He struggled to put down the glass without spilling the rest of the wine. "No, we'll live in our own home. That's a very old tradition. When Jesus told his disciples that he would go to his father's home and prepare a place for them, they understood that it was like the groom building a room for his bride."

"Whew! You scared me." The redhead folded her arms and, with a fake pout, said, "And, it's not nice to laugh at a severely injured person."

"Severely injured?" He snorted. "The doctor said you'll be released in a couple of days. I'll drive you to Toronto. Itsy said you could stay with her while you fully recover. I think that's a good idea, and I've got to go to Israel. There are wedding preparations I have to make in person. When you're ready, you can fly to Jerusalem with Itsy, Michael, John Steinberg's wife, Jean, and her son, Saul. You can see if Itsy's brother, Bobby, can get away from medical school to come too. I know how close you are to all those people. Don't worry about the money; I'll pay for everyone's travel and accommodations. My family has money put away for me and my siblings' futures."

He smiled widely with a gleam in his eyes. "I can't wait for you to meet my family. They're going to love you."

Her eyebrows rose in the middle. "I hope so. I'm nervous to meet them."

"If I'm happy, they'll be happy. Besides, what's not to love about you? You're smart, even more than I; not every person has a doctorate in biomedical technology, Dr. Welsh. You're caring; you insisted we rescue those people that Edward had enslaved. You're brave; not many people could go undercover for seven months working for a murderer. You're a loyal friend; Itsy, Bobby, Michael, and Jean can attest to that fact. You're incredibly beautiful; I love your alabaster skin with a sprinkle of freckles and long red hair. I can scarcely believe you want to marry me. And most importantly, you are a follower of Jesus. Since most of my family also believe in Jesus, they will like that part. Should I continue?"

"Hmm! I think you might have missed a few attributes, like geek, socially awkward, obsessive about my work, and head over heels in love with you."

"Well, that last one might be a strike against you. It shows a serious lack of judgment on your part." He laughed as he leaned over and kissed her on the lips. Then he straightened and said, "We need to get married soon!"

Breanna sighed, "I concur, Dr. Abrams. Maybe we can find a job to work on nanotechnology together since that is our common area of study. I'd love to read your thesis when I get out of here, and I'll let you read mine."

"Oh! I love it when you talk sexy to me."

"Ha-ha! We really do speak the same language." Breanna held Joshua's hand. "I still can't believe it. We're free to be together. No more Edward Connor."

He picked up her hand and kissed the back of it. "No more Edward Connor."

3

IN THE BIOMED Department of Tel Aviv University, Breanna and Joshua worked in tandem, backing up their research. Despite their relative youth—Breanna was twenty-nine, Joshua thirty-two—they had both secured contract teaching jobs at TAU. It could take several years before either of them found a tenured position as a professor, but it didn't concern them so long as they could continue together in the field they loved.

When Breanna was beside Joshua, she spoke quietly. "I suppose I should have known that the antichrist from the Bible couldn't be killed by human hands, at least not the one in the books of Daniel and Revelation. Edward must be that one because he suffered a fatal head wound and is miraculously alive, like the prophecy." She placed a hand on his arm. "I never thought for a minute that any of the program would survive the virus you and I planted—foolish me. I should have known Edward and his sister Lucinda wouldn't leave all the data in one place. But still, who would have the foresight to keep some of the nanobots in a syringe ready to use with the laptop, complete with my and Lucinda's program on it, and bring it on the plane that day? Tell me there isn't some kind of spiritual interference behind our physical world."

"That's what the Bible says. Somewhere along the line, Edward made a deal with the wrong side."

She shook her head. "But it was my program that allowed him to heal rapidly. Lucinda's program for rapid muscle growth in Edward's soldier project didn't work until they added mine to it. Even though Edward survived the crash, the laptop with the two programs was lost, so Edward will need to replicate them."

Joshua said, "What if he replicates the God Factor program? Then he could kill people at will with nanobots, like he did with Dr. Steinberg. Anyone who resists him will die."

Breanna stared at her husband, and, at the same time, they said, "We need to contact Hakeem."

Dr. Hakeem Sahal had performed eye surgery on both Joshua and Breanna using nanobots to enhance their vision. Microscopic nanobots were now visible to the pair. In the past, it had saved Breanna's life when her food was tainted with them. Those nanos were programmed to cause her to have a brain aneurysm. Nanos had been used in John Steinburg's insulin and caused a heart attack in her professor. Unfortunately, John was not able to have nanos placed in his eyes, or he would have seen them in his medication.

However, Hakeem had performed the same surgery on many other people around the world who were involved in trying to prevent the misuse of nano-technology. They were all part of secret organizations dedicated to preventing a one-world government ruled by a dictator called the antichrist. Joshua and John belonged to the Toronto cell. Breanna joined by default after John's death because Edward headhunted her to work for him for her high-level skills. It was the only way to protect Breanna from Edward, and she provided eyes inside his operation. Itsy and Michael joined after all the Edward drama was thought to be over.

"Hakeem needs to ramp up his operations and provide the same surgery to more people around the globe in case Edward begins his God Factor program again. The doctor should probably teach it to other surgeons as well." Joshua finished copying his computer program. "I'm going to pick up a burner phone to contact Dr. Sahal. Can I meet you at the hotel for dinner?"

"Maybe I should go with you," Breanna said.

"No, I have to go by myself."

"I'm not comfortable being alone right now. I'll be seeing Edward or his goons around every corner." Breanna felt her stomach knot and tried to calm her nerves. She pulled out a cracker from her bag and munched on it. It seemed to help with her nausea.

Joshua took her in his arms. "We just saw him live on television, and he was in Ireland. He's not coming for you right now, if he's even coming at all."

The heat rose from her chest to her cheeks. She shook her body, removing herself from his hold. "What are you talking about? You know he'll come for me. Who else can replicate the programs as quickly as I can? I wrote half of it and worked with the other half." He went to reach for her again, but she backed away and snapped at him. "Don't try to placate me or reassure me that everything will be fine. It is not fine. It will not be fine. This guy can't die. I will never be safe."

Joshua folded his arms. "You're right. I'm sorry. I didn't want you to worry. But that was foolish."

"Yeah, it was stupid. We need a plan, not platitudes."

"I've never been accused of being stupid."

"Not you … what you said. I should stop using that expression. It's not nice to call people names. Sorry."

"No, it isn't nice. I forgive you if you forgive me. Still, did anyone ever tell you that you're scary when you're mad?"

Breanna puffed air out of her nose. "I've been told a few times. Seriously, we need a plan."

"I'll drop you at the hotel so you can be with Itsy and Michael, then I'll get in touch with my contact and grab four burner phones. I'll return right afterwards." This time, when he reached for her, Breanna allowed herself to get some comfort from him. "There has to be a way to stop Edward. We'll find it."

"I really think I should come with you. I would feel safer."

His cheeks twitched as he tried not to clench his jaw. "You'll be with Itsy and Michael while I'm gone. Stay in public, well-lit areas. I'll be back soon."

"I don't really like it, but I can tell by your face that you won't budge on this. Promise you'll hurry back. This whole thing is terrifying. The only thing holding me together is you and Jesus."

Joshua kissed her gently on the lips. "Jesus is the only thing keeping all of us together."

4

"YOU'RE MOSSAD?" BREANNA shook her head. Mossad was Israel's equivalent of the CIA. "Of course. It makes sense, doesn't it? How else would you get burner phones, bug-blocking devices, tranquillizer guns, and machine guns? Were the men who stormed the factory Mossad agents?"

"Yes."

"That's all you have to say for yourself. I asked you when we met if you were a spy, and you said no."

Joshua shrugged. "I wouldn't be much of a spy if I admitted to it because a pretty girl asked." Breanna slapped his arm. "Ow!" He rubbed the spot, although it really didn't hurt.

She turned away from him and went to sit down. "I can't believe you lied to me. Maybe at the beginning it made sense, but now we're married. When did you plan to tell me?"

"I don't know. Someday. Never. I hoped that maybe I wouldn't be needed in Mossad, and I could quit. When the Chinese Christian underground cells found out about the human trafficking operation at the nano factory, I reported it to my handler at Mossad. We needed help to free the slaves."

"I guess after the Holocaust, that's something Israel would be interested in."

"Well, yes and no. The Israeli government wanted in on the super-soldiers promised by Edward. Given our precarious position here in the Middle East, it's understandable that we would want the same thing our enemies have in terms of weapons. However, human trafficking was a priority too. If no one was going to have access to the soldier program, then that was a moot point."

Joshua pulled a chair up to sit beside his wife. "It's not safe for you to know that I'm an agent. I was trying to protect you."

Breanna folded her arms and shifted, facing away from him.

"Bree, honey, I love you. You know that."

Tears threatened at the corners of her eyes. She blinked them back. "Do you? Don't you trust someone you love? You know that I was undercover for over half a year inside Edward's organization. That was dangerous. I didn't tell anyone about you or the underground cells. You should've trusted me." She swivelled in her seat to look at his face. "If I hadn't followed you this afternoon, would you have told me?"

He said nothing but pressed his lips tightly together. She knew from the twitch in his cheeks he was pondering what to say.

They were sitting in an interview room in the Mossad headquarters. Breanna had followed Joshua in a cab when he refused to allow her to accompany him. She wanted to know where he was getting the burner phones, in case she ever needed to buy one or other spy objects, since Edward turned out to be alive. She expected an out-of-the-way store, not for him to waltz into Mossad headquarters, show ID to the guard, and walk through the security check. Breanna came in the front door behind him. In her anger, and before Joshua could disappear into the building, she yelled out his name. When he saw her, his eyes bulged, and he muttered something under his breath. He returned through security, grabbed her arm, and led her to this room.

She waved her hand in the air. "And what does it mean for the Toronto nanotech organization cell? Were you spying on them for Mossad? What about the New York cell with your professor? Were you spying on them too? How about the Israeli cell you recently connected with? What about all these hidden underground watchdogs? What about you spouting the importance of Christians undermining the antichrist and the one-world government? Was it all a game?"

Joshua remained silent.

Breanna shook her head in disbelief. "You were spying on all of them. They trusted you. Who are you? You're not the man I thought you were." She covered her eyes with her hands. Another thought hit her. "Did Mossad get us jobs working at the university together? Did they think we would replicate the soldier program for them?"

He winced as if she had stabbed him.

"They did."

Joshua's eyes suddenly turned darker. "Be realistic. I had to promise them something if they came to help free the prisoners and shut down Edward's operation. It's not like we'd be building killer nanobots. Israel needs protection. She is surrounded by countries swearing to annihilate her."

"It's you who needs a reality check. Instead of Edward building his army and selling them around the world, only Israel would have them. But you know the Bible. Israel makes a peace deal with the antichrist, who is probably Edward. So, in the end, he gets the program anyway."

She grabbed the arm of his jacket. "Is that what it's like to make a deal with the devil, Joshua? The ends justify the means?"

"You're getting hysterical." The moment the words came out of his mouth, he knew it was a mistake.

Fire rose from the tip of her toes to the top of her head. "Hysterical! Hysterical! Why is it that when a woman gets angry, she's hysterical? You're mad at me right now, but do I accuse you of being hysterical? You … you … sexist pig!" It was the worst thing she would allow herself to say. She folded her arms and glared daggers at him.

"I'm not mad at you but at myself."

"Why, because you're such a great spy, you didn't notice me following you?"

He huffed. It was aggravating that she knew exactly why he was upset with himself. Time to get this under control. "Breanna, I would have eventually told you, but I was worried you would react the way you are doing right now."

"Really? You didn't answer my question. If I hadn't followed you, would you have told me? When do you think you would have gotten around to it?"

He didn't answer.

"I've got to get out of here. I can't breathe." Breanna jumped up and tried the door. It was locked. She whirled around to look at Joshua, tears streaking her cheeks. "Let me out of here."

"We can't leave yet. I have to go speak to someone first."

Was the pain in her chest her heart breaking? Her stomach started heaving, and she ran over to a garbage can in the corner and threw up. He went to rub her shoulder, but she shrugged him off.

"Bree, it's not my choice right now. Let me go smooth things over, and we'll leave."

Joshua moved toward the door. He stared at her with his lips pressed tightly together. "I'll be back soon." He knocked on the door, and it buzzed open. Joshua slipped out, and the lock sounded behind him.

Breanna reached into her purse for a mint. *Is no one who they appear to be? Lord, what is going on?*

5

BREANNA WAITED AT the edge of the outdoor venue with Itsy, her maid of honour, and Joshua's two sisters, Irene and Barbara, her bridesmaids. She was dressed in a slim-fitting white silk wedding dress. The bridesmaids and maid of honour wore slim-fitting deep indigo satin dresses that complemented the bride. The ladies held white roses with baby's breath bouquets. The whole space was dripping with white wisteria garland hanging from pots, poles, and gazebos. White lace material was draped around the perimeter and had fairy lights woven into the fabric, providing an atmosphere of purity and light.

At the pre-wedding reception, Joshua covered Breanna's face with her veil in the *badeken* or veiling ceremony. Joshua told her it was to demonstrate he was not only interested in her looks but also her inner beauty. His parents, Ruth and Caleb Abrams, along with Jean Steinberg, her surrogate mother, blessed them both as bride and groom. After this, these family members and the groom proceeded to the chuppah without the bridal ladies. The chuppah was an ornately decorated wedding canopy woven with gold thread. The guests filled the chairs surrounding it.

The music began when everyone was seated. It was an unfamiliar, slow, and melodic Jewish song. Breanna's stomach fluttered, and she shifted her weight between her feet as she waited. Bobby, Itsy's brother, was giving Breanna away. He had always been like a little brother to her, and she smiled nervously at him. Bobby patted her hand and leaned into her ear. "You are the most beautiful bride I have ever seen, Bree. Joshua is lucky to have you."

Breanna was thankful that Barbara, a movie makeup artist, had chosen colours that complemented her skin and hair because Breanna knew next to nothing about it. Barbara had added hair extensions to Breanna's already long hair so that red waves fell to her waist. To top it off, Barbara had added a weave of baby's breath to her hair under and through the white lacey veil.

Joshua had explained to Bree and her Canadian friends that they would follow the ancient Jewish tradition where the groom's father would give the signal for the ceremony to begin. "It would be like a thief in the night, just as Jesus said he would come for his bride," he said. Joshua had his father, two brothers, and Michael at the wedding party. He and Michael had become friends after the kidnapping episode. It didn't hurt that Michael had proposed to Itsy, and they planned to marry the following month in November. Joshua didn't have to be jealous of Michael's old crush on Breanna any longer.

Finally, Caleb Abrams announced to the guests, "It is time." The groom and his groomsmen all began blowing small shofars, and they walked towards the ladies. When they reached Breanna, they helped her onto a seat, and they, along with Bobby, carried her to the chuppah. Joshua had told her, "This is a Galilean tradition when the bride goes flying to meet her groom. It is a symbol of the rapture or snatching away of Jesus's people, his bride, to be taken to heaven to celebrate the wedding supper of the lamb—Christians as his bride and Jesus as the groom."

Under the chuppah, the wedding party held lit candles in lanterns, and the Messianic rabbi performed the ceremony. The rabbi said the chuppah represented that the bride and groom would reside under one roof under God. Then he recited the marriage contract, which was the traditional Bible verses and marriage vows in a Western ceremony. Joshua said his lines and placed a wedding ring on her finger beside his grandmother's ring, which he had given her for their engagement. She put a ring on his finger after she said her vows. They each drank from a glass of wine that the rabbi had blessed; then the glass was wrapped in a thick napkin, and Joshua stomped on it and broke it. The rabbi announced to the guests who were unfamiliar with the custom that it was to remember that no matter how happy you were, you should always remember the destruction of Jerusalem and long to return there. All the guests yelled, "Mazel tov!"

The tables had already been set up. White and indigo linen dressed the tables, and white and deep blue flowers formed centrepieces. White plates with crystal glasses were used for the settings. Breanna thought it looked like a layout for a bridal magazine. Nothing was out of place or missing. When the guests sat down at their tables, the food was served. After the meal, there was dancing, some traditional and some modern. She marvelled at how Joshua had put all this together with minimal input from her. It was every little girl's dream of what her wedding would be like when she grew up.

The honeymoon was just as spectacular. Joshua planned it all, and she was pleasantly surprised by everything. He booked a lovely bohemian-style hotel in Tel Aviv on the beach. The room had Moroccan-style arches and brightly coloured walls. He carried her over the threshold and swung her inside their room. For the first several days, they didn't venture outside.

On the third day, Breanna woke before Joshua, showered, wrapped herself in a towel, and went out onto their balcony for the first time. It was early in the morning and already hot. She stretched out on a chaise lounge and allowed the rising sun to warm her. When she heard the sound of running water coming from the room, Breanna knew her husband was awake. It brought a smile to her heart that drifted to her mouth as she thought about him. She closed her eyes and cherished every moment. Then she felt the chair sink beside her as Joshua sat. He leaned in and kissed her, starting with her mouth, and slowly worked his way down to the nape of her neck.

Breanna murmured, "I would love to stay here forever."

"Oh, would you?"

"Umm! Wouldn't you?" She pulled him closer.

He stayed in her arms, gently kissing her neck and nibbling on her ear, breathing in her lavender scent. Finally, he said, "Well, I have a proposition."

She turned on her side, propped up on her arm. "Do you, now?"

He sat up but kept a hand on her waist. "How would you like to live here?"

"What do you mean?"

"I have a friend at Tel Aviv University, and he says there are two openings in their biomedical department. We could continue our work on nanobots, but this time together."

"I'm definitely listening," Breanna said. "That university is one of the partners of the University of Toronto. I've always been impressed with their investment in equipment and their dedication to the research. Should we apply?"

"I think so." He kissed her again.

Breanna couldn't believe how fortunate she was to have a husband like Joshua. She ran through his attributes in her head. He was intelligent; he had obtained a doctorate in biomedical technology, like her. He was caring; he rescued all those slaves from the factory. He was brave; he rescued her from a kidnapping by sneaking onto a plane and diving out of that plane after she was shot. He was handsome; he had dark skin and dark eyes that could see into her soul. He was loyal and trustworthy; he followed her to Ireland when she went to work for Edward Connor. He was a Christian, and he had introduced her to Jesus. He was the first man she ever loved and the only one she wanted to spend the rest of her life with. Now they might work together on their passion to use nanotechnology to cure cancer and other diseases.

I am the luckiest woman alive.

6

WHEN JOSHUA RETURNED to the interrogation room at Mossad headquarters, Breanna had quieted down, but she was devastated by his betrayal. In one day, the perfect life she believed she was living had shattered like broken glass, and the shards were ripping apart her insides.

Edward was still alive. He was a product of the soldier program she helped write. Not only was he a mass of muscles, but the nanobots inside him made him practically indestructible. Now he would be looking for a way to force her to rewrite the program. She could only hope he no longer wanted Breanna as a wife. To top it off, Joshua had betrayed her and all their friends in the Toronto watcher cell. He was a spy and wanted her to rewrite the program for Israel. She had no way of knowing if he'd married her because he loved her or to use her for her ability to build these soldiers.

Joshua said, "We can go now. I smoothed everything over. You have to keep what you learned here quiet, though."

She brought her brows together. He was insane for requesting her silence and complicity in his lies.

"Please, Bree. It puts my life in danger and yours too."

"The watcher cells are Christians, not murderers. The ones in Toronto are our friends … my friends."

He shook his head, "I didn't mean from them, but there are others."

"My life is already in danger from Edward, remember?"

"Of course. I could never forget that. We need to plan to keep you safe." He held the door open for her to exit. She breezed by, careful not to touch him.

Once outside the front door, Joshua pointed. "I parked down there. Although you probably know that since you followed me." He started walking towards the car.

Breanna didn't move.

He waved. "Come on. We should get to the hotel and meet with Itsy and Michael."

She shook her head and walked straight ahead toward the road. Joshua marched over to her and took her arm, which she shook off. "Don't touch me. I don't know if I ever want you to touch me again."

"What?"

She waved her arms, "What did you expect? You lied to me. You betrayed me."

"I love you, Breanna. Despite all the rest of it, that is true. It's been true since the first time I saw you." His brows knitted together.

"You have a funny way of showing love."

She moved to walk past him, but he stepped in front of her. "Don't leave. We can work this out. I told you that the Bible says that when we get married, we become one person. In Jewish tradition, we become one soul before God. If I didn't love you, would I have married you and joined myself to you for eternity?"

Bree looked into his eyes, forcing herself to show no emotion. "I don't know. I don't know what you would do, Joshua. You lied to me so easily, you could still be lying. You're a great actor. Bravo! You had us all fooled." She clapped her hands like she would at a play.

Joshua looked wounded and shook his head.

"I'm going to catch the bus. Leave me alone."

"How can I protect you if I'm not with you?"

"How can you protect me from you?" Breanna saw a bus pull up across the street. She pushed past him, ran to it, and climbed on board. Joshua was blindsided by how fast she moved, and as he tried to follow, several cars went by, blocking his way. The bus merged with traffic and left before he could get across the street. He ran toward his car, but it was parked on the road a block away.

Bree pressed her forehead against the cold glass as she watched Joshua struggle to get to her. He was running as the bus rounded the corner, and she lost sight of him. "Goodbye," she whispered, and the tears ran freely.

She exited after a couple of stops when she saw another bus waiting in front of this one. Transferring, she hoped to throw Joshua off her trail if he tried following her on the first bus. She did the same, switching two more times until she was lost in the city. The way she was feeling, it didn't matter. Breanna never realized that anyone could physically feel heartbreak, but she was living proof of it. To top it off, her stomach was doing somersaults and not in a good way. She was happy she had already emptied the contents of it, or she was sure she would be hanging over a garbage can on the streets. Joshua had ripped out her heart, thrown it on the ground, and stomped on it, trampling her dreams, her hopes, and her love.

Jesus, you are the only one who can handle this for me because I can't do it. It's too much. Must I lose so many people that I love? My parents, John, and now Joshua. How can I go on? Where do I go? What do I do? Do I run to Itsy and Michael? If I do that, do I put them in danger again from Edward? Tell me. I need to hear from you. Help!

7

WITHOUT PAYING ATTENTION to where she was going, Breanna instinctively caught buses that took her to Itsy and Michael's hotel. *I guess this is where you want me to go, Lord. Maybe I can get some peace of mind from my friends. Itsy always knows what to say.*

Breanna moved to the front of the bus, intending to get off in two stops. Looking out the large window, she saw her best friend come out of the front of the building. Warmth flooded Breanna's heart, but then it froze. A man jumped out of a car and grabbed Itsy's arm.

Breanna gripped the pole she held on to and cried out, "No!"

Itsy twisted herself out of the large man's hold. She jumped up and did a roundhouse kick, connecting to his head.

"You go, girl." Breanna leaned forward. *Those MMA fighting lessons are paying off right now.* She no longer thought Itsy crazy for taking the martial arts training for the last five years.

The man quickly recovered and grabbed Breanna's friend. Itsy pivoted and punched him in the head three times in quick succession. He grabbed her hand when she went for the fourth time and twisted it, but Itsy dropped using her body weight to throw the man off balance. Breanna saw blood running down his face as the bus drove past the fighting people. She heard the driver radioing for the police, but she didn't take her eyes off her friend. Itsy punched the man in the throat, and he held the spot, gasping for air.

Breanna's pulse was pounding in her head as she rang the bell to exit. When the bus stopped and the door opened, she didn't step down because she saw Michael and Joshua come racing out of the hotel towards Itsy. It barely registered to Breanna that the attacking man jumped into a waiting car, and it ran past the bus. The air sucked out of her lungs as if Itsy had hit her. The only face she saw was Joshua's, and she wasn't ready to talk to her husband yet.

She heard the driver call out, "Lady, are you getting off?"

"No, wrong stop!" She moved to the closest seat and sank into it. Itsy was safe from the assailant, and although she probably didn't need his help, Breanna felt better that Michael was there. *They'll be all right without me complicating things.*

As the bus rounded the corner, Breanna saw a taxi sitting in front of a different hotel. She rang the bell and got off.

Arriving at her apartment building, Breanna asked the cab driver, "Can you wait for me and keep the meter running?" She handed the woman double what was owed. "I will be maybe ten minutes tops."

"Sure. Are you all right, honey?" The middle-aged driver looked in the mirror, and Breanna could see the concern in her eyes. "Do you need help? Or someone to talk to?"

Bree fought the tears. "Maybe when I get back. Please don't leave without me."

"Okay, you got it, honey." The woman's voice was soft, even though it was gravelly from years of smoking.

Breanna ran into the building and took the stairs two at a time to get to the second floor. Inside their apartment, she saw Joshua's and her briefcases on the floor of the kitchen. He had obviously gone there looking for her. *Good!* She turned on their laptops and let them boot up as she ran into the bedroom.

In the back of the closet, there was an old backpack from her student years, and Breanna began shoving a few changes of clothes and toiletries into it. She opened the safe. Inside was the burner phone Joshua gave her last year, complete with charger. They had both forgotten about it. She saw the small tranquillizer gun with darts that he used during the raid on Edward's factory, her passport, and a large sum of money, American, Canadian, euros, and shekels, the currency used in Israel. All these things she shoved under her clothing in the bag.

When that was complete, Breanna extracted the memory stick with the virus used in Edward's factory from the safe. She moved quickly into the kitchen, plugged the virus into Joshua's computer, then hesitated as she considered what she was about to do. Shaking her head, she typed in the code and let the virus infect his laptop. When it was finished, she restarted his machine so it would take effect. The same was repeated on her computer. Breanna grabbed the virus stick and all the backup copies of their programs that they had copied that afternoon and threw them into her bag. She resolved to destroy them later.

Breanna took out her cell phone and turned it on. She texted Itsy, "I need some time to myself. Take care of yourself. Love you. B."

She also sent one to Joshua: "Don't try to find me. It's better this way."

True to her word, Breanna returned to the cab within ten minutes, minus her cell phone, which she left on the table with two laptops running the virus. She knew Joshua would have Mossad track her phone to their apartment, and that would give her time to get away.

The driver asked, "Where to, honey?"

"I need to get to the Benedictine monastery in Abu Ghosh. Any suggestions on how I can go about it?" Breanna had never been there, but she had heard about it once. Nuns and priests lived in the monastery and offered hospitality to visitors. "Also, I am leaving an abusive husband who has many connections in this country, so no one can know where I'm going. Can I trust you?"

The woman nodded, "I've been there, done that, and have the T-shirt. You can count on me. But are you sure you don't want to go to the women's shelter?"

"No, he'll find me. I need to disappear for a little while."

"You got it. I'll take you myself and we can be there in less than an hour." The cabbie hit the gas, and as Breanna stared out the rear window, the apartment building where she had built what she believed was a dream life disappeared from her view. She turned to face forward and let the tears fall.

Goodbye, Joshua!

8

SAUL, THE REAL estate broker, came to pick them up at the hotel where they were honeymooning. "Shalom, Shalom."

Joshua said, "Shalom, shalom."

"Why do you say it twice? I notice a lot of people do it here in Israel." Breanna pulled her purse high on her shoulder as she stood up from the comfortable chairs in the lobby.

Joshua took her hand, "You are wishing someone perfect peace or God's perfect peace."

She squeezed his hand and leaned closer so their arms touched. His dark eyes seemed to embrace her.

Saul nodded approvingly at the newlyweds. "Are you two ready to look at some places to live?"

"Absolutely." Joshua led Breanna out of the hotel beside the broker.

"Good. It's a bright, sunny day, although a little cooler than it has been."

Joshua laughed. "That's probably a good thing if we are going to be running in and out of homes. I wouldn't want to get too hot and sweaty." Then he winked at Breanna, and she felt her cheeks go red. He laughed a little harder.

Saul didn't seem to notice the couple flirting, and he kept up the pace as they headed to his small car. Joshua helped Bree into the front passenger seat, and he sat behind her. Saul handed her six pages with one listing per page. When she finished with them, she gave them to Joshua. "Right," Saul said. "Is there a specific one you want to start with, or should I go in order of neighbourhood and work our way around directionally?"

Breanna said, "I think it makes sense to see the ones in one area and then proceed from there. Do you have appointment times for any of them?"

"Three have specific times, and three are whenever we get there. If you don't like any of these, we can always look at more tomorrow."

She half turned in her seat so Joshua could see her face. "We've got to stay close to the budget we gave you. We haven't got the jobs yet, although we applied."

Joshua interrupted her, "But I have money saved, so if we need to go over to get something nice, that's okay."

She flattened her lips and shook her head. "We talked about that. I don't like extending ourselves until we know how much we're going to make or if we're going to work longer than one semester. We need to be frugal." He reached his hand through the opening between the bucket seats and laid it on her arm. "Don't try to sweet-talk me."

"Why not? It worked when I tricked you into marrying me."

All three of them chuckled.

"You're hopeless." Breanna gazed at him. She sighed as she stared at his face. *He still takes my breath away. I can't believe we're married.* His eyes seemed to look into her soul, and she felt loved completely.

"Hopelessly devoted to you-ou-ou!" he sang, out of tune.

Her eyebrows rose in the middle. "That will never convince me."

Saul had been driving to their first apartment viewing during the couple's banter. "Here we are now. This is a two-bedroom, one bathroom apartment." He parked the car and looked over to the sheets. Pointing, he said, "This one."

Breanna grimaced. "Only one bathroom."

"It's in the budget," Joshua pointed out sarcastically.

"Fine, let's go see it." She shrugged and opened the car door.

They continued to see the rest of the listings, but the second viewing was too far away from the university. The third was a large house that was too expensive for Breanna. The fourth one was way too small, and they would go crazy in such a small place. The fifth needed lots of repairs. The last apartment was the one that both Breanna and Joshua liked because it had two bedrooms and two bathrooms, and it was clean and roomy enough for them both.

Outside that apartment building, Joshua said, "Give us a minute, Saul."

"Take your time. I'll sit in the car. I have to make a call." He left them.

"You have to admit, this one is perfect."

She held her purse on her shoulder and leaned against the wall. "It is, except …"

"I know, it's a little over budget, but I know we can afford it. We might never find another one this perfect, this close to the university, this size." He ran the back of his hand against her cheek. "Say yes."

"I ... I ... stop looking at me like that and trying to seduce me. It's not fair." Goose bumps rose on her arms.

Joshua pressed his advantage and kissed her. "I have the money. Don't worry."

"That's your money. We should live off what we earn."

He put his hands on her shoulders and became serious. "What's mine is yours. We are one now. Everything we do from now on is together as one. There is no more yours and mine. Before God, we are joined forever."

"But—"

"Say it. We are one, joined forever."

She sighed as she stared at him. "We are one, joined forever."

9

BREANNA FOLDED HER arms and cried as she said goodbye to that apartment and her life. The cab driver let her cry it out without interruption. *I'm sorry, Jesus, if I lied about Joshua being abusive. But isn't it controlling if your husband lies to you about everything to get what he wants from you? It's a type of abuse. Does he even love me? Has he ever loved me? Does he act so much with this spy business that he doesn't know the truth anymore? And what about those times he's gone for a few days to a week? He says he's at a conference or dealing with a family problem. Were those times he was doing a job for Mossad?*

Lost in her thoughts, she didn't notice the time passing. The tears eventually stopped, and she stared out the window silently. Then she came up with another plan.

"Would you mind if we stop at a pharmacy? Hopefully, there is one still open." Breanna looked at the time on her watch. It was ten to eight at night.

"Sure, honey. I'll put it on my GPS."

In less than ten minutes, the cab pulled into a drugstore parking lot.

"I'll be right back." Breanna ran in and quickly bought the supplies she needed.

Once in the cab again, she made small talk with the woman driving and discovered that she had two adult children from her first marriage. He had been an alcoholic and become abusive over time. The woman said she left him countless times but always ended up back with him when he promised to change. "It's hard when you're financially dependent on someone and you have a couple of children."

Breanna felt sorry for the woman.

"Eventually, it got so bad that I decided I had had enough. The children were suffering while watching him beat me. I packed them up after a bad night, and when he passed out, we caught a cab. That driver took me to the woman's shelter." She smiled in the mirror. "A year later, I was divorced from the first man and married to a nice driver. It was the best thing I've ever done. He loves me and my children. He helped raise them as his own."

The woman slowed the cab as they came up the driveway to the monastery. "This is it, honey. How are you doing?"

Releasing the breath she felt she had been holding for the entire drive, Breanna said, "Not too great. But I'm strong, like you. I'll be okay."

"That's the spirit. Take it one day at a time, and you'll do fine. I hope you find some peace in here."

Breanna gave a weak smile at the cabbie and handed her twice what the meter read.

"No. I can't take that. You're going to need it."

"You've taken over two hours of your night because you still have to drive home. Take it. My husband can afford it." Breanna shook the money she held over the front seat.

"Well, since it's his money—" The driver grinned as she took the cash. "Do you want me to wait until you're inside?"

"Yes. Thank you. Shalom, shalom."

"I'll sit here until I see the door close. Shalom, shalom."

Breanna put the store bag into her backpack and then exited the cab. She hoisted the pack onto her shoulder and walked up to the large wooden door. A priest answered her knock, and Breanna said, "I would like sanctuary."

The old man nodded and stood to the side to allow her to enter. Breanna turned and waved at the cab driver, who then pulled out of the driveway.

Inside the austere hallway, she looked at the priest. "Is it still done these days? Seeking sanctuary?"

He gave a lopsided smile. "Not usually. People do come to stay from time to time as they travel the Jerusalem-Emmaus Road. You are welcome, though."

She responded, "Thank you." Breanna stared at the priest. He looked like he was in his late sixties or early seventies, gray-haired, clean-shaven, and with a bit of a tummy. She imagined Friar Tuck from Robin Hood would look like this man, except for the tonsure. This man had a thick head of hair, although cut short.

The priest could see that she was nervous and didn't know what to do. He said, "I am Father Rolly. I am one of the senior priests here, in more ways than one. I came here as a novice priest in 1985, and I have been here ever since, forty-five years."

"Hi, I'm Bree." She didn't want to give him her full name, and she didn't want to lie. "I'm here for some time of prayer and reflection. Would it be all right to stay for a few days?"

He said, "Yes, Bree. That would be fine. Are you hungry?"

Her stomach did a kind of knotted flop at the mention of food. "I'm not overly hungry, but I haven't eaten since lunch, so I probably should eat something."

"Follow me." Father Rolly turned and led her down the brick hallway. The décor became only slightly more ornate in that part of the monastery. They arrived at a large kitchen, and the priest led her to the industrial-sized refrigerator. When he opened the door, Breanna saw small containers of milk and juice, fruit, bread, muffins, and vegetables. "What would you like?" he asked as he took a muffin for himself.

"Could I have a container of milk and a muffin?"

After getting their food, the priest took her out to a large dining hall with long wooden tables surrounded by chairs. The Father sat on a chair near the kitchen door, so Breanna planted herself on one beside him. She felt a little self-conscious as she nibbled on the muffin, willing herself to swallow with the lump in her throat.

"Bree, if there is anything you want to talk about, priestly vows prevent us from discussing it with others. Anything you say would be kept in the strictest of confidences unless you plan to endanger yourself or others."

She nodded and lowered her head. *Should I talk to him? Can I talk about any of this without breaking down right now? Should I betray Joshua's confidence? I never want anything bad to happen to him.* "Maybe tomorrow, Father. I'm tired tonight. It's been a tough day."

He rose and took the muffin wrappers to the bin. "I'll show you to the nun's quarters. We have strict rules about men and women staying on their own side. Even husbands and wives sleep on separate sides when they come here."

"Thank you."

Once Breanna was deposited with one of the nuns, Father Rolly said good night. Breanna followed Sister Beatrice to a room. She was surprised at how few nuns seemed to be in the dormitory. Sister Beatrice said, "We don't have many visitors right now. We get more in summer. You'll have this room to yourself, and the bathroom is attached. We don't have much in the way of possessions."

Breanna looked around the stark room with four single beds and a couple of mismatched dressers. "This is perfect, Sister. It has everything I need—a bed, bathroom, and a place to spend time with God."

"Well, it is that for certain." She smiled at Breanna. "If you need anything, I am staying two rooms down to the right. I share a room with my biological sister, who also happens to be a nun. Sister Evangeline. Goodnight."

Once the door was closed, Bree took out her drugstore bag and headed to the washroom—it was time for some changes.

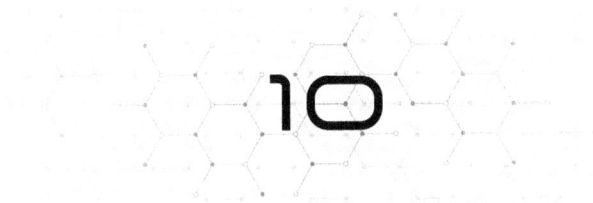

10

JOSHUA KISSED HER softly. She stretched out and wrapped her arms around his neck.

"Breanna, you've been a naughty girl." The voice was not Joshua's. Her eyes flew open, and it was Edward's face in front of her. He looked angry with eyes black as coal. "What have you done? Destroyed my nanobot factory. Let my workers go. I paid good money for them. Tried to destroy my nanotechnology. But Lucinda and I tricked you. She had sent me some of the nanobots and copied the program onto the laptop for the enhanced soldiers. Good job, we did too. It saved me. Aren't you happy, Breanna? Your work saved my life."

She tried to move, but he had her pinned down on the bed. "It's futile to struggle. I'm bigger and stronger. A better me." He tossed his head back and laughed an evil sound that echoed in her brain. "I'm indestructible now. There is more of me to love." He stared her in the eye. "And you will love me eventually. After a few babies, you will accept your fate, like the Celtic women of old. I will be the most powerful man in the world, and you will be at my side programming my killer nanobots and making supersoldiers."

Breanna struggled, writhing on the bed, trying to get away.

"We will do great things together, Breanna. We will raise the dead."

"Rebuke you, Satan, in Jesus's name. Ahhh!" Breanna screamed and sat up. She was covered in sweat, and her heart was pounding. It took a minute for her to realize she had been dreaming. She found herself wrapped up in the blanket on the bed, which was why she couldn't get away.

There was a knock at the door. "Bree, are you all right?"

Breanna went to the door and opened it. "Yes, Sister Beatrice. I'm so sorry. I had a nightmare, but I'm fine." The sister stared at her for a minute with wide eyes. Breanna touched the top of her head. "Oh, my hair. I cut it off last night and dyed it dark brown. I wanted a change."

"Ah!" The older nun smiled and nodded. "We are having mass in half an hour in the chapel. We have it every morning at seven a.m., and then we go for breakfast. Get ready, and I'll come by in twenty minutes to bring you to the church. You can meet my sister then." With that, the nun turned and walked towards her room.

Breanna closed the door and leaned on it, still shaken up from the dream. *Lord Jesus, are these nightmares going to plague me again?* She rubbed her eyes like she was trying to erase the memory of Edward.

Breanna grabbed her clothes and went into the washroom. Her hair looked as short as Itsy's used to be. She dabbed the gel she had bought onto her hair, working it through to make it spikey. Now she understood why Itsy played with her hair when it was in the pixie cut. It was a little fun and something to fidget with to placate her nerves. Her skin looked pale next to the dark colouring in her hair. *Once I put on dark foundation, makeup, and glasses, people I know will find it hard to recognize me. I'll give Joshua a run for his money in the spy business ... at least the disguise part. But I don't need makeup in here.*

Breanna had never been in a Catholic church. She liked the stained-glass windows depicting the life of Jesus. There was something that felt holy about the chapel, like there was a tangible presence of God in the place. Never having attended a mass, Breanna followed the two old sisters who sat beside her. She particularly liked kneeling on the small piece of wood with a pad provided for that activity. It seemed fitting to kneel before the King of kings.

When the service was done, the elder sibling, Sister Evangeline, who looked to be in her eighties, chatted away to Breanna about her and Sister Beatrice's childhood in Maine. She finished their brief family history by explaining how they became nuns. "Beatrice was the true beauty. She had many suitors, but she was only interested in one. Billy Scatton, a brown-haired boy with a face like an angel. Unfortunately, he was sent to Vietnam in 1972 and never returned. At only eighteen years old, Beatrice was crushed. She resolved to join the convent. I had already chosen that vocation. Now all these years later, here we find ourselves, living outside Jerusalem where Jesus walked."

Sister Beatrice had been involved in a brief exchange with Father Rolly and turned to hear the end of her sister's story. "Hush now! Bree doesn't want to hear all that ancient history."

Breanna smiled at the younger sister, in her mid-seventies. "I don't mind at all."

With a faraway look in her eyes, Beatrice said, "I can't even picture his face anymore." The younger of the two nuns brushed the front of her frock like she was dusting off the cobwebs of history. Her eyes focused on the young woman with her, and she said, "Let's get something to eat. I'm hungry. Are you?"

The thought of food turned Bree's stomach. She nodded but wondered how she was going to get a mouthful down. In the dining room, there was a flurry of activity, but Breanna was surprised that so few people were there. She expected to see many more priests and nuns. As if reading her mind, Sister Evangeline leaned over and said quietly, "This is not as popular a vocation as it once was, as you can see. We are an aging population." Breanna felt sad hearing that bit of information. It was like the end of something special, the end of an era.

"There are still some new novices around the globe. God calls people from all walks of life and all ages," Sister Beatrice added on a more cheerful note. She looked at Breanna's engagement and wedding rings, and the young woman realized she still wore them. She thought for a moment and decided to keep them on for now. They made her believe there was still a thread of hope, and she wasn't willing to allow herself to fall into the depths of depression about the end of her short marriage yet.

Breanna found that she did not have an appetite, and she picked at the food. The sisters chatted with other priests and nuns, including Breanna in the conversations. She was experiencing waves of nausea, so she finally had to excuse herself.

As soon as she arrived in her room, she headed to the toilet and promptly threw up the small amount she had eaten at breakfast. She felt her forehead on fire, so when she was finished, she lay down on the cold tile floor. A few minutes later, she was shaking with cold, and the bed was calling to her. Within minutes of crawling under the covers, she fell asleep.

This time, she dreamed of Joshua. They were holding hands, walking down the street on a sunny day. He was pushing something, but she was focused on his face. She wanted to remember everything about him—the small wrinkles that branched out from the corners of his eyes when he smiled, deep brown eyes with long black lashes, the straight bridge of his nose that ended at a perfect angle, lips that were not too full or too thin but very masculine, olive skin that became darker when they spent days at the beach, and a smile that melted her heart when he stared into the depths of her.

She woke up remembering every detail about him and how safe she had felt when he held her in his arms. Tears leaked from the corners of her eyes as she wondered if she would forget how he looked, the way Beatrice had with her boyfriend. Then the nausea struck again, and she ran to the bathroom.

11

THE FOLLOWING DAY was not much better. Breanna began to wonder if she had been poisoned by Edward somehow or if she had contracted a terrible flu. She went to church in the morning but ate only crackers and drank a little water for breakfast. Even the thought of having a cup of her beloved coffee turned her stomach. The crackers helped somewhat, so she returned to the chapel to pray. Kneeling before the Lord, she prayed and poured out her heart. *Where are you, Lord? Why don't you answer me? So many other people say they hear you all the time ... and sometimes I have, but now, when I really need you ... nothing.*

Day after day, Breanna continued with this routine, praying as often as she could and trying not to be sick the rest of the time. On her fifth day at the monastery, she was again in the church praying when, after an hour, Father Rolly came into the chapel. He knelt beside her and asked, "Do you mind if I pray here?"

Breanna shook her head. "No."

"No, you don't mind?"

"I don't mind."

They prayed silently beside each other. After about ten minutes, he asked, "Would you like to talk about it?"

The familiar tears pricked her eyes, but she blinked them back. "I guess." *Maybe he's got an answer from God to my prayers.*

The father sat on the bench. Breanna did the same, and he swivelled to face her.

After a brief hesitation, Breanna decided to tell him some of her heartbreak. "I've only been married six months. I'd known him for about a year.

He seemed perfect for me. He was sweet and loving. Then, five days ago, I found out he lied to me … from the start, he lied to me. The man I thought I loved was an illusion. We had a huge fight, and I left. How can a man who professes to be a Christian lie to his wife?" Breanna thought it best to leave out the details.

He sat silently. When she was done, she wiped the tears off her face that had come despite her best effort to prevent them. He handed her a handkerchief. "It's clean."

When she finished, the cloth was a bit of a mess. Embarrassed, she said, "I'll wash it and return it later."

"Keep it." The priest looked up briefly, then asked, "Would you like some fatherly advice?"

"I think I need it."

"You never solve anything by running away. You have to face it to fix it, if it can be fixed. And you'll never know if you don't try."

"Do you tell everyone that solution?"

"No. If your husband physically hurt you, I would not tell you to go back. I would say run as far as you can. Abusive men don't often change, unless Jesus changes them. But you said he already knows Jesus. Bree, I say this as a priest, but also from years of counselling couples. Marriage is hard. It takes work. It takes communication. In the end, it can become something beautiful. Something God created to make life better for men and women."

"Can I ask you a question?"

"Depends." A lopsided smile crept across his face.

"Why didn't you marry?"

"Because I felt like my life belonged to Christ. I believe he called me to this vocation."

She said, "You're good at it."

"Thanks." Father Rolly patted her hand and then left her to her thoughts.

Breanna whispered to God, "I guess that was my answer."

In her room, Breanna nibbled on another cracker. It seemed to keep her from throwing up. She pulled out the burner phone and charged the battery for half an hour. While she waited, she debated whether to call Joshua first or Itsy first. Maybe her best friend could calm her nerves about calling her husband. She didn't want to fight anymore.

She dialled her best friend's number. It rang several times and went to voicemail. "Hi, Itsy. It's me. I'll call back in a few minutes."

The crackers didn't work for her nerves, and she went into the washroom and emptied her stomach.

It was time to call Itsy again. The phone rang several times, but this time a male voice answered. "Bobby?"

"Bree?"

"Yes. Where's Itsy? I need to talk to her."

"She was taken."

"What do you mean, taken?"

"She and Michael arrived in Toronto yesterday." Bobby sounded terse. "Thank God, I agreed to skip class. They sounded cryptic on the phone, so I knew I had to meet them in person. When I got here, Michael was unconscious, shot, and bleeding out. I performed basic triage and called 911. The police came with the ambulance, and Itsy was nowhere to be found. Michael's suitcase was still in the hall, but not her bag. It has taken some doing, but I convinced the police that Itsy did not shoot Michael and run away. They're looking for her now."

"Who else knows?"

"I contacted our friends to let them know to pray for the two of them and put out feelers to find her."

She knew Bobby was referring to the Toronto underground organization or Toronto cell, as they called themselves. "Does Joshua know?"

"Yes!" He paused. "Bree, where are you? Joshua said you were missing and that Itsy and Michael returned home early to be here in case you came here."

"Is Joshua on his way there?"

"No, he's working on something else." She knew Joshua was trying to find her for Mossad. Their priority would be getting the nanotechnology programs from her.

It occurred to her that she had forgotten to ask. "How is Michael?"

He said, "He's in a coma on life support. It's not looking good. Go to Joshua or come home here. You need to be with people who love you."

"I'm safe in hiding where I am. It's safer if I stay away."

Bobby snapped back, "No one is safe who knows you."

That cut her to the bone. She started to cry but tried to keep it quiet.

"I'm sorry. I didn't mean that, Bree. It's just … I'm worried about Itsy, about Michael, and about you. This is not your fault. None of it is."

"No, I'm sorry. I love you, Bobby, and Itsy. I'll see what I can do to find Itsy."

"Leave it to our friends. They can help better than you. You need to stay safe. Promise me," Bobby pleaded.

"Okay. I'll call again when I can." She paused, then added, "And I'll pray."

When she hung up the phone, she sank to her knees on the floor. *The Toronto cell can't help Itsy, but I can. Lord, help us.*

12

BREANNA CONSIDERED DIFFERENT scenarios for accomplishing her goal. Between her upset stomach, the lack of food, and the frequent dreams disrupting her sleep, she was coming up short every time. Mossad would find her. There were too many checkpoints and too much security. Her head was pounding, so she decided to lie down again for a little while.

Before her head hit the pillow, she thought of a perfect plan: *keep it simple and make him do all the work.*

She pulled out the burner phone and dialled the number she'd hoped to forget. *I wonder if it's the same.*

"Hello, Breanna. It's about time you called." The deep voice with the Irish accent made her skin crawl. "I was getting concerned that you didn't get my message."

She kept her voice flat, void of any emotion. "I only received it a few minutes ago."

"Hmm, good."

"I propose an exchange."

His voice rose but remained measured. "Do you, now?"

Her hands were shaking, and she balled the one not holding the phone into a fist to keep it steady. It crossed her mind that she'd like to use it on the man on the phone. "I have what you want, and you have what I want. I will trade the nanotechnology programs for Itsy."

"I want you, Breanna. And I want the technology. Your friend Isabella is my guest until you bring yourself and your work here."

"I doubt she would see it that way. Kidnapping her and shooting her husband doesn't sound very hospitable for a host."

His voice became hard. "That snivelling worm, Michael, tried to dismantle my trade deals as if he could thwart my plans. He got what he deserved. The man had no vision."

Bree could feel her face burning. She blurted out, "What vision? A one-world government ruled by you as the supreme dictator? Killing anyone who gets in your way, like Michael and John?"

He began to laugh, but not the light, musical one he'd had in the past. This one was menacing and evil. "That's it. Now, instead of exchanging barbs, tell me how you plan to do this exchange. I'm a busy man, and your friend might run out of time while you stall."

A fist clenched around her heart. "Don't hurt Itsy. I'm on the outskirts of Jerusalem, but I can't leave the country without alerting security everywhere."

"And you wouldn't want that. Your husband is running to save you but sacrificing your best friend in the process." He sounded hard again. "You did have me fooled, though. I must say that was well played. Poor Michael was a patsy in your plan to destroy my factory, and all the time, you were involved with a different man. And I, I was strung along until you could accomplish your goals. You really are an Irish fairy … an evil one. Playing all the men against each other."

"It wasn't like that." *I'm not evil, am I? It was unintentional, mostly. I did string Michael along, but how was I to know Edward would try to hurt Michael to get to me?*

"Yes, it was exactly like that, Breanna. But don't worry about it now. Everything will be made right when you're here by my side. Tell me where you are, and I will come get you."

She hesitated. *Lord, is there any other way?* Nothing came to mind.

"Now, Breanna. If you want your friend back in one piece. I have been patient long enough."

"Her for me and the technology."

"Fine."

She gave him the address.

"Pack, I will be there in eight hours." The line went dead.

Breanna gagged. There was no food to empty from her stomach. *Maybe if I'm lucky, it will turn out that I have a deadly plague and I'll take him with me.* She packed her few things and went to say her goodbyes, pretending to be happily reuniting with her husband. *These precious people don't deserve to be dragged into my drama. Bobby had that right. I'm not safe to be around.*

Slightly more than eight hours later, a black limousine pulled up to the front door of the monastery. With his private jet on his private landing strip at his home in Ireland, he must have left immediately after the call ended. It made sense to her that he would have it ready to go on a moment's notice. Breanna was outside with her backpack. A large bodyguard got out of the front seat and opened the rear door of the car. He held out his hand, and without a word, she handed over her bag.

She peered into the car. "Where is Itsy?"

Edward made a grimacing face. "What have you done with your hair?"

"You're talking hair? Where is my friend?"

"I hate your hair. You will dye it back to your normal colour, and then you will grow it out again."

"I don't care about my hair. I care about my friend."

"Get in," he ordered. "You didn't think I would bring her so you could double-cross me again. No, she remains at my home until we get there."

Breanna knew she had no choice. She slid into the seat as far from Edward Connor as she could sit. He grabbed her and pulled her close to him. "We will work together again. Isn't that wonderful?"

She looked at him like he had two heads. "You're insane."

"That's your fault. That technology that saved my life also caused me a great deal of pain. The plane crash caused burns all over my body and injuries that should have killed me. Even with your healing program, the nanobots were spread thin trying to repair everything. It took months instead of seconds."

"If you hadn't tried to kidnap Michael and me, your plane wouldn't have crashed."

He put his face right up to hers so that she felt his hot breath. "You killed my sister."

"You killed her. You and your evil plan."

Edward slapped her face. He didn't use much effort, but with the bulging muscles the nanobots built, he packed a punch. Breanna felt her lip split and knew she would have a serious bruise on that cheek. Despite her efforts to restrain them, tears fell. He pulled a tissue from the box and snapped, "Wipe the blood. This car is a rental."

She dabbed the blood and managed to slide away from him. Edward didn't try to stop her. From the front passenger seat, the bodyguard held up her passport and dart gun.

"Where's the phone?" Edward asked her. When she didn't respond immediately, he lifted his hand. "Don't make me use force, Breanna."

She flinched and capitulated. "In the hair dryer."

"And the virus program?"

She pulled a memory stick out of her bra. "Here."

"For your and Itsy's sake, it had better be."

Breanna was initially surprised he didn't ask for her current work, but then she guessed he wanted her to use it.

On his new plane, Breanna kept her distance, and Edward ignored her while he conducted business by phone. She wasn't sure if he acted like that because he felt bad for hurting her or if he was actually indifferent to her. Most likely the latter since he had threatened to hit her again. Either way, she was happy she didn't have to fight him off. The plane had a small kitchen like the last one, and she retrieved ice cubes, wrapped them in a cloth napkin and held them on her lip and cheek.

An employee brought out food, but as soon as Breanna smelled it, she ran to the bathroom and threw up. *Deadly plague take me and Edward.* When she was finished, she returned to her seat.

"You look like death itself. What is wrong with you?"

"I've been sick."

"How long?"

"A week, maybe two. It's just the flu."

Edward shook his head. "Maybe morning sickness."

"No," she replied, but as soon as he said it, she knew it was true. *Pregnant.* Breanna remembered the night she forgot her pill two weeks ago. When she realized, Joshua said not to worry. It was only one time, and it usually took a month before the pill wore off. Her breathing quickened, and her chest burned. *It's all Joshua's fault. I'm pregnant! Why do I listen to him?* Even while her mind raged at her husband, she knew it was irrational. It wasn't his fault she forgot her pill. It was her mistake. Still, he had a part in making the baby. That thought caused her heart to melt a little. *I'm having a baby. God creates babies, but Lord, this is crazy timing.*

Edward watched her face closely and saw her moods change rapidly in a short period. "You are pregnant."

"I guess I am."

"We can arrange to get rid of it."

Her throat constricted. "No, never. I can't kill my baby."

"A baby doesn't fit with my plans." He said it in a matter-of-fact tone, like it was another negotiation they were discussing, not a life.

"Why? You said you would get me pregnant like the old Celtic way of marriage. You don't have to worry about it. I already am."

Edward's eyes narrowed, and he glared at her. "My baby is not some other man's. We will get rid of this baby. You can have others with me."

"If you kill this baby, I will never work for you, whether you kill Itsy or everyone else I know. You will have to kill me, too. Nothing, not a minute of work from me." She folded her arms over her belly and reclined in the chair. *Jesus, do something. Don't let him murder my baby.*

He stared silently at her for a long time. Eventually, the Irishman said, "Have the baby. As soon as the baby is born, we will find a family to raise it. Then we will begin our family. But you will work for me. Remember, abortion can be done right up to the moment of birth, and then murder can happen anytime afterwards. The baby for your work."

She choked back the lump in her throat and nodded her head like a bobble figure. *Thank you, Lord.*

13

JOSHUA KISSED HER belly button above her swimsuit bottoms, then he rested his chin on her stomach. "Lots of babies. We need to have lots of children."

"Okay. How many?"

He pushed himself up to lie on the beach blanket beside her, propped up on his elbow. On this unusually hot day, they had decided to go to the beach. "Maybe a dozen."

She half sat up. "A dozen?" She started coughing as she choked on the words.

He ran his free hand lightly up her face and tucked a loose strand of long red hair behind her ear. She shivered as goose bumps rose. "Maybe more. My cousin's cousin has seventeen children. Of course, some had grown up before the younger ones were born."

"No. I would spend my whole life being pregnant."

He moved his hand to her stomach. "I think I would like you pregnant."

"Stop teasing me. Tell me you don't really want to have a dozen children." Their wedding was in two days, and she worried because children were not something they ever discussed. What if he really did expect her to have that many?

He roared at her reaction. Then his finger traced the scar still healing from the bullet wound in her abdomen. "I want some. How many do you want?"

"More than one. I was an only child, and it was lonely sometimes. Then, when my parents died, I found myself with no family. You have two sisters and three brothers, so you wouldn't know how it feels."

"You're right. I wouldn't know." He looked serious and placed his hand under her chin. "You never have to be alone again. You have me, and soon you'll have my crazy family." He leaned in and planted a quick kiss on her lips. "I want what you want, Bree. If you want one, that would be fine. If you want six, that would be fine too."

"What if I said none?"

He scrunched up his nose. "Could we talk about that?"

Breanna laughed. "I want some. I was just checking if you would still want me if I said I wanted no children."

"I will always want you, no matter what."

She became serious. "What if that bullet made me infertile?"

He shook his head, and the black hair that had grown a little longer fell on his face. She reached up to brush it off, and he grabbed her hand and kissed the palm. "The doctor said it didn't hit any of your vital organs, which means your uterus, too."

Breanna felt her face go red when Joshua mentioned that body part, although it seemed silly to her. They were medical scientists after all. It was only that no one had talked about her uterus before except her doctor, much less a man she was dating.

When Joshua saw her cheeks colour, he chuckled. "I love it when you blush. Those cute freckles stand out."

"Stop. You know I don't like my red hair and freckles."

"Freckles. Freckles. Uterus. Uterus." He laughed hard, and she pushed him over off his elbow. He stayed where he landed, flat on his back, but he kept hooting.

She joined him. "Why do I have to love the weirdest people? Itsy and now you."

He reached over and pulled her beside him. "Now I know what you find attractive about me. It's my peculiar personality."

"Strange. Odd. Unusual. Bizarre."

"Bizarre? Now you've gone too far." Joshua gave her a little tickle, but when she winced, he stopped. "Are you all right? I forgot you're still healing."

"I'm okay. I'll be fine."

"Good, because once we're married and you're healed, we might want to work on our first baby."

"So soon? Maybe we should get to know each other first. Like, wait a year or two before we start."

"I have a plan. I'll begin right away, and you can wait a year or two."

She frowned. "That makes no sense."

"Sure it does. You take the pill until you want a baby, and I'll keep trying until you decide it's time and stop taking the pill." They both giggled. "I'm joking. I will respect what you decide and agree to whatever method of birth control you want." Then he raised his brows. "But I really like my first idea."

Breanna rolled her eyes. "You're something else, Joshua Abrams."

He sat up and kissed her. "And so are you, Breanna, soon to be Abrams."

14

BY THE TIME they had boarded the plane, it was getting dark outside, so they travelled overnight on the plane. The early morning was misty and grey when they landed on Edward's private airstrip next to his home in Ireland. Breanna followed him down the boarding stairs, and then he held the door to his waiting limousine for her.

As they wound around the drive to the house, Breanna took a keen interest in her surroundings in the hope of an escape in the future. Much to her dismay, she noted a number of armed guards patrolling the grounds with trained dogs. Some of them drove the grounds in Jeeps. No other employees were visible on the estate. The red and white stables appeared empty. No smell of hay or horses wafted through the air as they had on her last visit. The sound of those magnificent beasts was noticeable absent from that area.

The garage door stood open, and as their vehicle entered the large structure, Breanna saw a handful of cars, but compared to what was there before, it was a much smaller number. The office buildings previously used for Edward's businesses were quiet, with shutters closed and lights off. The only sign of life that Breanna could see was the guards roaming the grounds. *Perhaps everyone left when Edward was reported dead.*

When Breanna walked through the door of Edward's home, she flashed back to the first time she visited there. The home was beautiful, and a team of designers and historians had been restoring the twelfth-century castle and the subsequent centuries of additions. That time, she was in awe. This time, Bree entered with trepidation. She knew this would be her prison. The same stiff, grey-haired butler, Mr. Maxwell, met them at the door, greeting Edward. He said nothing to Breanna, yet his dark blue eyes narrowed on her, piercing her like daggers. *He no doubt blames me for the plane crash that killed Edward's sister, Lucinda, and burned Edward … but it was Lucinda who had the gun and fired it, bringing the plane down.* Breanna knew the truth wouldn't matter to either of these two men. Conspicuously absent were the maids, restoration workers, or any other visible employees. The building was silent and echoed the emptiness of her heart.

"This way." Edward made a half-circle motion to her. She followed behind like an obedient dog. He took her to the castle tower. Breanna had thought that when he said he would put her in the tower and keep her prisoner, he was being facetious. It didn't appear that way. The air was cooler in the tower, and Breanna shivered. Even with the draft, the damp castle smell caused her to swallow a new wave of nausea.

"When will you release Itsy?" She tried to sound braver than she felt. Speaking split her lip open, and it burned like a bee-sting.

"I thought you would like a reunion before she left. I'm sure she wants to see you," he snapped. Breanna thought it best not to provoke him further and didn't persist in her questions.

Edward walked up the uneven stone stairs that wound around the upper hall. Breanna was thankful for the railing that someone had drilled into the rocks, given the pitch and angle of the stairs. The room that he took her to was at the top of the keep. They passed floor after floor, five levels, each with a few doors leading off it. Breanna wondered what was inside these rooms and if any of them would provide a means of escape. She remembered Edward telling her and Michael the story of Aed in the hall at the bottom of the stairs. Her ominous foreboding when he told the tale of a Norman Lord attempting to kidnap the Irish maiden, Aed, and force her to wed him under Celtic law, turned out to be true. Before the plane crash, Edward told Breanna that he intended to make her marry him, even though she was not consenting. He was like the conquering nobleman in the story of Aed. Now she was in Edward's clutches again, and a sense of hopelessness gripped her heart.

Reaching the top floor, Breanna gasped when she saw four armed guards sitting outside a door. The muscular men sporting tattoos, shaved heads, and army fatigues stood at attention when they saw Edward and his prisoner. One of the guards pressed a code for the metal lock. Breanna was vibrating so badly that her teeth felt like they were chattering. It wouldn't be long before she threw up again, so she decided to hurry past the men into the room.

There was a brief hesitation until Breanna's best friend recognized the short-haired brunette. "Bree!" Itsy sprang to her feet. "Why did you come? You should've stayed away."

She flew into Breanna's arms. Then Bree held her shoulders and gazed into her eyes. "I'm here to rescue you."

Itsy drew back and asked, "What happened to your face?"

"What happened to yours?" Breanna saw that the blond woman had bruises on her face and a black eye that was starting to open.

Itsy began to cry. "They shot Michael. They hit me with one of those darts. I woke up on a plane with Edward and tried to fight. Unfortunately, that supersoldier strength was too much for me. It didn't matter; Michael was dead, and I didn't care if he killed me. Then I was stung by another dart and woke up here. That was a few days ago. They put food through the slot, but no one talks to me or tells me a thing." She broke down crying in her friend's arms. "He's dead. He's dead."

"Touching reunion," Edward cut in. "I'll leave you girls to talk."

Breanna whirled around. "No. The deal was to release Itsy."

He glared at her and hissed, "I lied. Just like you. How does it feel?" With that, he left the room. The guard slammed the steel door and locked it before Breanna could reach it.

She banged on the door and called, "Let Itsy go! You have me. You know I'll work for you. Edward!"

There was no answer and no noise from the other side of the door. Itsy pulled her away from the door. "They don't answer."

"I'm so sorry, Itsy. If it weren't for me, you wouldn't be here. I thought I could make him send you home."

"Home to what?" Itsy's voice cracked.

Breanna leaned into her friend's ear. "Bobby came home right after you were kidnapped. Michael is in intensive care in an induced coma. He's still alive." She squeezed her friend's arm and whispered, "We should be careful. This room is probably bugged."

The short woman hugged Breanna tightly. "Alive. Praise God. I prayed like I've never prayed before. Thank you, Jesus."

"Thank you, Lord," Breanna agreed. "We need to keep praying for him and believing in a miracle."

When Itsy finally let her friend go, she asked, "What happened to your face? Let me guess: Edward?"

Breanna nodded and then placed a hand over her mouth. She cried out, "Bathroom!"

Itsy dragged her friend around the corner where a toilet, sink, and open shower were squeezed into a small space. Breanna got on her knees and had dry heaves. There was nothing left in her stomach. Her friend moistened a cloth and wiped her forehead.

When Breanna stopped, Itsy asked, "Are you okay?"

Tears tumbled down her face. "I'm pregnant."

15

"OKAY, I DIDN'T expect that. Lots of other things, maybe, but … you're pregnant."

Breanna raised her shoulders.

"Why would you give yourself up if you're pregnant? Bree …." Itsy rubbed her friend's back. "I should be saying congratulations, but this is hardly the time or place."

"I didn't know I was pregnant. I thought I had the flu and that I was upset finding out Edward was alive and fighting with Joshua. It was Edward who suggested it shortly after he picked me up." Breanna began fidgeting with her short hair. "I still would offer myself for you any day. This is such a mess."

"Does Joshua know … no, of course, he doesn't. What am I thinking? He was going out of his mind looking for you. He said that you took your passport and the money, and we thought you might be headed to Toronto. Michael and I agreed to go there to see if we could find you. Joshua stayed behind in case you showed up somewhere in Israel. What were you thinking, taking off like that, and right after we saw Edward on television?"

Breanna pressed her lips together and decided not to tell Itsy about Joshua being a Mossad agent. Edward's castle was not the place to talk about it, and if she was completely honest, she didn't want Itsy to hate Joshua for deceiving all of them. Breanna held on to a sliver of hope that he really did love her, and they would reconcile, however unlikely it seemed at present.

She said, "We fought. He said that Edward probably wasn't after me, and I was being paranoid." He did say it, although he retracted it afterwards. "I told him he was stupid. Well, you know what my temper is like. I lost it, and

I wasn't thinking rationally." Breanna tried to stick close to the truth in every other aspect. "Then I took a bus to the hotel and saw you fight off an attacker, and when I went to get off the bus, I saw Michael and Joshua. I knew you'd be all right, but I didn't want to face Joshua yet. I figured you guys would be safer without me, and I went to a monastery seeking sanctuary for a few days to think about what to do. After several days, I called you to talk, and Bobby told me what happened. Then I called Edward to propose a swap, me for you."

"That guy that you saw was one of Edward's men. He was trying to kidnap me. Only he didn't expect me to have MMA combat training." Itsy stood and offered a hand to Breanna to stand. "Let's go sit in the other room. It's more comfortable than this tile floor."

Breanna grabbed her hand and followed her into the other room. It had been modernized. The walls showed some of the stone on the interior walls, but the exterior had been drywalled and, Breanna hoped, somewhat insulated. There was a stone fireplace with a gas insert. It was on, and heat emanated from that direction. Two stuffed chairs were positioned facing the fire with a small table between them. There were two single beds against one wall, complete with large duvets and fluffy pillows. The only window in the room was a narrow rectangle high up on the wall, so the women had no access to an outside view.

Beside a dresser was Itsy's silver suitcase. Breanna glanced at the door, and there was her backpack where it had been placed to the side. On another wall was a small refrigerator and microwave. Beside them was a sink with a few dishes on a shelf above. To the other side was a coffeemaker, mugs, and a shelf of snacks, easy-to-make food, and coffee. It was as if they were staying in a cozy hotel suite rather than prisoners in a castle.

Breanna said, "Two of everything. Like he never planned to release you."

Itsy said, "Just what I was thinking." She brought Breanna to the chair in front of the fireplace. She went to the fridge and returned with two bottles of water. "Edward has meals delivered, but we have some things here in the room." Itsy opened one bottle and handed it to her friend, who was paler than normal. "You don't look too good. Maybe Edward would let you see a doctor."

"It's morning sickness. How long can it last?" Breanna gave a half-hearted chuckle.

Itsy raised her voice. "Breanna needs a doctor. She needs something to stop this vomiting. Some crackers wouldn't hurt, too." Smiling at her friend, she added in a normal voice, "There, that should help." When she saw Breanna shiver, Itsy went to the bed, grabbed one of the extra blankets at the end of it, and covered her friend.

"Thanks, Itsy. I'm sorry Edward didn't release you, but since he didn't, I'm selfishly glad you're here. There is no one I'd rather be with as a prisoner."

Breanna felt overwhelmingly tired all of a sudden, and she fought to keep her eyes open.

"Ditto, sister." Itsy could see Breanna's eyes fluttering. "Why don't you go over to the bed and have a nap? I've got a few books here that Edward left for me to read. One nice thing."

Breanna wrapped the blanket around her and plodded over to the bed, which Itsy pointed to as hers. When she woke later, she could see that it was dark outside the window. Her friend sat in the chair reading.

"Hey, sorry I slept so long."

Itsy's head poked around the chair. "No problem. Some food was dropped off and this." She held up a bottle of antinausea medication. "I read the label, and it's used for morning sickness, so it's safe for use during pregnancy. You've got to be able to keep something down, or you're going to lose the baby from lack of nourishment."

Breanna dragged her feet to the chair in front of the fireplace. Itsy opened the safety seal and handed her the pill bottle. After checking the instructions, warnings, and dosage, Breanna took the medication. Within fifteen minutes, she felt ravenously hungry and ate some of the meal reheated by Itsy. When she went to wipe her mouth with the napkin, she noticed that Itsy had written on it. *The room is obviously bugged, like you thought.*

16

EDWARD DIDN'T BOTHER with the women for the next few days. Breanna suspected he was waiting for her to regain some strength after not being able to eat much for almost a week. The antinausea medication helped enormously, but she hoped she would be able to stop using it soon. She would give it a week and then begin to wean off it.

She and Itsy were quieter than normal. It was awkward knowing that everything you talked about was being monitored. If they wanted to communicate about anything private, they wrote it in brief cryptic notes. One thing they did out loud and unashamedly was pray. They prayed several times a day and reminded each other of Bible quotes. They prayed for whoever was monitoring their conversation that the Holy Spirit would minister to them.

On the evening of the third day, Itsy and Breanna were on their knees beside the bed, praying together, sometimes quietly. Itsy leaned over and whispered in Breanna's ear. "It's awful not knowing how Michael is doing. Is he alive? Do you get any answers from the Holy Spirit? Do you hear anything?"

Breanna shook her head no. She, too, was not getting any answers. She whispered to her friend, "I know how you feel. How is God going to use this situation for our good?"

They were both such new Christians that they had never faced testing of their faith. They had more questions than answers. The mood between them was sombre for the rest of that night, and they went to bed early.

On the morning of the fourth day, a note was placed on the tray of breakfast croissants and coffee. It was addressed to Breanna. *Be ready to begin work by 9 a.m. A guard will come for you.*

The women looked at each other. Breanna leaned over to her friend and whispered, "Can I ask him to have you work with me as my assistant? I can train you."

Itsy nodded. "Beats being stuck in here with nothing to do. I hope I can catch on."

Breanna winked at her. In a loud voice, she said, "Ask Edward if Itsy can come with me as my assistant. I could use her help, and I can train her. Some of the information she already knows from working in the Biomedical Department at the University of Toronto. Tell him we'll behave and not fight or try to escape."

An hour later, the metal door lock scraped opened. Two armed guards stood at the door holding handguns. The tallest one said, "Both of you. Come this way."

Itsy grabbed two water bottles from the shelf and followed Breanna and the men. They held on to the railing against the wall as they descended the stairs of the tower keep. The women were surprised to be led to a newer section of the house. Breanna remembered that she was told it had been added in the early twentieth century and updated over the years. They were escorted to the basement. The guards stopped at a metal cart outside a locked room. The ladies put on the provided lab coats, foot coverings, goggles, and gloves. Afterwards, a guard hid the keypad and pressed a code, opening an automatic door. Breanna and Itsy found themselves in a large laboratory.

Normally, Breanna would have been delighted with all the technology in the room, like a girl in a candy store. However, given the circumstances, she found the prospects of working here disagreeable. Itsy working with her was a source of pleasure and pain. Breanna was happy for her friend's company but sad that she, too, was a prisoner.

Itsy was feeling bad for Breanna. Here she was, pregnant with Joshua's baby and unable to tell him or be with him. Her friend revealed to her in a note that Edward intended to remove Breanna's baby from her care after he or she was born and then force Breanna to be with him. Itsy also felt sorry for herself. Would she ever see Michael again? What if Edward decided she was expendable? Itsy was under no illusions that Edward wouldn't think twice about killing her if it suited him. But there was no point in dwelling on that prospect. She needed to be brave for her friend. *Even though I don't hear from you, Lord, I know you're there and we are in your hands.*

Breanna told Itsy to follow her. She introduced her friend to the equipment, explaining what each unit were for and how to use them. Itsy was familiar with all the basic information about nanotechnology and understood everything Breanna was telling her. Breanna explained what she would need from her in terms of support. Itsy caught on quickly, and they were able to move to the work that was saved on the computers. It appeared to be everything Edward's people had put together up to that point without Breanna or Lucinda's input.

Reviewing some of the nano programming, Breanna said, "They're further along than I thought they would be."

Itsy nodded. "I suppose that's a good thing." She was able to help her friend with the basic technician's role. "Do you want me to print some of this for you to review? I found what appears to be important documents."

"Hmmm ... yes." Breanna clicked her nails on the keyboard as her mind began to process the data. When she analyzed what Itsy handed her, Breanna raised her brows. "This is perfect. You picked it up so fast. Some master's-level university students have trouble with this. I told you before, you're smarter than you pretend."

"Well, in all fairness, I do have a bachelor's degree in computer science, and I have a friend who has a doctorate in medical bioengineering. I work in that department office, and I have a brother who is always talking about his medical courses. It's not like I haven't heard about this stuff for years and years and years ..." Itsy droned on, emphasizing her vicarious indoctrination into the field.

The women giggled, and the sound echoed in the empty lab. This was the first time they had laughed since coming to the castle. It felt comforting yet sad at the same time. They stood staring at each other, knowing what was on both of their minds.

Bree broke the silence first. "All right then. Let's get to work, Itsy. We've got a lot of ground to cover. We've got to evaluate everything done up to this point. Then I'll know where I need to fill in the gaps and where I'll need to come up with new ideas. After we've gone as far as we can here, I'll see if there's anything new on Joshua's and my copied work from the university. The University of Toronto gave us access to Professor Steinberg—" She stopped and remembered that Itsy had worked with the professor also. "John's and my work for healing nanobots, but I was trying to remember how I got them to work so fast, like I had for the supersoldier bots. I will need to get a sample of the nanos inside Edward to test. There's so much work to do. It will take months, maybe longer."

In her quirky manner, Itsy pointed a finger at Breanna and said, "Well, it won't get done by talking about it. Let's giddy-up and go."

17

EVERY DAY FOR three months, Itsy and Breanna were escorted to the lab to work for eight to ten hours. Food, water, herbal tea, and coffee were left in the adjoining break room for them so they wouldn't contaminate the lab or nanobots. They saw only their guards. It was as if the house were deserted except for them and their armed escorts. They were usually so tired at night that they said prayers and fell asleep immediately afterwards. Other than praying for their loved ones, they refrained from talking about their husbands or the outside world because they would get depressed. It was better to keep the talk to work and occasional silliness to lighten the mood.

One evening, as Breanna was changing for bed, Itsy pointed at her. "Look at your belly. You're starting to show. Do you feel any movement yet?"

Her friend placed a hand on the little bump and rubbed. "I think I felt a fluttering a couple of times, but I didn't know if it was gas or the baby."

"Ha-ha. Wait until I tell your baby someday. Your mama thought you were gas."

Breanna almost laughed but caught herself.

"Oh, I'm sorry, Bree. I wasn't thinking." Itsy put her arm around her friend. She whispered, "God will work it all out. Don't lose hope."

Breanna tipped her head to the side.

Itsy noticed her friend's hair was its normal red colour and it was already touching her shoulders. "I'm surprised how fast your hair grew back. It took me six months to get mine an inch or two below my shoulders."

Breanna said, "Remember the movie *Little Women* when the one sister cut her hair, the other sister said ..." Itsy and Breanna finished the sentence at the same time. "Your one beauty." They both snickered.

"Don't worry, Bree, you have more than hair as your true beauty." Itsy laughed some more, and it felt good.

"Thanks, and same to you. I like your hair both ways, short and long."

"Michael asked if I would grow it out because he liked long hair on women. He would love me either way, but I figured why not keep my husband happy?" Her voice trailed off at the end.

Breanna repeated what Itsy had said to her. "Have faith in God. Don't lose hope."

The next morning, the guards took Itsy and Breanna to the lab like every day. At the door, one guard told Breanna not to put on the lab coat but to follow him. Itsy was told to go to work, and Breanna would join her later. The women sensed there was no use arguing about it, so they separated. Breanna glanced behind to see the guard lock her friend in the lab and station himself on a stool outside the door. Breanna was escorted upstairs into the library, where she and Michael had first met a charming Edward Connor.

She was instructed to sit in the same seating area as on the first day. The leather crunched softly as she lowered herself onto a chair. Breanna closed her eyes, remembering how enchanted she was with Edward. She knew now that he could wield some kind of supernatural power over people who were not Christians. It no longer worked on her since she accepted Jesus as her saviour. The spell had been broken.

Edward's voice behind her made her jolt in her seat. "How is your work going, Breanna?"

Attempting to get her breathing and heart in check, she stuttered, "F–fine."

He leaned over her and kissed the top of her head. Breanna forced herself not to bolt. As he came around to face her, it took a second to remember this version of Edward. Her mind thought of him as he was before the nanobots morphed him into this hulk of a man.

He sat beside her and ran his hand through her locks. "I like your hair like this. I'm glad it's growing back." He smiled at her, but she remained stoic. "You really do glow in your face. I think pregnancy agrees with you." He looked down at her baby bump and frowned but caught himself quickly. Smiling again, he said, "Don't worry, we will have plenty of babies."

A cold hand gripped her heart. This was nothing like the talk about having children with Joshua. This was creepy, and she sensed the evil coming off this man. *Lord, how am I going to endure this? I've got to be careful so he doesn't kill my baby or my friend. Help me, Jesus.*

Edward jumped up and changed seats to sit opposite her. Breanna wondered if it was because of her prayer. *Thank you, Lord.*

"We have much to discuss, you and me. I will have a doctor remove some of the nanobots in my system so that you can work with them. We will need them replicated, as you know. How is the programming coming?"

She remained professional and reported, "I've made some gains. Luckily, I have my copied files from the university, and I have the other Dr. Abrams's work, as well. I haven't looked at them yet, but when I finish with what your scientists and programmers have come up with so far, I'll move on to them."

Edward's brows knitted together at the mention of Breanna's husband. Then he relaxed his face. "Why did you leave your husband? Was he not what you were expecting? A disappointment." Edward sounded smug. It was as if he hoped to hurt Breanna with his words, and it took all her effort not to show him it was working. When she didn't answer him, Edward continued, "I know you left him. My sources tell me you discovered a secret about him. He used you and lied to you to recreate the enhanced soldier program."

She gasped. *How could he know? I didn't tell anyone, not even Itsy. Is he testing me? Does he want me to expose Joshua? Say nothing. Don't respond.*

"Come, come, now. We will be united as one soon enough. There's no need for secrets between us."

At the words *united as one*, Breanna jumped up from the chair and moved over to the shelves to her right. She gripped the shelf and leaned into it. It was the same thing Joshua told her. *Why do these men get to play with my heart? They say things they don't mean. They say things that hurt.* She was angry with Edward, but it also brought up her anger with Joshua.

"I see that I struck a nerve. Maybe I should tell you what I know. Come over here, Breanna." It was an order.

Breanna took a few deep breaths and then returned to her seat. She gripped the bottom and forced herself not to rock.

"You discovered he was a Mossad agent. A spy. He lied to you. All that time, he lied to you. What kind of man marries a woman under pretenses? He pretended to love you to get what his country wanted from you."

It felt like he stabbed her heart when he voiced her concerns about Joshua. She fought the tears as Edward's words ripped apart the fabric of her marriage. The emptiness of her life was laid bare once more. She went from having a family to not having a family again. This theme was destined to replay itself over and over in her life. Her parents, John Steinberg, and now Joshua.

Edward could see the effects of his words. He continued his onslaught in an attempt to crumble all her defences. Only then could he build it back up with him at the centre. "I'm sorry that he hurt you like that, but it was his job. Joshua Abrams is a Mossad spy. They're trained to be the best of the best. Few are able to escape their traps once they're laid. Mossad teaches them to be masters of disguise. They can infiltrate anywhere. You are not the first victim of the romance scheme. Several of their spies were married to their mark for many years and had children also." He looked at her pregnant belly. "Yes, like this one. He would have you hooked with professions of love and having children. One after another, so long as it kept you working for their government and blind to his true purposes. Perhaps he goes off for days at a time for other trysts with lovers, saying they are business trips."

Tears burned trails down her face as she remembered the business trips he took once a month or so, speaking engagements for the university, he claimed. When she found out he was a Mossad agent, she thought it was spy work. Now a seed was planted that maybe they were not either. Then there was the week she couldn't reach him when she returned to Toronto. Was he with a woman at that time? Another lover?

Satisfied with the damage he inflicted, Edward decided it was best to let these suggestions fester in her brain. He would pick the scab off the wound once in a while to keep her off balance. He was certain that in the end, he would destroy any love she had for Joshua Abrams.

"I'm sorry to hurt you. At least I can say that I was always honest. I told you I wanted you to work on my enhanced soldiers and my medical nanotechnologies. I was honest with you when I said I wanted to marry you. Maybe it was not the way you desired, but at least I was truthful."

Edward gave her a box of tissues and left her in the library to gather herself before being escorted to the basement.

Once inside the locked lab, Itsy asked, "What was that about?"

Breanna couldn't bring herself to talk about it. She had just managed to pull herself together. "I met with Edward. He is going to have a doctor extract the nanobots from his body so we can work with them."

"All of them?"

"No. There would be too many, and he wouldn't want them gone. He needs them for self-regeneration. We will get a few."

"He could have you do it."

"He'd never trust me."

Itsy leaned over and whispered, "Good call."

Breanna wondered. *Edward was right about one thing. He never lied to me about wanting to marry me or wanting me to work for him.*

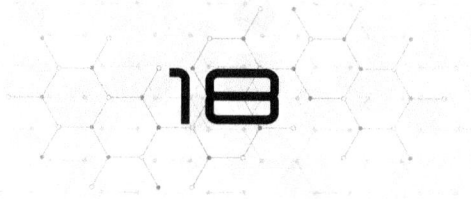

"BREE, WAKE UP," Joshua said softly. Breanna opened her eyes, and he was lying beside her. They were in the apartment in Tel Aviv.

"Where are we?"

He laughed, "Where do you think? We're at home. Were you dreaming again?"

She stretched out on the bed. "It was a real crazy one this time."

He raised an eyebrow, "Edward?"

"Yes." She remembered the baby and felt her stomach. It was flat. Disappointment flooded her heart. "I was pregnant."

"With his baby?"

"No. Silly. With yours. But Edward held me prisoner … and Itsy." She sat up in bed. "It seemed so real." She twisted to face him. "You were working for Mossad. Your marriage to me, our jobs, all of it was part of an elaborate spy game to get me to build supersoldiers for Israel." She snickered. "Silly, right?"

Joshua didn't laugh. He betrayed no emotion behind the dark eyes.

"Tell me it's not true, Joshua." She rolled onto her knees and faced him fully. "Tell me that I'm wrong."

"Bravo, Breanna. You really are brilliant. You figured it out," he snapped. She shook her head in disbelief. "It couldn't all have been a lie."

He sat on the edge of the bed. "Israel needs to be able to defend itself. You know that. You know she is threatened at every border."

The heat hit her head, and she allowed the flames full rein. She snapped, "I'm not talking about Israel right now. The two of us are what I care about. Whatever happened to *We are now one under God?*"

"We are legally married, so it's true." Joshua sounded dispassionate, like the marriage was a business transaction. "When you finish the soldier program, we can divorce. We'll be free."

Breanna felt as if he'd punched her in the stomach. She gasped for air and doubled over. When she was finally able to talk again, she barely whispered, "You mean, you'll be free."

Joshua reached out and patted her arm. "It doesn't mean we can't have some fun while we're together. Besides, if you want, you can date other men. I certainly have not stopped seeing other women. In fact, there is one really hot lady I'm seeing now."

Without thinking about it, she began to slap him repeatedly as she screamed, "Liar! Liar!"

"Bree." She felt someone shaking her. "Bree, wake up. You're dreaming."

Breanna slowly grew conscious that it was Itsy's voice. She opened her eyes and was surprised to find that her cheeks were wet. The light between the beds was turned on, and her friend sat beside her.

"You were dreaming," Itsy reassured her. "You were crying and calling out, 'liar.'"

She propped herself up on her elbows. "I'm sorry I woke you."

"You want to tell me what your nightmare was about?"

"I don't remember," she lied.

Itsy was hurt. She knew her friend wasn't telling her the truth. Without another word, she returned to her bed, lay down, and pulled the covers up. "Okay then. Goodnight."

The redhead stared at the back of Itsy's head, aware that she was angry. But Breanna felt she didn't have the emotional reserves to tell her best friend anything. Breanna still hung on to a thread of hope, even if it was tenuous right now.

Tears dripped over the bridge of Itsy's nose and onto the pillow. She worked hard to conceal the fact that she was crying. *Where are you, God? I'm worried about my friend. I'm worried about my husband. What's going on with Edward? Is he going to kill me? Talk to me, please. I don't hear you, and right now, I don't even feel you. Without Breanna to talk to, it's like I'm living in my private hell.*

Lying back down, Breanna pulled the covers up to her neck. She pressed her hand to her stomach and rubbed the growing baby inside her. *One good thing. This baby is a gift from God. Will Edward allow me to keep my baby? He says I have to give it up when the baby is born, but maybe I can convince him to let me keep it. He plans for me to have lots of his children, so what's one more? If I play along and I'm nice … maybe. I want to keep my baby, Lord.* Breanna quieted her thoughts. There was nothing but silence. *Lord, are you there? I don't hear anything from you. I don't feel your Holy Spirit. Are you even real, or did I imagine you? Talk to me, Jesus.* She waited in the stillness until she fell asleep.

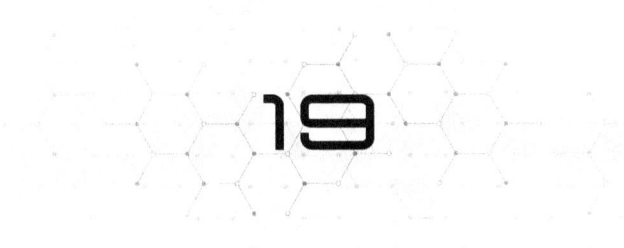

THROUGHOUT AUGUST AND into September, Breanna was escorted to Edward's dining room for dinner every night after work. Itsy ate in her room alone. Each day, Itsy watched her friend withdraw further and further from her. Working in the lab was torture, with Breanna focusing solely on work and limiting the conversation to nanotechnology.

Itsy couldn't get Breanna to reveal what she and Edward discussed during those meals; each day, Bree would say only that the conversation was about how their research was progressing. Itsy knew her friend well enough to know she was withholding from her. The blond woman was sinking into a depression, as it seemed her friendship was slipping away. To make matters worse, she didn't know if her husband was dead or alive. There was also the worry that Bobby might neglect his medical studies to go searching for her. Always on her mind was the possibility that Edward might retaliate against her or others she loved if she said or did something wrong. She needed her best friend, who was increasingly emotionally absent.

Several times, she attempted to have Breanna pray about what was bothering her, but Breanna kept her prayers short, saying she was tired because of the pregnancy. Itsy could surmise only one conclusion from the change in her friend: Edward was playing mind games with her emotions.

One day, Itsy dropped a vial in the lab, and when the glass shattered, the contents scattered across the floor.

"Be careful," Breanna barked.

Itsy banged the vial holder on the counter. "That's it. I've had it," she bit back. "This is total crap. I don't care if you're pregnant. I'm tired of tiptoeing around so I don't upset you."

Breanna whirled around on the stool, belly bulging against the lab coat, pushing the buttons to their limit. Her eyes flashed at her friend. "Tiptoeing around me? You sulk around here every day, licking your wounds like you're the only one hurting."

The blond woman's eyes went wide, and she put her fingers to her mouth as if she was trying to prevent what might come out. "Enough! No more blaming me for coming here. Brave Breanna rescued her friend." She stomped across the floor to stand in front of the scientist, her voice raised. "Edward is the bad guy. He's the one to blame for all of this. I don't know what lies he tells you every night when you eat supper with him. But he's doing this to you, not me … not Joshua. Him!"

"You don't know anything. Don't talk to me about Joshua. He lied to me about everything."

Itsy shook her head. "Is that what Edward tells you? It's not true, Bree. Joshua loves you."

Tears began to flow over Breanna's freckles. "No, he doesn't. It was all part of his spying job for Mossad."

Itsy was incredulous. "Don't believe Edward. He wants you to stop loving your husband." She wrapped her arm around Breanna's shoulders.

"Joshua told me."

"What?"

Breanna reached for a tissue from the box on the desk. "The day I ran off. I followed him to Mossad headquarters. When I confronted him, he admitted it all. He was a spy. The whole time I've known him, he was a spy. Mossad needed me to recreate the enhanced soldier program; hence our jobs at the Tel Aviv University. It was Joshua who lied to me. In fact, he spied on all the watcher cells."

The shorter woman was having a difficult time processing this information.

"He asked me to keep it a secret so that I wouldn't put him in danger. That's why I didn't tell you. Plus, we know we are being listened to all the time. But Edward knows. His spies found out everything, so it doesn't matter anymore. I'm sorry, Itsy, that I didn't tell you even after I learned Edward knew. I couldn't bring myself to say it out loud. My marriage was a lie. It was all part of his assignment.

Itsy put a hand on each of Breanna's shoulders and held her at arm's length. "You listen to me, Breanna Abrams. I saw the way the man looked at you. I saw how worried he was when you went missing. He loves you. He's not that good of an actor; no one is."

"I hoped … but sometimes he goes away for a few days at a time. I think he has a girlfriend." Tears dripped off Bree's chin and landed on her lab coat.

"Business meetings, whether for Mossad or the university. You will never convince me that he would be with anyone but you. I'd have to see it with my own eyes to believe it."

Breanna leaned over her belly to hug her best friend. "You're so loyal to me. You're the only one I can trust."

"Did Joshua admit he was seeing anyone else? Did he say that he didn't love you?"

"No, of course not. He wouldn't, not when he wanted me to work on the program."

"Did he tell you he loved you?"

"Yes. But what was he supposed to say?"

"Maybe you should give your husband the benefit of the doubt."

Breanna closed her eyes. She was so confused and conflicted.

Itsy moved close to Breanna's ear. "Don't trust Edward. Don't listen to him. Remember he murdered John Steinberg and the two other professors, Peter whatshisname from Cornell University, and Dr. Landry."

The two women hugged for a bit longer, both happy that they were together. That night, when Breanna returned from her dinner with Edward, she was open with Itsy and talked to her about what had been discussed. It became clear to Itsy that she had been right about Edward making things worse for Breanna.

Breanna rubbed her belly as she sat in the chair in front of the fire, which counteracted the dampness from the rain outside. "One good thing happened tonight. Edward told me he would take me to see an obstetrician. I can make sure my baby is doing well." The baby kicked under her hand. "Oh my. Itsy, feel here quick." Breanna lifted her shirt.

Itsy placed her hand on Breanna's bare skin. They both watched as her stomach rippled with the fetus moving. Itsy put her mouth beside the baby bump, "Hey, little one. It's your Aunt Itsy. I'm going to talk to you all the time, so you recognize my voice." A smile spread across her face. "I read once that babies can hear in the womb. It is one of the earliest developments. Talk to your baby."

Breanna felt a little silly but said, "Hi, sweetheart. It's your mama." She rubbed her stomach. "I'm going to try to do everything I can for you."

Itsy went back to what they were discussing before the baby kicked. "So he's going to let you see a doctor? Where?"

Breanna said, "I think it'll be in Cork. But I had to agree to pretend that Edward was the father. I hope it means I'll be able to keep the baby. There's one other thing. Any mention of being a prisoner, and I'll never see the doctor again … and ..."

"And?"

"He'll punish you."

20

TRUE TO HIS word, Edward took Breanna to Cork three days later. It was the second week in September, and the day was sunny and hot for Ireland. With Edward's permission, she opened her car window and leaned against the side, feeling the wind on her face. She inhaled deeply and smelled the county scents of the season. Her awareness of the sights became sharpened. The countryside shimmered, with colours appearing brighter as they travelled past emerald pastures, livestock, hedges, hills, settlements, and towns. Breanna thought about how much she had always taken her freedom for granted. She could go anywhere, anytime. Now everything she did was by Edward's leave. She breathed in again. *Enjoy the present. There might not be a tomorrow.*

When the driver parked the limo, Edward grabbed Breanna's hand and helped her exit. "We will go shopping first. You need maternity clothes that fit properly."

He held her hand gently as if they were a couple on a leisurely day out on the town. He gazed lovingly at her and began chatting about the history of Cork like a tour guide. When he pointed to the landmarks they passed, she followed the direction of his finger and listened attentively. Breanna found herself absorbing everything. The whole experience was surreal. Instead of a maternity shop, Edward held open the glass door of a jewelry store. Her brows rose, but she didn't utter a word. He put an arm around her shoulder in a possessive manner and led her to the display of engagement and wedding rings.

Breanna had removed the rings from Joshua, but she wore them on her cross necklace around her neck. Edward had ordered her to take them off several weeks prior. He said they were a reminder of the betrayal she experienced and the one who had been disloyal to her.

The owner of the store, a short, heavyset, middle-aged man, met with them and took them to a private viewing area in the back. Breanna thought he looked like a leprechaun and suppressed a disbelieving laugh at the absurdity of the situation. It turned out that Edward had made an appointment, and a velvet-lined tray with a variety of gold rings was already laid out for them. Breanna felt disdain that all had exceptionally large diamonds in their settings. The way the two men spoke, Breanna realized these were prechosen by Edward. Her heart fluttered in her chest like a captive bird. There was nowhere to run, nothing she could say, and no help for her.

When Edward asked for a minute, the jeweller left the two of them with the engagement rings. Edward whispered to her, "Don't look so shell-shocked. Smile. This is a happy occasion. We must be engaged if you are having my baby. That is what I told the doctor. Your pregnancy dates from the day I picked you up outside Jerusalem, April 25. That's the official version. The paparazzi and news will run with that story." He placed his index finger under her chin and brought his face close to her. "That's the story, right, Breanna? You know the consequences otherwise."

She mutedly nodded her head. Edward removed his hand from her face as the jeweller returned.

"I think this one." The billionaire pointed to a large rock that Breanna thought too gaudy for her tastes, but she knew none of this was for her.

The chubby little man appeared thrilled. She wondered if it was because of the price tag. Edward picked it up and held his hand out for Breanna's. She placed her hand in his like she was about to have it cut off for stealing. Her new fiancé placed the ring on her finger.

I shouldn't be surprised it fits. No doubt he found a way to measure my finger or find out the size of my other rings. She plastered on a fake smile. *For Itsy and my baby.* "It's beautiful, Edward. I love it." She flexed her fingers, staring at the ring.

Edward placed a hand on her face and lifted it to kiss her on the lips. She closed her eyes and willed herself not to recoil.

When they were through with the first purchase, Edward took her down the street to a maternity shop. They stayed another couple of hours in the store buying clothes suitable for her entire pregnancy. Breanna was tired and hungry when they departed. She wore a new, better-fitting outfit. One of the two bodyguards who accompanied them on the shopping spree took the remainder of the bags back to the car.

Breanna became aware of people taking their photos from across the street. *The paparazzi. Did I imagine one with black hair and dark eyes?* She scanned the area again, but the man she was hoping to see was nowhere to be seen.

Edward led her into a restaurant, where they were ushered to a window seat. *Why here in full view? Did he want the photographers to take pictures? The world will see. Joshua will see.* The large muscular man she sat with reached for her hand and admired the ring on her finger. As he leaned across the small table, he brought her hand to his mouth and kissed it slowly, never taking his eyes off her. Breanna couldn't do anything but stare at him. She willed herself to smile again. *He wants Joshua to see this. Maybe it won't matter to Joshua anyway. It might only be my heart that's broken. I can't torture myself. This is my life now, especially if I want my baby to live with me.*

Everything Edward ordered was delicious, and she was ravenous. He was animated as he chatted about events in the world. His ability as a storyteller had not diminished since becoming a muscle-bound man. He told her about current events in the world. Many storms and natural disasters continued to kill millions. Several countries were experiencing wars. People were tired of so much death and destruction. As Edward spoke, Breanna wondered if this was his reasoning for a one-world government, although he never came out and said he wanted to be the supreme dictator. When she couldn't eat another bite, she leaned back in her seat.

"You don't eat as much as you used to." Edward's eyebrows furrowed. "Are you well? It's been a while since you needed your morning sickness medication."

She waved a hand in protest. "I'm fine. The baby is taking up a lot of room; there is only so much I can eat at one time."

Satisfied with her answer, he finished his meal before they went to visit the obstetrician.

The doctor was a woman who might be in her early fifties. She was tall and willowy, with salt-and-pepper hair and a pleasant manner. Breanna was happy Edward chose her.

"I see by the date you listed that you're shy of five months along. You should have seen a doctor before this. It's best to start maternity care immediately upon discovering you're pregnant."

Edward spoke up. "As I told you, my fiancée was adamant she didn't want to see a doctor. I have been nagging her all along, but trauma regarding her parents' death made her reluctant. But we are here now, right, dear?" He raised one eyebrow at Breanna.

"Ah … yes." She was caught off guard. Turning to the obstetrician, Breanna added, "Sorry, but I'm ready now."

"Well, I'm glad you came. Can you take off your clothes and put this on? I'll be back in a couple of minutes to examine you." The doctor held out the hospital gown, and Edward removed it from her hands. He placed it on the examination table for Breanna. The doctor left the room.

Breanna stood awkwardly, staring at Edward. He said, "Come now. Do you need help?"

"No. I need privacy. I'm not going to change while you're in the room." She took a step backwards.

Edward leaned in. "You think I'd leave you alone for a minute. I know your treachery, remember."

She shook her head no. "I will not take off my clothes with you watching me."

"Eventually you will, fiancée." He emphasized the last word. With a sigh, he said, "I will turn around." He faced the wall.

With no other option, Breanna removed her clothes but put the gown on to cover herself as quickly as possible. The man did not attempt to steal a glance as she finished and lay down on the table.

Edward stood near her head to watch. Breanna kept the gown in position to cover her breasts, and the sheet covered her bottom. Only her belly was exposed to the doctor, but she was still embarrassed by Edward's presence.

The doctor measured her stomach. "You're a little on the large size, but not too bad. It might be a big baby. Everything else appears to be fine. Let's order an ultrasound for next week."

ON THE WAY back to the castle, Breanna fought sleep. It had been a long and emotional day. Edward, true to his word, had allowed her to see a doctor, even if he never left her side for a moment. She tried the wind on her face from the outside world, but even that didn't succeed in keeping her awake.

"We're here." She felt a slight shaking of her shoulder.

It took her a moment to get her bearings. Edward was beside her in the back seat of the car. The car door was open, and a bodyguard stood beside it. Breanna reluctantly moved. She entered Edward's home, past armed guards who didn't look in her direction.

"Go to your room, and take the rest of the day off. Tomorrow you can work again." Edward left her in the care of two guards who escorted her to the top of the keep, one of them carrying her shopping bags.

When the metal door closed, Breanna headed to the washroom. Coming out, she noticed Itsy on her bed. Rushing over, she knelt beside her friend. Itsy had a large, nasty gash across her right cheek, a black left eye with some blood trickling at the edge. Her lip was split and swollen. There was a damp and bloodstained cloth on the table beside the bed.

"I'll get some ice. I'll be right back," Breanna told her friend. She went to the fridge, placed some ice inside a cloth, and returned to Itsy.

When the ice touched her eye, the blond woman flinched.

"What happened?" Bree asked.

Itsy's turn of her head was almost indiscernible. "No more talk about Edward. I've been warned."

Breanna felt heat rise to her face. She wanted to unleash on Edward. He'd obviously ordered this beating because of what Itsy had said to Breanna about trusting their captor. There was nothing she could say that wouldn't make the situation worse, especially for her best friend. Instead, she nursed the injuries as best she could with ice, cloths, and cold water.

That evening, the two women didn't talk. Breanna, because of the emotional insanity of the day, went from experiencing kindness to suspicion and terror for her friend Itsy—for fear of another thrashing or worse.

As Itsy closed her eyes, she shuddered as the trauma replayed in her head. After Breanna had been whisked away for a day at the doctor, the door opened again, and Itsy thought she was to be escorted to the lab to work. Instead, four guards entered the room. She knew they weren't there to talk. Fear fuelled her reflexes. While she hadn't worked out as frequently as before being kidnapped, she tried to do some of her martial arts training in the early morning or late at night.

Itsy went on offense. She roundhouse kicked one guard and jumped onto the shoulders of another and hit him in the head. Before she could make another move, something hard hit her on her back, and she fell to the ground. Before she could jump up, she felt the metal tip of a boot slam into her stomach. Then another. Two of the men grabbed her arms and dragged her to her feet while she gasped for air. She felt a backhand across her face, and a ring on the man's hand ripped her cheek open.

That man growled, "No more talking about Mr. Connor. Keep his name from your lips, or next time you won't be so lucky. Mr. Connor wants you to know, it's not only your life you risk but also Breanna and her baby and your family. He has a long reach."

After he said that, two punches landed on her face, first her left eye, then the left side of her mouth. She felt a tooth as it dislodged, and she spit it out. One of the men grabbed a handful of her hair and banged her head against the wall. Itsy woke up on the floor sometime later, head pounding, ribs aching, and barely able to crawl to the bathroom. She wet a cloth, then lay on the floor and lost consciousness again.

Itsy came to before Breanna came home. Finding herself crumpled on the cold tiles, she managed to crawl to her bed, her whole body screaming all the way. Now that Breanna was here, Itsy felt a small sense of security. Her friend would look after her.

Breanna moved the small table between their beds out of the way. Then she dragged her bed over beside her friend's. They lay in the dark holding hands.

A scraping sound let them know a tray of food had been pushed through the slot on the bottom of the metal door.

Breanna patted Itsy's hand and got up to see what was offered. She switched on the lamp, still perched on the bedside table, and retrieved the evening meal. There was a meal supplement drink with a straw. *Generous of Edward to provide this for Itsy after ensuring she could barely open her mouth.* Even though she would rather throw it into Edward's face, Breanna held the straw for her friend and encouraged her to drink. Tears dripped down Itsy's face, but she tried her best to slurp the liquid up the straw with her swollen mouth. When she was finished, Breanna ate a little, not for herself but for her baby.

Lord, forgive me for plotting revenge on Edward. I am trying not to hate the man. He's made in your image ... with a little enhancement. Somehow, I will thwart his plans. I don't know how, but I'll figure it out. Breanna started going through different ways to sabotage the work that would keep the two women and the baby safe.

———————

Itsy knew her friend's mind and that she would be planning some kind of retaliation, and she was afraid for them both. When they retired for the night, Breanna said the prayers.

Moving as close as she could to Breanna's ear, Itsy said quietly, "Don't do it."

Breanna moved her mouth to her friend's ear. "Shhh! Don't worry. I'll play his game. We have no choice." *For now. I will protect you, Itsy.*

22

THE NEXT DAY, Breanna refused to go to work so she could care for Itsy. Edward didn't communicate with them, but didn't force her to leave her friend. Breanna knew Itsy had a concussion and most likely one or more cracked ribs. Calling out in the room, she asked for a doctor, but none was sent. With ice and vigilance, she treated Itsy as best she knew how. *This is my sister, Jesus. Please help her.* Neither mentioned Edward or the ruthless beating for fear of further retaliation for Itsy. Breanna asked to stay with Itsy the following day, but this time the guards insisted she follow them to the lab—Mr. Connor's orders. Itsy assured her friend that she was feeling better, although her head pounded, and it hurt to breathe.

"My beautiful teeth are broken. No more nice smile to attract the men." Itsy tried to joke, although she was really upset about losing one tooth completely and having another one on top chipped slightly. *In the big scheme of things, I'm happy to be alive.*

Breanna tried to play along and feigned a look of horror. "Your one true beauty."

That did cause Itsy to laugh and then wince as her lip split again. Breanna handed her the cold, wet cloth.

The next four days, Breanna worked in the lab on her own. Edward didn't summon her for meals. Perhaps he knew she would unleash her anger on him. *He's a brute and a monster. Beating innocent women, threatening unborn babies, murdering people who stand in his way ....*

Pouring herself into the work took her mind off her worry for Itsy. After completing the work on what Edward's employees had already accomplished, she pulled out her memory stick from Tel Aviv University. It included the work she and Professor Steinberg had completed before his death. She had also managed to remember some of the program she had written for Edward in the Chinese plant, so she was able to copy that over to the mainframe. She took Itsy's laptop and her tablet and copied the work over.

As usual, she lost herself in the work with nanotechnology. Edward had provided vials of the microscopic nanobots manufactured elsewhere. He said he would later provide her with the micro-robots from his body so she could examine the programming for the supersoldier. First, she needed to reinvent her program.

The time flew by as she tried different options and codes. It would've been easier with Itsy's help, but she was in no shape to leave the bedroom. Breanna tried to do the work of two.

On the fifth day, Breanna inserted Joshua's memory stick into the computer. Her mouth dropped open. She stared at the screen and typed in a few commands. Breanna read the program. Page after page, she scrolled through his work. This was not the information she had seen at the university when they worked together, yet she believed this was the stick from their hurried copying job.

She replayed the scenes in her mind, and it hit her. The stick she had given him at the university was blue. This one was red. Where did this one come from then? She had grabbed it out of his briefcase when she was escaping. Did she take the wrong one? When he was away at conferences or speaking engagements, was this what he was working on?

Breanna copied the data to her tablet but not to the mainframe. This might come in handy later. For now, she would say nothing to Edward. She would work on it privately and not involve her friend either.

The rest of the day, Breanna worked on the information she had from her work combined with that of the other biomedical engineers.

That evening, Breanna found Itsy healed enough to eat a normal meal. She took small mouthfuls and chewed carefully not to reopen the cut on her lip. The bruises were turning green and yellow, but her eye was opened, although still swollen underneath.

"Do you think you'll be well enough to join me in the lab soon?"

"I think I should come tomorrow. I'm bored here, locked up all day. Do you think Edward will allow me to go?"

Breanna waved around the room, knowing their conversation was relayed to their kidnapper. "I guess we'll find out tomorrow when the guards come."

Itsy asked, "Anything new happening in the lab?"

Nodding, her redheaded friend said, "I've added my research from TAU. I'm getting close to replicating my part of the enhanced soldier program ... the rapid healing of injuries."

The blonde chuckled sardonically, "Any chance it would work on my body right now? My head is killing me."

Breanna's lips went flat, and her eyes looked pained. "Not yet. I'm sorry."

"No worries. I know you'd help me if you could."

Guilt washed over Breanna. She was miserable that her best friend was suffering because of her work, and she was unable to do anything about it. *Soon Itsy. Sooner than you think.*

After their evening prayers, Breanna had trouble going to sleep. She wondered about what she had discovered in the lab that day. He had accessed her work and gone further. *Joshua, how did you recreate my program? The night of the raid in China ... did you somehow access most of the soldier program? How else could you be so far ahead of me? So close.* Then she became agitated as she thought about it. *Another lie. Why? For Mossad, of course. Did you know I would disapprove? Did you think I would sabotage the work? Maybe I would have, but now I can't. I've got to continue.* She closed her eyes and remembered Jesus. *God, help me forgive Joshua as well as Edward.*

23

MARCH 2030

JOSHUA CAME UP behind Breanna in the lab at the university. Putting his hand on her back, he said, "How is my lovely wife doing with her programming?"

She twisted into his arms and kissed him. "It's coming along." He kissed her back. Breanna returned to her computer work.

He hesitated for a moment, then he said, "I've got to go again. I'm sorry, but the university wants me to go to Paris for another conference."

Heat rushed to her cheeks as she whirled around. "Why you? It's always you. It seems like once a month you're running off somewhere." He brushed her hair off the side of her neck and kissed it. Goose bumps rose on her arm, and a shiver ran down her back. "Tell them to send someone else. We're still newlyweds, for pity's sake."

His hands circled her waist. "It's such a good opportunity. It will help me get tenure. Then we can stay here permanently." He spoke softly in her ear. "I'll make it up to you, I promise. You can spend some time with my sisters. You enjoy shopping with them."

"I love them, but they're not you. I don't sleep very well when you're gone." She decided to try her most seductive tactics and kissed his ear.

Joshua laughed and held her. "We can continue this at home, and you can try your best to convince me. I'll be a willing victim."

"Humph. Later. I have to finish here. Besides, you have no intention of letting me talk you out of this. We've only been married for five months, but I know better." Breanna turned back to her work, trying her best to ignore him. She was still angry.

"Okay. I have some more work to do and a class in an hour. I should be finished by five. We can take this up again then." She shrugged. He knew she was upset. "Bree." She kept her back to him while she pretended to work. "Come on, Bree."

She huffed again, frustrated by his constant trips. Minutes later, their department head confirmed to her that Joshua was the only one suitable for the job. Breanna didn't understand that because they were not senior professors, but he was their supervisor, and their employment rested on his shoulders. "Fine. I'll see you later." She waved him away. Breanna knew she needed a little time to cool down.

Joshua tried a peace offering. "How about I take you out for dinner? We can talk about anything you want … nanotechnology … our friends and family … completely up to you."

"Maybe we should talk about moving back to Toronto if we can get jobs at the U of T. They won't send you all over the world to conferences. They only send tenured professors."

He was silent.

"Don't want to talk about that?" She was still snippy.

"Why don't we talk about it later? This is not the place to discuss it." He made a beeline for the door.

Breanna said curtly, "Go ahead, run away. You're right. I'm not good company right now." As soon as he left the lab, she was sorry for being so rude to him.

Why, Lord? Why do they keep sending him away? He's gone three or four days a month, then when he's here, he runs off to help his family or friends. Someone always needs him, but I need him too. Am I being too needy, too clingy? I don't want to be that kind of person. Maybe it's because I've lost my family and I'm so far away from my friends. Help me, Jesus. Help me be better.

That night at dinner, Breanna made an extra effort to be nice. She didn't mention his leaving, and he didn't talk about it further. They spoke about work, family, friends, and world affairs, anything to keep from fighting. Joshua was attentive and romantic. This is what Breanna chose to focus her attention on. She was completely in love with her handsome husband.

24

ITSY WAS PERMITTED to go back to work with Breanna the next day. They were happy to be together again. It felt less lonely and frightening. They didn't talk about much beyond the programming and nanotechnology.

Breanna found that Joshua's contribution put them much farther ahead. She copied some of his work into her program. She kept wondering how he'd managed to save part of the soldier project without her seeing it. *It had to be in China … but how?*

Three times that day, Itsy jerked her hand towards her left eye and forehead as if someone had punched her again. Itsy said it was a sharp, sudden stabbing pain. Breanna stopped work each time and examined her friend's eyes. The pupil didn't dilate properly where she was hit, and Breanna was concerned that the damage was more serious than they initially thought.

That evening, Breanna was escorted to Edward while Itsy was returned to the bedroom. She took the engagement ring out of her pocket and placed it on her finger before entering the dining room.

"Come sit." He patted the chair beside him at the large table. He sat at the head, and she was seated to his right. The plates were set out and, as usual, Mr. Maxwell brought out the food. She never saw a maid or a cook or any other employee except the butler and the guards.

"Tomorrow we will take a trip into town for your ultrasound. The doctor said you must drink a lot of water. It's at ten o'clock, so you'll have to begin drinking early and continue in the car." He cut his steak and began eating.

Breanna looked at him like he had two heads. How could he not mention what he had done to Itsy? She debated the wisdom of challenging him. Would he be angry and cancel her medical care? Would he have her friend beaten again?

He raised his eyebrows and pointed at her food with his fork. "Eat, Breanna. You've got to keep your strength up for the baby."

"Itsy needs a doctor. She's having complications from the concussion." Breanna knew she had to try to get help for Itsy.

"Tsk!" He clicked his tongue. "Those men were reprimanded. They went too far. I said, warn her, not kill her." Edward gave Breanna a wide-eyed gaze. "I think a doctor is out of the question, though. You'll need to get your part of the programming done faster so you can help her."

"But what if it's not soon enough?"

"It will have to be." He shook his head, then ordered, "Now eat."

Breanna contemplated the steak and vegetables on her plate. The knot in her stomach at Edward's lack of compassion for Itsy threatened to rob her of her appetite. But for the baby, she would have refused to eat. She picked up her knife and fork and began to cut. She chewed the tender meat but found it difficult to swallow. A gulp of water helped it go down.

"Tell me, how are you progressing with the project?"

Raising a finger as she chewed, she was able to say after she swallowed, "I think some of it is close, but other parts I'm having trouble with the programming. It might be a few weeks before I can test the nanobots."

"Speed it up, and Itsy can be your first volunteer."

Her mouth dropped agape. Breanna remembered the first volunteer she had seen used in the soldier program. The man was ripped apart before her eyes. She repented for her part in his death, but she couldn't absolve herself of the guilt. She put down her knife and fork. "I don't know when it will be ready for human testing."

Edward waved a hand dismissively. "I'll decide that part. You don't have to worry about it. I'm sure if Itsy is as sick as you say, she'll be happy for you to test them on her."

"Please, no. Not my friend."

"I heard her ask you, Breanna. You would deny your friend healing." He referred to the bugged conversation in the bedroom.

"What if it kills her?" She tried to keep the image of the dying man from her mind.

Edward's eyes narrowed, and he leaned towards her. "You will make sure it doesn't. You won't be able to trick me with her life on the line."

Breanna fought to compose herself. He pointed to her food.

Then, as if this conversation had never happened, Edward announced in a cheerful voice, "After dinner, I have a surprise for you."

WITH EDWARD, THERE was no way of knowing if it would be a good surprise or a devastating one. Her stomach felt like a flutter of butterflies was on the loose inside. She ate as much as she was able to get down.

When he was satisfied that she had eaten enough, Edward stood and put out a hand for her. She took it and allowed him to lead her out of the room, still holding her hand. "I'm pleased to see you wearing the ring."

She remained silent.

Edward escorted her to an area of the estate that she had never entered before. It was on the second floor of the eighteenth-century addition. The door to the room had four armed guards and required Edward to use his eye for an identity scan and then punch in a code that he hid from everyone's view. He held the door open for her to enter.

The space was large, and the operating room was clean. Everything was white or stainless steel and minimal. The only thing in the room was what appeared to be long metal tubes, a little larger than coffins. Breanna had heard of people using them to freeze themselves after death.

"What do you think?" He sounded pleased with himself.

"Ah, I don't know. What are these?"

"Cryogenic chambers. You must have heard of them before. These are ones that I had made for my family and friends ... the friends who could pay, of course."

She stared at her host.

"After the plane crash, my injuries began healing immediately. I crawled from the wreckage and was able to get a horrified passerby to call emergency services, as well as Mr. Maxwell. My butler is a trusted assistant who has been with me since I first began to make money. He had been instructed that should any accidents befall my sister or me, our bodies would be transferred to these chambers as soon as possible.

"Mr. Maxwell called a Montreal cryogenics company and had my and Lucinda's bodies picked up immediately. Mine was not required since I painfully and slowly began to recover. Lucinda, on the other hand, was frozen and then transferred here to my home.

"Look." He pulled Breanna by the hand to stand beside one chamber on her left. "This is Lucinda."

The tube was stainless steel with controls attached to the side. It had a glass window the length of the coffin-like structure, and inside was a mangled and burnt body, impossible to identify. Someone had pieced together an arm and both feet like a Frankenstein creation. Breanna swirled away and heaved into the garbage can Edward had placed nearby and rapidly produced for her. *Did he expect this reaction? Is that why it was placed beside the chamber?* She glanced around the room but failed to see any other cans.

Edward didn't acknowledge her reaction. Instead, he began to speak quickly and wave his hands in the air. "When your program is working and successfully tested, we will use it on Lucinda. We will raise her from the dead, Breanna."

She couldn't believe what he was saying. The thought horrified her, despite the knowledge that rich people had been freezing themselves for several decades in hopes that they could continue living in this life. The room was spinning, and she felt faint.

When she found her voice, she said, "Her spirit has left her body, Edward. She is dead. If there is a miracle that the nanobots can repair her body and brain, it wouldn't be her. Some demon would possess her body."

Edward began to laugh in a deep voice, his entire body shaking. "My dear Breanna. That happened years ago. How do you think I made my billions? Where did I get the insight into what stocks to invest in? How do you think I know about things like nanobots?" He glared at her, and his eyes changed from dark blue to almost black.

His voice changed to someone else's voice, something evil. "Why do you think people do my bidding? You think I can put a spell on them with my power? Tsk! Foolish, naive girl. It's only some Christians who can resist. Lucinda also made the same deal years ago. It's all about power and control. So you see, it doesn't matter to me."

———

"Breanna ... Breanna ... Breanna." It was Edward's voice. She was lying on a sofa in a lounge area they had passed through earlier. There was a cold cloth on her forehead. "Are you all right? You fainted after you threw up. I'm sorry. I should have realized it would be a shock to see Lucinda's body."

"Wh ... what? You said ...." She had difficulty recalling if it was a dream.

His eyebrows furrowed. "What did I say?"

Did she imagine it all? Was he a demon, or was it a trick of her imagination, the old dreams resurfacing?

His eyes were their normal colour, and he appeared perplexed by her question. "I don't know what you thought you heard, but you went down right after seeing my sister's body."

She shook her head. *Could it be? What about raising the dead? What about the demons?*

Edward flipped the cloth on her head to the cooler side. He was kneeling on the floor beside her. "I'm worried about you. I'm going to carry you to your room." With that, he slid one arm under her back and one under her legs. He lifted her off the sofa like she weighed nothing. The muscles on his arms flexed as he carried her, and Breanna marvelled at the results of her and Lucinda's program in action.

He mounted the stairs with her in her arms, murmuring comforting words about her health and the baby. It was all so surreal, and it made Breanna wonder about her sanity.

When Edward placed her on her feet at the door, the guards unlocked it and stood to the side. He gave her a nudge towards the room and said, "We have an early morning tomorrow. Goodnight, Breanna."

When the door locked behind her, she grabbed for the closest wall to steady herself. *What just happened?*

26

AFTER BREANNA STEADIED herself, she moved into the room and noticed Itsy was already asleep. It was about nine in the evening, which was early for Itsy to retire. Breanna crept across the room to the bed. Both beds remained side by side so the women could hold hands during prayer and sometimes for comfort during the night. Kneeling on her side, she examined Itsy's face for any concerning signs. It was definitely a concussion, but it could also be a fractured skull and any number of complications.

"Itsy." Breanna gently shook her friend's shoulder.

A moan escaped from Itsy's mouth as she opened her eyes.

"I'm sorry to wake you, but I'm still worried about the injury to your … Itsy?" Breanna noticed that Itsy was staring straight ahead but not responding to her voice. She reached over and placed a hand on the blonde's forehead and found she had a fever. "Itsy?"

Her friend's mouth began to move, but no words came out, and the stare remained.

Within a few minutes, Itsy blinked a couple of times then looked over at Breanna. Recognition slowly returned to her eyes. "Bree?"

She removed he hand from Itsy's forehead and shook her head. "You need to see a doctor." Then Breanna said it much louder. "Itsy needs to see a doctor." It was unknown if Edward would respond, but she would keep trying.

"I'm really tired," Itsy said.

"I know." Breanna pulled the covers up over Itsy's shoulders. It was common for people to feel tired if they suffered a seizure, and Breanna suspected that was what she witnessed.

Itsy closed her eyes and quickly nodded off to sleep.

The pregnant woman began to pray in earnest. There was a desperation in her pleas to God for her friend. *Where are you? Itsy really needs your help. Please, please don't desert us. Even if you need to send her home, I will miss her terribly, but I'd rather she were safe and I were in this mess alone. Don't let her die or have serious brain damage. Lord Jesus, I don't feel your presence. I don't feel your peace like I did in China. We are surrounded by darkness and evil. Where is your light? Why can't I hear you?* Breanna's legs were going numb from kneeling on the bed. With one last glance at Itsy, she stood and let the circulation flow.

The coolness in the stone tower was welcome for Breanna's hot pregnant blood. It wasn't damp in the room, so she knew it wasn't raining outside. She turned Itsy's chair to face hers and, kicking off her shoes, she put her feet up on it. As her mind wandered through a multitude of problems, she unconsciously bit her lower lip.

What if Edward doesn't let Itsy see a doctor? Seizures can get worse over time and cause serious brain damage. Can I finish my programming of the nanobots to heal Itsy? How and when did Joshua get a copy of the two programs? Why aren't either of them complete? It had to be in China. As angry as I am at him for having the copy, it could help Itsy. Even without Lucinda's rapid muscle growth programming, my rapid healing one is enough for now. But I won't have months to test it. It's needed right away. I hope I can remember the missing parts.

Then her mind flipped to the experience she had with Edward after dinner. *He mentioned raising someone from the dead during the television interview. Did he say it again tonight, or did I dream it? It seems unbelievable that he would turn into a demon. If it had been real, why wouldn't I remember getting to the sofa or the wet cloth on my forehead? It couldn't have happened. It must be my overactive imagination.*

Oh Joshua. I wish you were here to talk to about all of this. You would make sense of it. She began rubbing her baby belly. *Why did you lie to me? Was I a project for Mossad? It felt so real. I believed you when you said you loved me. Sweet baby, will you ever get to meet your father? Will you even get to meet me?* When the salty wet streams touched her lips, she realized she was crying.

27

IN THE MORNING, Itsy was humming a modern Christian tune while she carried the delivered breakfast trays. Breanna swung her legs over the side of the bed and managed an "Ugh!"

"Wakey, wakey, sleepyhead."

"What time is it?"

"Time to get up. The guard said you had to be ready in an hour to leave for an ultrasound."

Breanna rubbed the sleep out of her eyes. She wondered how long she had sat up the night before. "I didn't get a chance to tell you last night."

Itsy said, "I guess the tray with several glasses of water is for you."

Holding up one hand with her fingers spread wide, Breanna said, "Give me five minutes in the bathroom. I need a shower."

When she returned to the room, Itsy grinned at her. She didn't appear to have any residual effects from the seizure the night before. Breanna debated mentioning it to Itsy or waiting until she had a chance to talk to Edward later. She decided not to withhold it from Itsy. "Last night, I think you had a seizure. You stared straight ahead and mouthed words, but nothing came out. Afterwards, you said you were tired and went back to sleep."

The smile faded. "I guess we'll have to watch if I have any more. Maybe it was exhaustion."

"Yeah. Maybe." Breanna pressed her lips tightly together. After the two stared at each other for a few seconds, she said, "I'm going to ask Edward again if you can see a doctor."

"Again?"

"I asked him last night. He told me to hurry and get my part of the program completed, and you can be the first person to get healed."

"Guinea pig."

"Yes. I told him I was against it. I don't want to test the program on you." She reached out for her friend's hand. "We'll make him see reason."

Itsy took Breanna's hand. "If my headaches don't get better, and I have more seizures, I'm going to volunteer. I trust you. I know how brilliant you are and if you say it's ready, it will be."

"Itsy—"

Itsy pulled her hand away and placed a finger on her lips. "Shhh! Let's wait and see."

"But—"

Her friend interrupted her. "No more discussion about it." There was a knock at the door. Itsy stood up and said, "You've got to leave, and I have work to do in the lab. Come on."

Edward led Breanna to the limo waiting outside. Instead of heading toward the front gate, the car took the road out to the hangar and runway on the estate. When Breanna swung her head toward Edward, he said, "We don't have as much time to get to the appointment, so a helicopter will take us." He handed her another bottle of water. "Drink."

"I'm going to float away."

"Drink. The doctor said you had to drink all that water so they could see the baby."

Breanna reluctantly sipped on the water. She finished off the two large glasses at breakfast. When they arrived at the building where Edward's plane was hangared, there was a shiny black helicopter parked on the runway out front.

She followed Edward, clutching her bottle and purse. She climbed a couple of stairs to board the helicopter, and the pilot handed her a headset, but Edward took it and put it over her ears. Once his was on his head and he'd buckled them both in, the pilot asked, "Are we ready to leave, sir?"

"Yes, go ahead."

Breanna was surprised that they could converse through the headset. It was for more than blocking the sound of the engine. Edward lifted the bottle of water towards her lips. She'd never felt less like drinking water, and she hoped she didn't have to wait once they were there to use the washroom because she didn't think she'd make it. When he scowled, she dutifully took a sip.

The flight was much shorter than the drive, and for that, she was thankful. They landed on the hospital helipad and debarked. The pilot told Edward to call when it was time to return home, and they would meet at the airport.

When they were descending from the rooftop, Edward explained, "We have special authorization to land on the hospital roof as long as there are no emergency needs for the helipad. I couldn't get permission for my pilot to wait here for us, though. We'll meet him a little later."

On the second floor, the couple exited the elevator. In front of them was the sign for the imaging department where the ultrasound was located. The nurses whisked them through the line, and Breanna went into a changing room to put on a hospital gown. She had to remove everything except her underwear, and it dawned on her that Edward planned to watch the procedure. The heat rose from her chest to her face, but she had no choice if she wanted prenatal care. *Put on your big girl pants, Breanna. You can do this. You have to do this.*

28

WHEN BREANNA EXITED the changing room, she held the back of the hospital gown together despite the ties covering up her back. Edward was waiting with a young nurse who was hanging on his every word. The pretty brown-haired woman dressed in flowered scrubs was standing close enough to Edward that his arm touched hers. Breanna noticed the goose bumps on the nurse's arms. The nurse let out a nervous giggle at something Edward said to her in a low voice. His eyes flashed at Breanna when she joined them. "Here is my bride-to-be," he announced to the brunette, whose face dropped at that statement.

What did she think? He's here with a pregnant lady to get an ultrasound. But Edward does it to all the women on purpose. He flirts and they fawn. His ego knows no bounds. And I was once like this poor woman.

Edward took Breanna possessively by the arm, and the nurse led them into the adjoining room where the technician was waiting.

"Lie down on top of the examination table. Place the sheet over your lower body and pull your gown over your stomach."

Breanna struggled with her big belly to get on the table, and Edward lifted her the rest of the way. He gave a wink to the technician. "I'm so excited to see my baby finally." Then Edward helped pull up the hospital gown, exposing her baby bump.

Breanna cringed inside but said nothing. "I'm excited too, but right now all I can think of is that I have to go."

The technician said, "We'll take a few pictures and then I'll let you empty your bladder, and we can take a few more." He shook his head. "Every woman feels the same way." He played with the imaging machine for a minute, then picked up the jelly. "This is going to feel cold." The man squirted the slimy goo on her stomach and began moving a rectangular wand over it.

She watched the monitor in amazement as her baby took shape before her eyes. God's creation was wonderous to behold, and she forgot about everything else, including Edward, for a few minutes. The technician clicked pictures and pointed out body parts.

Edward asked, "Can you tell if it's a girl or a boy?"

Breanna wanted it to be a surprise for her when the baby was born, but before she could say anything, the lab tech said, "I can't be sure because of the position, but I think it's a girl." She was disappointed not because the baby was a girl but because she didn't want to know, and she didn't want Edward to know ahead of time.

"A mini-you, Breanna. It's wonderful." Edward bent down and kissed her quickly on the lips. "She'll have your red hair and green eyes."

"Like Ireland herself," the ultrasound operator said.

Edward looked at him with wide eyes and a smile that stretched across his face. "Exactly."

But what if the baby looks like Joshua, with dark hair, brown eyes? Will you let me keep her then? Breanna suddenly felt naked in front of the two men. "Can I go to the bathroom now?"

"A couple more pictures." The computer clicked as he pressed the buttons. "There now. It's the door past the changing rooms. Come right back so we can finish up."

Getting off the table was slightly easier than getting on, and Breanna waddled to the bathroom with Edward on her heels. *Does he think I'd run away and leave Itsy behind? How far would I get anyway?*

After they finished with the ultrasound and were leaving the hospital, Breanna saw the limo waiting for them at the hospital entrance along with a lineup of paparazzi flashing photos of them. Edward stopped Breanna, squeezed her hand, then leaned in and said, "Smile." She did as she was told. "Now look into my eyes like a woman in love. Itsy needs you to sell it." Her stomach lurched, but she stared into his eyes and imagined Joshua.

One man yelled out, "Are you excited about having your first child, Mr. Connor?"

"I couldn't be happier. My fiancée and I are thrilled." He bent down and kissed her, parting her lips with his tongue. Trying not to gag, she heard the camera snapping photos, and her heart sank, realizing Joshua would see these in the news. She became suspicious that Edward had set the whole press thing up, and this was the real reason the helicopter couldn't wait for them. He continued to play to his audience. Edward swiveled her back to face the camera and placed a hand on her belly. "We are having a girl. And as you can see, she's a healthy size."

A woman in the group asked, "Isn't your fiancée already married?"

His grip tightened as he pulled Breanna towards his side. "She married on the rebound, thinking I had died in the plane crash, like the rest of the world. Things fell apart quickly in her marriage when she discovered I was still alive. And here we are, together and in love. She will be divorced soon, and we can be wed." He twisted Breanna towards him and, holding her head in place, ensured the photographers took pictures of another intimate kiss.

Edward began laughing as if he didn't intend to get carried away. She held onto him because her head was swimming from the emotional onslaught. Her mind was reeling. *Divorce? He's going to force me to get a divorce. Joshua is going to want one when this hits the news. Dear Lord, I don't know if it's bad or good. I'm so confused. I still hope I'm wrong about Joshua.*

29

AFTER THE HELICOPTER landed and they were in the limo for the short drive to the castle, Breanna tried begging Edward to let Itsy see a doctor. He refused. He said Breanna's finished program would be what would help her friend. She persisted until his eyes flashed out a warning that she pressed him too far. His pupils dilated and his brows knitted together. Grabbing her arm, Edward snarled, "Enough. If you keep going, I will send Itsy down to the old dungeon of the keep. It's rat-infested, damp, and cold. There are no niceties down there." He leaned closer, "Is that what you want for your friend?"

"Please, no," she offered meekly. When he released her, she rubbed where the bruises would show up later. He had defeated her again. It seemed Edward had the upper hand and played all his cards to win this time around. The man swung from charming to nasty and cruel, without batting an eyelash. She knew better than to test him. The consequences for Itsy and her were too great. The last time she and Itsy angered him, Itsy was badly beaten. Her friend couldn't handle another thrashing. Breanna was quiet and submissive the rest of the way to the house.

She was escorted to the lab by the guards that Edward had assigned. He didn't say another word to her after his outburst. Once she hung up her coat and got suited up, she joined Itsy in the lab.

Her best friend took one look at Breanna, and her eyebrows raised an acknowledgement that Breanna was upset. All had not gone well.

The bubble in her throat displayed some of the emotion. "It looks like I'm having a girl."

Itsy came over and hugged her friend. "Congratulations."

"It seems I'm also to get a divorce." Tears pricked Breanna's eyes, but she stared at the ceiling to keep them at bay.

A mouth that formed a perfect O was Itsy's shocked reaction. Her heart hurt for Breanna. *What choice did Bree have? What choice did either of them have in any of this? Obviously, Edward was going to make this permanent, at least for her friend.* Itsy shuddered to think what his long-term plans were for her. *Don't go there.*

"He refused to allow you to see a doctor. He said I needed to complete my program and heal you." Breanna shook her head. "I'm sorry. I tried. I really did, then he told me to stop or else …."

Itsy knew exactly what that meant. He could threaten to kill the baby, and Itsy was obviously expendable. Breanna winced when she touched her arm. Itsy knew better than to ask anything about it that could be overheard. "Thanks for trying." Then she went to her workstation and picked up a stack of papers. "I've printed out all this information. There are some promising results here."

With a big sigh, Breanna cleared her mind of earlier in the day and focused on the task at hand. She began reading what Itsy had printed. As it took on a life of its own, her mouth dropped open. "I think you found it, Itsy. This is one of the missing keys. I have to put it all together, but I think this is it." She whispered to her friend. "Joshua had copied some of my program somehow in China, and with this, it might make it possible. Maybe within the month I can have it working. It could heal you."

Itsy's eyes filled with fluid. As much as she tried to stay strong for her friend, she was worried about herself. She said quietly but not in a whisper, "I think I had another mild seizure today. I lost a couple of minutes, then I had to lie down on the sofa in the lunchroom because I was exhausted right afterwards. This can't come soon enough."

It was Breanna's turn to hug her friend. "I'll work as hard as I can. If all goes well, we can begin some tests in the next two or three weeks."

"Right before you hit the six-month mark." Itsy placed a hand on Breanna's belly. "Do you hear that, Bella? Your mama is going to save me."

"Bella?" Breanna chuckled.

Itsy laughed, "Of course, you'll name her after me. My full name is not my nickname. Isabella … Bella."

"I like Bella. It's a great name for my daughter."

"It means beautiful in Italian. She will be gorgeous … and smart, like her mother."

"Let's hope her mother's smart enough to recreate this program again."

"She is." Itsy made a silly face, and Breanna reciprocated.

30

THE FOLLOWING DAY, they worked for ten hours with barely any breaks except three unexpected ones. Itsy had two seizures and had to lie down for about an hour each time. Then Breanna had a mild contraction and took a long break. When no other pains occurred, Breanna chalked it up to gas. Those events were upsetting, but when one of them was out of commission, the other kept working. It wasn't until Edward sent the guards that they reluctantly stopped for the day.

The women were split up, with Itsy escorted to their room for her dinner and Breanna brought to their kidnapper. Bree was tired, but she pulled the engagement ring out of her pocket and took the elastic out of her hair to let it hang down. It wasn't as long as it had been, but it was getting close. These were two things Edward insisted on, and she didn't want to bring out his dark side.

Shuffling into the dining room, she made for her assigned seat beside Edward. No sooner did she sit down than he commanded, "Look at me, Breanna." The tone of his voice was sharp, so her head snapped up. His eyes were dark and narrowed as he stared at her. The lump in her throat threatened to choke her, while the sudden increase in her heart rate threatened to give way to her fear. Her instinct was to run. It always was in a fight-or-flight situation. Fighting was out of the question, and flight would have been preferable, but also impossible. She gripped the edge of the table as she returned his gaze.

"What do you think is wrong?"

Was it a trick question? She had no idea, so she shook her head.

He leaned over until his face was less than a foot from hers and grabbed her left hand. "Think. Think hard." His gripped tightened.

"Ow!" The pressure didn't subside. Crying out, "What did I do? I don't know." Not releasing her hand, he stopped squeezing it.

"Whispers? What did you whisper to Itsy yesterday? I reviewed the footage today. Whatever you told her made her very happy. She said you were going to save her." Edward kissed the hand he hurt, then said, "Make me happy and tell me, Breanna."

The man kept her on an emotional roller coaster. *I was foolish to think I could keep anything from him. Lord, help me behave better so I won't upset him anymore.* "I told Itsy that when I plugged in Joshua's memory stick, it wasn't the one I expected." She looked at the large hand that was massaging hers. *He holds our three lives in his hands.*

"Go on," Edward said.

Her throat felt dry, and she licked her lips. "It contained most of my program—the one from China. I don't know how he was able to copy it. We destroyed your mainframe together. He wasn't alone then. There was no time for him to download it, and if he had, he would have had the complete one."

"Well. It seems your betrayer had more secrets. Perhaps his business trips were to work on the program for Israel." Edward released her hand and leaned back in his chair. "I wonder if he copied Lucinda's also." His eyes flashed to her face, and he saw something there because his lip twitched before he said, "He did." His hands went to a praying position, and he tapped his mouth several times, his telltale thinking move.

Breanna bit her lower lip as she wondered what Edward would do with the information she withheld. Before she could react, he pulled her over into his lap and kissed her as he had for the photographers. There was nothing she could do to escape as he held her firmly in place. "Kiss me back, Breanna," he ordered. So she did, all the while fighting the tears that threatened to flow.

He ran his fingers down her face and stopped at her throat. Breanna knew her pulse was racing out of control, and her mind went to the day on the plane when he choked her. It was all she could do to will herself not to move. The corner of his mouth raised. Did he think her reaction was attraction? Did he care? *Or was this a threat to remind me?*

"No more secrets," he said.

Breanna managed a barely discernible shake of her head, unwilling for him to firm up his grasp on her neck. His message was received loud and clear.

"Our meal is here," he announced as he pushed her to stand.

The bird was released from the hand of its captor. *Dismissed as quickly as directed. He keeps me unbalanced ... just like he wants it.* Even while she thought this, Breanna breathed a silent sigh of relief. The table steadied her as she returned to her chair. As they ate, Edward talked excitedly about how much further along Breanna would be because of Joshua's deception. It didn't escape her notice how much Edward emphasized Joshua's duplicity. *He wants me to hate him, but I don't. I'm mad at him, but I can't hate the man I love. But it probably doesn't matter since I won't see him ever again.*

31

THE NEXT SEVERAL weeks flew by without Edward summoning Breanna, which provided her with a much-needed emotional respite. After advising Itsy about their orders to refrain from whispering for the recording and camera, the two women worked together with the common goal of getting Breanna's portion of the project running as soon as possible so they could heal Itsy.

Itsy's seizures now occurred two to three times a day, but thankfully never developed into a grand mal seizure.

In Breanna's case, she could not believe how good she felt. She marvelled, "I don't know if I've ever felt this healthy. I've got this baby bump, but every other part of my body is energized."

"It's got to be Bella. She's your good luck charm … I mean blessing. You know what I mean." Itsy laughed because old habits and expressions die hard. They'd both had some setbacks since becoming Christians last year.

Breanna said, "Here it is, the middle of October. It's been a year for you since accepting Jesus."

The blonde became serious. "Fat lot of good it's done. My husband's been shot and might be dead. I've been kidnapped, beaten, and threatened with worse. I have a huge scar on my cheek and a missing tooth. And now, to top it all off, I'm having seizures." She folded her arms. "I don't mean to be ungrateful for salvation, but couldn't I have a few more blessings and not so many curses? Where's God in all this, Bree?"

Breanna lifted her eyes briefly and sent up a prayer. *Where are you? What do I tell Itsy? We could use some good news.* "I don't know. But I do know that

God is ultimately in control. Think about what the disciples suffered because of their witness."

"There you go. You always talk about how others have it worse as if that makes my suffering less somehow. It minimizes my feelings."

"I didn't mean it that way. Sorry. You're right."

"So are you, but still."

Breanna pressed her lips together. What could she say to Itsy? Her friend had suffered a lot because of her, and there was nothing she could do to help except work on the program. "I've heard of the night of the soul. I wonder if this is it."

Itsy didn't want to dwell on the negative. They couldn't change anything. "Let's talk about Bella. How far along are you? Let's figure it out. Then we can figure out your due date."

Breanna shrugged. "I'm guessing that it was the second week of April that I got pregnant, before my six-month anniversary on April twentieth."

"Hmmm! That was memorable." Both ladies raised their brows. It was the day they saw Edward on television, very much alive. Itsy looked at the calendar, and they counted together. "Twenty-six weeks. You'll be due the middle of January 2031." She paused and stared at her friend. "And next week is your first anniversary."

Tears pricked Breanna's eyes.

"Sorry, Bree. I know you're suffering too. You have every reason to cry." As soon as Itsy said it, the two of them broke out laughing. It struck their funny bone that instead of saying not to weep, Itsy said she should give in to it. When they were able to stop, Itsy continued, "God better know what he's doing because otherwise the enemy is having a field day with the two of us." Itsy stared off for a moment.

"Hey, are you all right, Itsy?" Breanna was worried her friend was having a seizure.

Her friend smiled. "Yes. I was thinking. I heard somewhere that we should count our blessings by saying what we're thankful for. We can try that exercise to cheer us up."

Breanna said, "I'm thankful for you. I wouldn't want anyone else here with me."

"Even Joshua?" As soon as she said it, Itsy worried what Edward would think that she brought him up.

"Not kidnapped. He'd get us both killed with his temper."

Itsy said, "Michael, too. I'm glad to be with you also. I wouldn't want you to go through this alone … the kidnapping … the pregnancy. Even with the bad stuff. I'm thankful you're my friend."

"I'm thankful for the bed and food and clothes and the little prenatal care I've received. Lots of people in the world would love to have their basic needs met."

"Sad but true. There are so many disasters, wars, diseases, poverty, and evil out there. We can even count what we've received from Edward as a blessing." Itsy meant every word.

The two women became silent as they thanked God for these things. Finally, Breanna said, "Let's get back to work. The faster we finish this, the sooner you'll be cured."

Itsy pointed at Breanna and said, "Giddy-up and go."

32

THE WOMEN'S PEACE didn't last. Two weeks later, at the end of October, Edward sent for Breanna for dinner. As she entered the dining room, she was surprised to find Edward drinking wine. The entire time she was with him, she hadn't seen him have any alcohol. It wasn't as if he didn't drink. She had shared wine with him in the past, but it seemed unusual that he should be drinking alone.

"Ah, Breanna. I've missed you, my Irish fairy." Edward patted the seat to his right, and she took her place. "Look at the size of Bella." He placed a hand on her stomach and rubbed. Then he bent down and spoke to the baby, "Hello, Bella. I'm your dad."

Breanna gasped. *He's not the father, no matter what he told the world.* Then she thought better about her reaction. If she played along, would Edward let her keep her baby? Would he adopt Bella as his own? Then she could be with Bella. She didn't care about the rest because the thought of giving up this baby frightened her. She thought she'd sooner have her heart ripped out of her chest. While it wasn't an ideal time or situation, Breanna found herself loving her unborn child. She couldn't help but ask, "Would you accept her as your daughter?"

His face smoothed out all lines, as his voice came across like a gentle breeze. "Would you like me to be?"

"And I could keep her?"

"She could live with the two of us as a family. The world already believes she is mine."

Breanna nodded. While she didn't want Edward, she did want Bella. She had no other choice.

"Say you want us to be a family, and it will be so." Edward smiled sweetly as if she had imagined all the malice from him in the past. He picked up her hand and kissed it slowly. "Tell me what you want, Breanna."

Why did he always make her say things? It hurt her heart, but she had to do it. "I want us to be a family."

"Music to my ears." He lifted her and placed her on his lap. He kissed her. This time, she knew that she had to kiss him back without being told. He nibbled on her ear and said, "I want to hear it again."

She closed her eyes and repeated the sentence.

Satisfied that he had made her capitulate, Edward lifted her back into her chair.

God forgive me for lying. I want to keep my baby. I should be thankful that Edward hasn't forced himself on me during the pregnancy. I can put up with a few kisses, but I'm going to need your help, Lord, if and when there's more.

Mr. Maxwell served their meal and left the room. Breanna knew that the butler was fully aware of her situation, and he didn't care that she and Itsy were prisoners. In fact, Breanna suspected Mr. Maxwell harboured animosity towards her for the betrayal of Edward and his plane crash. He never acknowledged her when he was in the room.

As they ate, Edward broke the silence by saying, "I've been away for meetings with heads of state and my affairs. I can't conduct all my work from home." He stopped and pointed to her with his knife. "During my regular business, I've managed to get things in order for you, too. We'll take care of it after dinner. In the meantime, tell me, how is the research going?"

What things did you do for me? She said, "I think I've finished. I'm running simulations now. It would help to test on an animal, but I hate that idea also."

He put down his knife and fork. "Wonderful news. I knew you could do it. You are a brilliant scientist." He placed his hands on the table. "The doctor contacted me and said the ultrasound was perfect. She said the baby is on the bigger size but healthy. All your tests came back excellent. Isn't that grand?"

Breanna smiled in relief. Her baby was fine. Probably not on the bigger size since Edward added two weeks to the date of the pregnancy to coincide with his acquisition of her in Israel.

"My Bella will be a healthy Irish fairy like her mother." Edward's voice sang.

Lord, please make Bella light-skinned and red-haired like me. I don't want Edward mistreating her if she looks like Joshua.

33

WHEN THEIR MEAL was finished, Edward took Breanna by the hand and led her to a room in the house she had never entered. Edward's office was enormous, much bigger than the one at the Chinese factory. The same dark mahogany wood panelling covered the walls that were not lined with mahogany shelves. There was a bar along one quarter of the wall on one side. It was fully stocked, more than many restaurants.

There were shelves with what Breanna assumed were priceless artifacts. Paintings lined the wall. She recognized Rembrandt, Degas, Renoir, and Monet as the most famous. It was as if she had wandered into a private viewing area of a museum. How he managed to procure them was a mystery. She wouldn't put it past Edward Connor to use illegal means if necessary. Without conscious thought, Breanna began to move around the room, admiring the art.

When she came to the bookshelves, it wasn't surprising to find that many old books lined the shelves. She had to ask, "First editions?"

He stood beside her and placed an arm casually around her waist, or what remained of it under the baby. "Nothing but the best."

She twisted her head toward him, and he held her eyes with his. Clearing her throat, she managed, "The books or art or—"

"You." He leaned in and kissed her.

It was all she could do not to push him away. Why did he persist? Could she continue this ruse day after day, year after year? *For Bella and Itsy, yes.* She kissed him back.

He played with her hair, twirling his fingers in the locks. "Come over to the desk, Breanna. We have things to take care of here."

Her brows knitted together as he led her over to the dark oak desk. Edward rolled out his chair and offered it to Breanna. Once she was in the chair, Edward pushed it back to the desk. He opened one side drawer and produced a stack of papers. She was watching his face, but he gave nothing away. "You need to sign these." He tapped the papers in front of her.

Following his hand, she read the top page. *Motion for Divorce.* Though she knew it was coming, she still wasn't prepared to see it in writing. Tears flooded her eyes, and she couldn't stop them as a few drops fell onto the page.

Edward crouched down beside her. "I know this isn't what you wanted. You wanted to live happily ever after like the fairy tales." His voice was soft and understanding. It confused her more. "But even if I hadn't taken you away, do you think you could have salvaged a marriage based on lies? Do you think he'd want to remain married after the enhanced soldier program was replicated? This was inevitable. Sad, but it would have happened anyway. I'm sorry, but he never really loved you, Breanna."

Edward handed her some tissues. She wiped her face and sniffled. "How did you know about Joshua's lies? How did you know he was Mossad?"

"I have friends who are employed in many levels of government. You must have known that from working with me in China, and I'm sure Joshua told you. My associates told me about Joshua and how his assignment was to convince you to work for Israel. I told you before, marriage was something spies often do during their work, and that was the best way to get you to cooperate. They can make you do almost anything for love. He doesn't know about your pregnancy, but I'm sure he would have used it to keep a tight rein on you. He wouldn't be the first spy to have children with their mark."

The word *mark* stung. Was that all she was to Joshua? Edward had infiltrated the Canadian spy agency, CSIS, so it wouldn't be a surprise if he had done the same with Mossad. Breanna's resolve not to listen to Edward about Joshua was crumbling. Her host didn't plant the seeds, but he watered them and nurtured their growth, and now it was time for the harvest. She tried to read the words that swam across the page. There was something about pretenses and betrayal in the documents, but she couldn't read them. She flipped to the back page and picked up the pen Edward had placed beside her. He pointed to the places for her to sign or initial. She could barely make out her writing through the tears.

When she was finished, Edward told her to dry her eyes and fix her face. He had his lawyer ready to witness the document. Breanna did as she was instructed, then put on a mask of impenetrable hardness. *No man will ever hurt me like this again.*

Mr. Maxwell showed up with a middle-aged lawyer in an expensive suit after Edward rang him through an intercom. Edward introduced him, a name that flew out of her head the moment it was said. Breanna shook his hand without saying a word. The lawyer looked over the documents and then asked, "Are these your signatures?"

She answered, "Yes."

He nodded and placed his witnessing signature and the date on the document. "Do you swear that this is the truth to the best of your knowledge and that this is approved of by you without coercion?"

Breanna felt her cheeks burning. "Yes."

The man didn't gaze in her direction. Instead, he gathered the papers and shook Edward's hand. He didn't even say goodbye to Breanna.

She flexed her hands open and closed, steeling her heart. *It's done.*

Instinctively, Edward knew not to press his advantage. Without any further conversation, he escorted her to her gilded cage.

34

"I'M DIVORCED," BREANNA announced flatly to Itsy.

Itsy choked on the gulp of water she had taken after her evening workout. Once she finished coughing, she said, "What do you mean, you're divorced? From Joshua?"

Breanna nodded and waddled into the bathroom. Itsy was right behind her. "You can't just say you're divorced with no emotion, no explanation, and leave me hanging."

"Can I have some privacy for a minute? I'll be right out."

"Fine, but I'm right outside the door."

Breanna yelled louder than necessary, "Where else would you be? There's nowhere to go. You're stuck here like me."

Itsy frowned. "At least anger is an emotion."

When Breanna came out of the washroom, Itsy was standing by the fireplace. She rushed over to her friend and put her arms around her. Whispering, she asked, "Did he force you?'

Shaking her head, Breanna said, "No. I agreed to the divorce. Why would I hang on to a pipe dream? Joshua lied to me. Once I finish this project for Edward, which will be soon, Joshua will have no use for me anymore. I'm making this easier and cleaner for both of us."

"But you love him." Itsy didn't try to speak quietly.

"So what? I'm here now forever. This is where my life will be. Edward agreed I could keep Bella, and we could be a family. I've got to think of the future and not dwell on the past." Breanna appealed to Itsy with her eyes for understanding.

She folded her arms. "I'm sorry, Bree. How I wish things had been different for you. I wish I could somehow make it happen."

Breanna bit her bottom lip. "I'm going to see if Edward will release you once the soldier program is complete. I'll marry him, and there'll be no need for you to remain a prisoner."

Itsy stared at her best friend. There was so much she wanted to say, but nothing would heal the wound in Breanna's heart. She knew her well enough. Then there was always the fear of Edward's vengeance if she went too far with Breanna. *Lord God, this is one big mess. I know Breanna loves Joshua, and I'd bet my life that he loves her. I know she doesn't love Edward, but she will do what she needs to protect her baby and me. She's going to need a huge miracle from you because we're helpless. Turn this whole thing around and use it for your good. Amen.*

In bed later, Itsy took Breanna's hand to pray. Breanna shook her off and said, "Not tonight, Itsy."

"What do you mean?"

"I'm mad at God … if there is one. Look at us and the situation we're in. If there were a God, would he let all of this happen? Would he let Joshua use me, and now I've got to get a divorce? I'm a scientist. I think logically. None of this God stuff is sensible." Breanna tried to roll onto her other side with much huffing and puffing.

Not letting it go, Itsy put a hand on Breanna's shoulder. "You can't be angry at a God that doesn't exist. Things are not looking good right now, but don't give up on God." It was on the tip of her tongue to go on about trusting Joshua and not Edward, but fear gripped her. She thought she smelled burnt toast. *I'm sorry, Lord, for failing you and Bree. I can't handle another beating. I can't.*

Breanna felt the bed vibrating in a jerky, uneven manner. "Itsy." No response. "Itsy. Are you okay?" The bed was still moving as Breanna laboured to roll back towards her friend.

Itsy was jerking her arms, and her back arched stiffly. Breanna didn't know what to do to help her friend. She sat up and called, "Itsy, I'm here." Her friend began foaming at the mouth, but shortly afterwards, Itsy stopped all movement. Breanna checked her pulse. Itsy was unconscious but alive. She went to get a cold compress. By the time she returned, Itsy was stirring.

In a weak voice, she asked, "What happened?"

"You had a seizure."

"Oh … I'm tired." She closed her eyes and fell asleep.

Okay, God, I'm sorry. Please help my friend. I didn't mean it when I denied you. "I'm here." Breanna wrapped her arm around her best friend and lay beside her. "I'll do the testing. We'll get it working this week. I'm so sorry, Itsy."

"REALLY, BREE, WHAT did you expect?"

She squinted her eyes as she tried to wake up, "What?"

"Come on, get up." Joshua was hanging over her.

Breanna rubbed the sleep out of her eyes. "I feel drunk."

"Could it be from the amount of wine you drank last night?" He sounded perturbed.

"I don't remember."

He rolled out of bed and opened the curtain. The sunlight assailed her eyes with a vengeance. She pulled the pillow over her head. "Stop. Why are you trying to kill me?"

Joshua laughed. "I'm not trying to kill you. I'm trying to wake you. We've got to meet Jean for brunch."

"Oh! Is that this morning?" Joshua left the room, and Breanna heard the shower running. *A couple more minutes.* She hugged the pillow.

She felt his arms lifting her out of the bed, and he carried her into the bathroom. When she realized what he was about to do, she began flailing. "Stop. Don't you dare. Joshua, stop. I will be furious with you." Breanna was carried into the shower, and the warm water flowed over them both.

"I'm awake now. Thank you very much," she hissed. Her head pounded.

"I realize it was your best friend's wedding, but I told you to be careful about how much wine you were drinking. But no, you had to keep going. You don't drink enough to have any kind of tolerance." He snickered. "You'd better have some coffee and take something for your headache."

"I hate you." She pouted.

"I love you." He kissed her cheek. Joshua put some liquid soap in his hands and began lathering Breanna's back. "Where's my loving wife? I know she's in there somewhere."

"No, she's not." She grabbed her head with both hands, attempting to keep her brain from spilling out. She wasn't really mad at him. "I only drank three glasses of wine."

"Try five or six."

"I'm going to die."

"No, you're not." He washed himself and lifted her hand, squirting soap onto it. "Finish up, and I'll get the hotel coffee-maker working; it's magic."

By the time Breanna finished her second cup of coffee and the medication took effect, she contemplated her husband of a month. He was handsome and smart and hers. She gave him a sheepish grin. "Remind me never to have more than one or two glasses, if I ever drink again."

He laughed. "I did last night. But you were having such a good time dancing with me, Michael, Bobby, Saul, and even Jean and Itsy, that you kept drinking."

"Dancing is thirsty work."

"Ha, ha! Try water next time."

She gave a slight wave of her hand. "There will never be a next time."

Joshua let out a deep belly laugh of total enjoyment. Hearing him caused Breanna to laugh.

When they finished the coffee and merriment, he stood up and offered his hand to help her rise. "We've got to leave. Michael and Itsy need to catch their flight for Barbados, and we promised to drop them off so they wouldn't have to pay for parking." He held open the ski jacket she wore to survive the November chill. She was already acclimatized to the weather in Tel Aviv. Toronto felt that much colder now, even though the true winter weather hadn't started. Itsy and Michael didn't want to wait to get married, and a month after Breanna and Joshua had tied the knot, their friends did the same.

"We all picked weird dates to get married. October 20 and November 17. What's that about?" Breanna chuckled as she put her arms through the coat sleeves.

Joshua leaned in behind her ear and kissed it. "It's called being Christian and not sleeping with someone before wedlock."

"Well, none of us wanted to wait too long." She turned around in his arms and kissed him on the lips. She murmured, "I love you, Joshua Abrams."

He drew back his head to stare into her eyes. "I love you, Breanna Abrams. Don't ever forget it. Ever, no matter what." He became serious for a minute, and it seemed he might say something more. Breanna waited, but instead of telling her what he was thinking, Joshua gave a deep sigh and jokingly said, "But if we don't leave now, we won't be going anywhere. We'll be making our apologies and paying for our friends' cab." He whirled around and bent his arm. She laced her hand through the opening and leaned against him as they left the room.

36

BREANNA WOKE UP from dreaming about Joshua. As she lay in bed for a few minutes attempting to wake up fully, she remembered the morning after Itsy and Michael's wedding. What was Joshua going to say? Was he going to confess his spy profession to her? She dismissed it so quickly then. Maybe her memory was faulty. He sounded so earnest when he said he loved her and told her never to forget it. *Why am I torturing myself? It's too late now. I signed those papers. Besides, I've got to focus on Itsy right now.* Breanna gave her head a literal shake as she swung her legs over the side of the bed.

She looked over her shoulder, and Itsy was sleeping soundly. *Let her sleep. She probably needs it after last night.*

Breanna showered, changed, and ate breakfast, and Itsy continued to sleep through it all. When the guards came to escort them, Breanna said that Itsy was sick. She asked that food be brought to her friend for lunch.

That morning, while she was working, the lab door opened, and Edward came in fully suited up in a white lab coat, shoe covers, mask, gloves, and goggles.

"I heard that Itsy was sick today, so I thought I'd offer my help."

Breanna stared at him like an alien beamed into the workspace. "Ah! Um! I guess I can show you what to do."

He came close to her. "I like it when a woman takes charge."

The hairs on her arms stood on end, and she had to grind her teeth together so she wouldn't recoil or snap at him that he didn't like anyone else but himself giving orders. She was glad he couldn't read her mind, or she'd be in trouble.

Breanna got down to business and reviewed everything with him. The one thing she had appreciated about Edward in the past was his comprehension of the complexities of the nano programming. Again, she was impressed with his knowledge. *If only the situation were different, and I could truly see him as an equal and not my jailer.*

By the end of the day, Breanna was exhausted, and she yawned.

"I see you're tired. What about a quick dinner, then I'll take you back."

She rubbed her hands together, and her voice quivered when she said, "I'm really worried about Itsy. I should go see her right away."

Edward's eyes flashed. "No. I think you need to eat first." His voice softened. "For Bella, as well as you. Pushing yourself at this late date could cause early labour."

Breanna wanted to scoff at that statement because she didn't think it was true, but she could tell he would get angry if she tried to insist. She let him lead her to the dining room. On the way, he suddenly stopped in mid-stride, and she walked into the back of him. He twisted toward her and grasped her wrist as she attempted to step away. Breanna froze. Edward held up her hand that should have had the ring on it. She fished it out of her pocket. While she did that, he removed her elastic. As her hair fell around her shoulders, Edward began to massage her scalp. Unintentionally, a moan escaped her mouth because it felt so good. She swayed and closed her eyes. His lips descended on hers, and his kiss was deep and passionate. Because of her fatigue, physically and emotionally, Breanna allowed herself to enjoy it. The fight was gone.

When Edward pulled his lips away, a triumphant smile spread across his face. It was as if he could tell the change in her reaction from pretending to succumbing. Breanna let her head drop down into the curve of his shoulder blade. He held her in his arms gently. As she gathered herself, she took a step back. Edward reached down and took the ring out of her hand and placed it on her finger.

"It's not so bad, Breanna. I can make you happy. You've only got to permit yourself."

She nodded mutely. *He's right. I can make this easy or hard on myself. Easy feels better.* But her conscience niggled at her. She was a married woman. Married to someone else. How would God view this situation? Would he say that she was now one with Joshua under God forever? What could she do about Bella and Itsy if she resisted? Maybe she had to play along until she could rescue them.

Breanna remained quiet throughout dinner while her mind replayed the broken record repeatedly. She was so tired that her eyesight became blurry near the end of the meal.

"I have something to ask you," Edward said near the end of the meal.

She nodded as she raised her eyes to his face.

"How can you see the nanobots?"

Her brain snapped awake, but she kept her body from reacting. "What do you mean?"

"I have great vision. Even better than before, the nanos healed my body. But I can't see them. Yet I noticed today you picked out one without the magnifier."

"Did I?"

He leaned over and studied her face. "Yes." It came out as a hiss.

Breanna knew better than to lie, but she couldn't reveal the whole truth. Shrugging her shoulders, she said in a matter-of-fact tone, "I had laser surgery a couple of years ago and now I sometimes see small specs, like pepper shakes. I think they're nanos. Before the surgery, I needed thick glasses to see. It was frustrating. Now I think it's better than 20/20, if that's possible." She wouldn't betray Dr. Hakeem Sahal. Edward might have him murdered to prevent the doctor from using nanotechnology in people's eyes, like hers and Joshua's. *If Edward decides to revive his God Factor project, killing any opponents with nanos hidden in food and medicine, then Dr. Sahal's operation could save hundreds of people.*

"Oh. I thought it was some secret weapon." He laughed.

"What?" She chuckled. *How could I have thought to trust this man? He's a murderer. How could I have forgotten he killed John? Lord, help me.*

Edward reclined in his chair. "From what I saw today and results from the simulations, I think your program is ready to test on a human."

Breanna bristled at this. "I'm not sure it's ready."

"I am. Your friend, Itsy, needs you to succeed. Another seizure could kill her. You know she's getting worse." He pointed at her. "Tomorrow, Breanna."

Lord, help Itsy.

37

ITSY HELD BREANNA'S hand. "I have faith in Jesus. Don't worry. Everything will turn out. Trust him, Bree."

Breanna didn't tell Itsy she had already made up with God. She couldn't stay angry with him. He was all she had to hang on to and all Itsy had right now. She squeezed her blond friend's hand, then let go and hooked up the medical equipment to monitor Itsy's vitals. "I wish there was more time to test this."

"Most of your original program was intact. You only had to fill in the rest. Edward is proof that it works, or at least your part of it. That's all I need to heal me." Itsy fixed the pillow behind her head on the hospital bed in the lab. She wiggled into a comfortable position.

Biting her lower lip, Breanna rechecked the hookups several times.

"Hey. Stop fidgeting, and don't worry," Itsy repeated. Breanna continued to stall until Itsy grabbed her wrist and widened her eyes. "Stop."

Breanna stared at Itsy like it was the last time she would ever see her in the land of the living.

"Now you're freaking me out." Itsy's voice was raised. "Just do your magic. I'll be here when you're done."

Her shoes felt like they were lead platforms. Breanna dragged herself over to where Edward stood, watching her silently and closely. He handed her the syringe filled with the programmed microscopic nanorobots in a harmless liquid. After she clicked a few keys on the computer, she was ready to begin.

Bree returned to her friend. "It shouldn't hurt, but the solution will feel cold as it enters your system. You might also be a bit uncomfortable, like you don't belong in your skin. I've tried to speed up the process in the programming, so it shouldn't be too long. We'll know if it's working within seconds."

Itsy nodded and smiled, but Breanna noticed her friend's hands were curled into fists. Both women sent up silent prayers for success.

The injection was put directly into Itsy's vein so her heart would pump the nanos throughout the body. When Breanna completely emptied the vial, she hurried to the computer and began activating the microcomputers. She looked up to see her friend squirming on the bed as the foreign objects surged through her body. The scientist turned up the speed of the program by 50 percent. Itsy began to cry out and convulse on the bed. The only way to help her friend was to turn the speed to full power. Itsy arched her back and then fell back onto the bed unconscious. The machines measuring the patient's vitals slowly returned to a normal, steady rhythm after having been off the charts through the short procedure.

The computer keys clicked a couple of times, and then Breanna turned from the machine and ran to her friend. "Itsy? Itsy?"

A soft voice slurred out, "Hey, Bree. I told you I'd still be here."

"I'm sorry I didn't have any sedatives for you. It would have gone smoother."

Itsy's blue eyes fluttered opened, looking clear. Breanna took a flashlight and checked her pupil dilations. They were lightning fast. "Am I fit for duty, doctor?"

She checked the monitors, and everything registered as normal. Breanna was happy to see that every measurement was perfect. Even Itsy's slight heart murmur was corrected. With a sigh of relief and a very large smile, she said, "You look wonderful. I'd like to run a couple of tests, but I think it was a total success."

"I knew you could do it. But you lied." Itsy's voice was strong.

"How?"

"It hurt like hell," she said.

"Yikes! Sorry. I was afraid of going too fast. I wanted to be able to shut it down if necessary. It made the process more painful." Breanna was suddenly brushed aside by Edward, who grabbed Itsy's arm and sliced it with a razor-sharp surgeon's knife.

Itsy yelled in surprise. Breanna screamed for her friend. The scientist tried to move the large, muscular man but couldn't budge him. Edward continued to hold her friend's arm. Then he picked up an edge of the sheet covering the bed and wiped Itsy's bloody injury. It was gone. No cut, no scar, no more bleeding.

He began to laugh. Releasing Itsy, he turned and hugged Breanna. "You did it. She has the healing nanos working in her body. This is it." He clapped and walked towards the door. "Now you need to finish Lucinda's programming, and it will be complete." He rapped, and a guard let him leave the lab while Breanna was left reeling from that unexpected event.

Itsy's hand flew to her mouth. "I feel something moving in my jaw. Look at it, will you?"

Bree picked up the light she used to check Itsy's eyes and peered into her mouth. She clicked off the light and stood up straight. "Your tooth." She shook her head. "Your tooth is regrowing before my eyes." Then she ran a finger across her friend's cheek. "Your scar is gone." Resting her thumb and forefinger under Itsy's chin, she swivelled her friend's face side to side. Her mouth fell open for a moment.

Curiosity got Itsy. "What?"

Breanna walked across the room and came back with a mirror used to put the nanos on during their work. Holding it aloft, Itsy gazed at her reflection. She ran a hand over her skin. "Flawless. Like a new baby's skin." No marks, scars, spots, dark circles, puffy eyes, crows' feet, wrinkles, lines, or any imperfections of any kind were visible. She checked her new tooth, which was completely repaired. Even her chipped tooth was fixed. "How can this be? It's like some kind of miracle." Breanna removed Itsy's vital sign wires.

"Trust me, even I didn't expect this kind of success. You look like a model. Did I accidentally discover the fountain of youth? If so, I could sure use it." They both giggled. "I wouldn't do anything until after Bella was born, of course. There is no way of knowing what it would do to a baby, but look at you." She stood, shaking her head in disbelief.

Itsy jumped off the bed and hugged her friend. "I know vanity is a sin, but I worried what Michael would think of me scar-faced and missing teeth. Thank you, Bree. Thank you, Jesus."

"It's early yet. I want to monitor you to ensure the seizures are cured, but it looks promising." Breanna rubbed her mouth. She was happy that this seemed to work on her friend. However, she didn't want to finish the enhanced soldier program for Edward, and this was the first half of the procedure. Any way Breanna could delay completing the second half would be welcome. "Also, we have to make sure there are no negative reactions." She widened her eyes in silent communication.

Itsy didn't catch the look Breanna shot her, and in her excitement, flapped her hand, "There won't be. You rocked this. My friend, the genius."

Breanna rolled her eyes and sighed.

38

THAT EVENING, EDWARD permitted Breanna to observe Itsy in their bedroom. It galled her to have to beg for every special favour, but she was able to argue it was for the sake of science and his program. *Not mine. Intellectual copyrights always go to the one funding the program.* She began to wonder; if he was tired of her at any time, who would meet with a tragic accident, Itsy or Bella or herself? There was nothing she'd put past him. Everything was by his leave.

It was nice to spend time with Itsy. She was back to her old self, funny and chatty. Breanna had worried she might never see it again since the seizures had taken their toll on her once vibrant friend. Now, Breanna relished seeing her friend healthy.

Talking to Breanna's belly, Itsy said, "Bella, if you grow any bigger, you're going to burst out of your mama's tummy." She rubbed the stretched skin, and a little hand or foot rippled across her stomach. Breanna and Itsy giggled. "See, she recognizes her Aunt Itsy's voice! Little girl, I am going to spoil you rotten. We'll go shopping and have spa days. I'll be your favourite. And I know lots of card games."

"No teaching my daughter how to gamble."

"I wasn't talking poker. Besides, Carol, Betty, and I play for dimes, not big cash. We're admins, remember. No big paydays for us." Itsy smiled, but the sides of her eyes slanted down, betraying the underlying sadness.

It remained unspoken, but both knew they wondered if they even had a future, never mind a so-called normal one. Would they ever see their family and friends again?

Not wanting to ruin the celebration of her healing, Itsy clapped her hands. "Oh, you wait, Bella, I'm going to teach you all the crazy songs your mother and I sing. I'll also have to teach you to dance because"—she pointed at Breanna—"that girl ain't got no moves."

"What are you talking about? I've got rhythm." She stood up and did a sideways shimmy, but the pregnant belly made it appear to be a bobbing balloon at an Easter parade.

"Ha-ha!" Itsy folded over at the hilarious sight. "You look a bit like Jabba the Hutt from one of those *Star Wars* movies."

Breanna stood with her hands on her hips. "Now you've gone too far. You hurt my feelings."

"Just one?"

"That's all I have left, and now you've crushed it." Breanna tried to fake a hurt look, but she sputtered, then it rolled into a full roar. She began coughing as she tried to catch her breath. Itsy joined her. "Seriously, if I'm six and a half months, I still have another two and a half left. How big is this girl? Maybe there are two of them in there."

"Actually, I know you feel big, but in terms of pregnant ladies I've seen, you look pretty average."

"You sure she's not an elephant?"

"Well, if she were, elephants are pregnant for about ninety-five weeks instead of the forty weeks for humans. Can you imagine double the weeks plus fifteen more?"

"Ah! No. Poor elephants."

"Well, look at the size of their babies. Bella will be perfect. She's not too big." Itsy rubbed Breanna's baby bump. "Bella will be a beautiful fairy."

The redhead's heart flew into her throat at the same time that her hand reached for it. "That's what Edward called her."

Itsy formed an O with her mouth but said nothing so that Edward wouldn't hear. *The man hijacks everything good.*

Raising her shoulders, Breanna decided to brush it off. She said, "I have to check all your vitals again." She pulled out the medical bag she had brought with her, including the laptop to record the scientific data.

"Only don't slice me like Edward." Breanna shook her head no. Itsy complied with all the testing, probing, and prodding until Breanna was satisfied. "What's your prognosis, doctor?"

"I think you'll live to work in the lab another day."

"Yippee for me." Itsy became quiet. "But seriously, thank you."

Breanna said, "It is such a relief that it worked. I was afraid."

"I could tell. But then so was I."

"I noticed."

Itsy hid her mouth with her hand like she was chewing a nail. She nodded toward the laptop and mouthed the question. "Are the two programs on there?"

Breanna nodded and mouthed. "Not on Edward's mainframe."

They both thought, *hopefully, we can keep it that way.*

39

"JOSHUA!" BREANNA WAS startled to see him sitting in the dining room at Edward's home. "What are you doing here?"

"Hello, Bree." His voice was curt. "Edward invited me."

She looked around the room, but Edward wasn't there. "I ... I don't understand. Why?"

"He thought we should talk." Joshua was sitting in Edward's seat at the table. He patted her usual chair on Edward's right. "Sit."

Feeling like a deer in the headlights, Breanna knew there was no way to run. An armed guard stood outside the door she had just been escorted through. She moved cautiously toward the seat.

Her heart was thumping in her chest. She didn't think she would ever see Joshua again, and here he was at the table. The heat in her cheeks burned as she laboured to control her breathing.

"Look at me, Breanna," Joshua ordered.

Forcing herself to meet his eyes, she saw a coldness in there she had never seen before. Even when he had been upset with her, there was always an undercurrent of love. Her body vibrated with the nerves she was experiencing. She waited.

He broke the silence. "Nothing to say? You usually have so much to chatter on about, and now not a thing."

Tears pricked her eyes. He had never sounded so cruel.

"Stop snivelling. Do you know how tiresome that gets? You're always crying about something. Grow up."

Breanna struggled to contain herself. *It's best to appease him. I don't want him to get angry and hurt the baby or Itsy.* She realized she was thinking of Joshua the same way she did with Edward, but he was acting identically.

"I came for the baby."

"Huh?"

"Edward said he didn't want my son around. He needed you to focus on having his children. After all, you're marrying him." There was disdain for Breanna in his tone.

Shaking her head, Breanna cried, "I don't have the baby yet, and she's a girl." Her hand moved to her stomach and found it was flat. She jumped to her feet. "Where's my baby?"

"Bree, you had my son a month ago. I came for him."

It was then that she remembered she had a baby boy. Was she so upset at seeing Joshua that she had forgotten momentarily? "You can't have my son. He's mine."

Joshua jumped to his feet and grabbed her by both wrists. "He's my son. Edward doesn't want him. You can have more."

"You can have more too. He's mine."

"There'll be no discussion. Edward is having Mr. Maxwell take the baby to my car." He threw her wrists down.

Breanna's eyes became saucers. "No. He's mine. You're a liar. You used me."

"It's already done. I used you; Edward used you—poor little Breanna. Enjoy your new life. Goodbye."

She grabbed his arm and hung on. "You will not take my baby."

"Bree." She felt shaking. "Bree. No one is taking your baby." Breanna felt someone shaking her arm, and Itsy's voice said, "No one is taking your baby. She's still here inside you."

"Oh, Itsy. It was awful. Joshua came to take the baby. He made a deal with Edward. Bella was not a girl but a boy." She ran a hand over her face and found it wet.

Itsy put an arm around her. "Hush. No one is taking your baby. We won't let them."

"In case you haven't noticed, we're not in a position to do much of anything."

Her friend rocked her gently. "Be patient. It will all turn out all right. I just know it."

"Well, I don't. I feel helpless. I'm at the mercy of Edward and Joshua, in some ways." She closed her eyes. "Why is this happening? What is God doing?"

"I guess Jesus felt the same when he was handed over to the religious leaders. He put up with torture, beatings, and death for us. He didn't have to, but he did. I feel like he's asking us if we can do this for him. I guess we have to pick up our crosses." Itsy was thoughtful.

Breanna pondered what her friend had said about Jesus. "I guess I can pick up my cross for him. One thing Joshua said to me in the dream was to stop being a crybaby. I think I need to work on that issue. Jesus didn't sob all the way to the cross."

Itsy smirked. "Maybe he did."

"You are too much." Breanna smiled. "I'm glad you are my friend."

40

THE NEXT FEW weeks were like the movie *Groundhog Day*. Each day was a repeat of the day before. Breanna started by reviewing what Joshua had copied of Lucinda's program. Then she examined what other biomedical engineers had come up with for Edward. None of those were even close to her and Lucinda's progress. This took an enormous amount of time. In the end, she decided to focus solely on the incomplete program Joshua had copied. It was frustratingly slow.

Itsy was healthier than she had ever been. She cut her finger in the lab, and the nanos healed it up in seconds. True to her nature, her best friend tried to be upbeat and helpful to Breanna. She was like a ray of sunshine in Bree's darkness.

As for Breanna, she was feeling tired most afternoons and took a twenty-to-thirty-minute nap each day. On November 16, Edward took her to another appointment with the obstetrician, and he played the excited father-to-be to a T. Bella was growing normally, and the doctor had no concerns about the baby. Edward told the doctor he was worried about Breanna because she seemed excessively tired and stressed. He wondered if she shouldn't be getting more rest. The doctor and he talked as if Breanna weren't in the room. When the obstetrician finally began asking her questions about Edward's report, he flashed a warning stare at Breanna from behind the doctor, so she confirmed everything he said. The doctor ordered her to get more rest and stated that if she didn't follow her advice, she would be on complete bed rest. Edward asked the obstetrician about travelling, and she said it wasn't advisable. As they left the doctor's office, Breanna wondered what that was all about. Was Edward really worried about her health?

Outside the building, Edward had Breanna pose for the paparazzi waiting for them. He gave a brief interview to a reporter about how happy they both were with the baby's development. Edward added that Breanna was not doing as well, and she was ordered to have complete bed rest. Why he lied to the man was confusing, but Bree said nothing.

The following morning, she commiserated with Itsy over not being with Michael for their first anniversary. Their mood was sombre, and both women got down to business rather than talk.

Edward had Breanna brought to his office in the middle of the afternoon. When she entered, he was standing in front of the bookcase. When he twirled to face her, his eyes were burning with rage. Breanna didn't know what had happened, and she was terrified to find out. Wringing her hands, she glanced toward the door. Fighting her instinct to escape, she stood perfectly still and waited for him to speak or summon her closer.

"Come here." Edward pointed to one of the overstuffed wingback chairs.

Dutifully, she followed his direction.

He sat down beside her and began massaging her knee. She was careful not to flinch or make any mention of the pain. The swelling in that leg had come down, but the bruises were still dark from the last time he was angry with her. "It's all right, Breanna. You didn't do anything wrong."

She exhaled the breath she had been holding.

"Unfortunately, I have bad news for you."

Her eyebrows knitted together. *What now?*

"Joshua is refusing to give you a divorce unless you come to court in Tel Aviv. His lawyer says he wants you there in person." Edward ground his teeth at the end of the sentence.

Dear Lord. I can't. "I don't want to see him."

This pleased Edward as the corners of his mouth twitched, suppressing a smile. It was how she truly felt about facing Joshua, but Edward's satisfaction at her response was a relief. His demeanour changed as he took on the appearance of contrition, eyebrows raised in the middle, a frown, and a soft tone. "I know. I'm trying to get my lawyer to deal with it. With your present condition and the doctor saying you can't travel, the divorce will have to proceed without you."

Now she had her answer. Edward had manipulated her and the obstetrician for this reason. His apparent anger today was another trick to have her say what he wanted to hear. He was transparent in his motives, but she didn't care. She, Itsy, and the baby were safe. *Let Edward celebrate his victory.*

He patted her knee. "I will take care of everything. Don't worry, Breanna. I'll get the doctor to send the court a letter through my lawyer." He rested his hand and gave her knee a little squeeze. It wasn't hard, but the message was clear. "How's Lucinda's program coming?"

The threatening maneuver ensured compliance. "Ah! Umm." The switch in topic served to snap her out of fear mode. She was in her element again. "I have eliminated all the work of the other engineers. None of them came close to her program. I've decided I'll focus on building her project partly from memory but mostly on logical progression." Then she added, "It's too bad that when Joshua copied the work, he didn't copy the whole thing to save us the trouble." She didn't hide the bitterness in her voice. It wasn't because she wanted Edward to have the program sooner; it was because of Joshua lying to her. *But let Edward take it as he will.*

Edward said, "I agree. But if anyone can do it, you can. I have every faith in you."

"Lucinda was brilliant. Her program was … is ahead of its time." She meant it, but as soon as it left her lips, she wondered if she had gone too far. After all, Edward blamed her for his sister's death. She held her breath as his eyes narrowed.

After a brief pause, he said, "When you get the program to work. My sister will be the first one I try it on."

Breanna's mouth went dry. She repeated the words she thought he had said the night he showed her Lucinda's burnt body. "Raising the dead?"

Edward leaned his face in closer to hers and sneered, "Like your Jesus."

41

WHEN THE TWO women joined hands before bed that night, Breanna slipped in the information disguised as a prayer. "Dear Lord, please let Edward get the doctor's note that I can't travel, so I don't have to testify in divorce court in Israel. I don't want to see Joshua."

"I am praying in agreement with Bree. Don't let her have to face Joshua. Let it go through smoothly." This was Itsy's way of confirming she understood. However, she wondered if it was the best idea. Maybe if Breanna saw Joshua, then things could work out between them. Itsy said a sincere prayer. "I ask that you heal Michael from the gunshot wound. If he has passed, let him be with you, Lord, and say hi from me."

"I pray for Michael's healing. I have faith that he survived and someday he and Itsy will be reunited." Breanna believed in her heart that he was alive. Then she added her other news. "I pray that I will be able to complete this soldier program so that Edward can try to heal Lucinda with it."

Itsy's eyes bulged. Itsy had been too sick for Breanna to tell her what she thought happened the night Edward took her to see his sister in the coffin-like tube.

Breanna continued, "Abba, you know that Lucinda is in a cryogenic chamber, and Edward has kept her frozen since shortly after the plane crash. He wants his sister back from the dead, Lord, and this program might be able to do it." *Lord, I am sorry for the false prayer. Don't let him raise a demon in that woman's body.*

"Amen," Itsy said, incredulous at the new revelation.

"Amen," said Breanna.

After the lights were turned out, Breanna lay awake in bed. She stared at the faint line from the moonlight peeking into the room from the window high on the wall. She smiled as she noticed for the first time that it was shaped like a cross. Was it because of the position of the moon this time of year? Why hadn't it shown up before?

Lord, are you there? Even though I don't hear or feel you, I've got to believe you have heard me and Itsy. I'm confused and hurt about Joshua. No matter what, I pray you bless him. I don't wish him any ill will. I forgive him, even though I don't know if I can ever trust him again. I don't understand why this has turned out the way it has, but I'm going to trust you in this storm.

Edward and Itsy don't realize how close I am to solving the soldier program. I have a gut feeling that I'm not going to turn it over to Edward, not yet anyway. King Jesus, I need your help to keep this under the radar. In Itsy's case, it's to keep her safe. For Edward, I don't think he should play god and give demons a body to inhabit, that's if the program will even work to raise someone from the dead. If you have other ideas, feel free to download them into my spirit or let me know in some other way.

How I wish you would send angels to release us from prison, like you did with Peter. But it's not my will, but thine.

―――――――――

The following weeks continued as every other day. Edward did not call for Breanna, so she guessed he was away on business again. It gave her a chance to breathe easier.

Meanwhile, little Bella was doing tryouts for the Olympics in Breanna's belly. She would wake her mother up in the morning, jiggling around, and if Breana rolled onto a side Bella didn't like during the night, she would push against the bed through the womb until her mama rolled over.

It was the morning of the first of December when Breanna complained to Itsy. "Bella is so demanding. She's not even born, and she directs in which position I can sleep and when."

Itsy chuckled at Breanna's report.

"Fine for you to laugh, you're not the one losing sleep. You wait until she's born. I'm going to put you on night bottle duty so I can get some rest."

"You're probably going to breastfeed, so I can't help you there."

"I'll supplement at night."

"You want something to drink this morning? Maybe some herbal tea? That might make you feel less cranky."

"I want coffee."

"Really?"

"Yes. But I'm not going to drink it because it's not good for Bella." Breanna huffed. "Fine, I'll have herbal tea."

Itsy made a face and used a baby voice. "Are you a Grumpy Gus, Princess?"

Breanna flashed angry eyes at her friend. "Yes, I am. I'm tired, and I'm as big as a horse."

"Bwahh!" Itsy moved over to the kitchenette area and filled the kettle.

"You are the least supportive person in the world. Everyone else would feel sorry for me. You mock me and poke fun at my suffering." Breanna arranged a small back pillow and plopped down onto the chair.

Her friend said, "I wouldn't do it if I knew you couldn't handle it. Besides, you always feel somewhat better if you laugh at yourself."

"I'm sure Bella is going to join you in the teasing when she's old enough. I think she's already started."

Itsy walked over with the tea. "Good. I need a partner in crime. I'll have a Mini-Me."

"More like an evil minion."

"No, an angelic one."

Breanna snickered. "Of course. She's part of me. She must be angelic." Breanna gave her friend a toothy grin.

"Okay. I can see you're feeling better already." Itsy sat in the other chair and sipped her coffee. When they were done with the pastries, fruit, and beverages, Itsy took the tray over to the door and placed it on the floor.

"Let's get to the lab, shall we?" Itsy knocked and called, "We're ready."

42

IT WAS ABOUT ten in the morning when a faint commotion came from outside. Both women stopped working and listened. It was like déjà vu for Breanna.

The scientist quickly started filling syringes with the newly programmed nanobots. Itsy gave her a questioning look but began to help without saying a word. While Itsy finished up what Breanna was doing, Breanna ran to the mainframe to put in the memory stick. She copied her work onto it, plugged the stick into her laptop, and typed the commands for the program to activate. Breanna grabbed the briefcase left in the room by Edward in October when he brought some of his nanobots in for her to test on the program. She and Itsy placed all the syringes filled with replicated nanobots in the briefcase, with foam wrapped around each one to ensure they didn't break. Then Breanna closed the lid of the laptop without shutting down the program in case it was needed.

She grabbed Itsy's hand and pulled her over to the side of the door to wait for whoever came through. There was no way of knowing if it would be friend or foe.

Bratatat bratatat. Bratatat bratatat. The machine gun fire was coming from inside and outside the castle. They could hear indistinguishable yelling in the house.

When the lab door swung open, Breanna's heart fell when she saw Edward's face. He motioned with his hand and said, "Quick. Come with me."

The noise and chaos could be heard above them while the two women ran behind their kidnapper. Itsy held the briefcase, and Breanna clutched the laptop. Edward led them through the basement until they reached the oldest part under the keep. He pointed to a tunnel as he hurried them forward. Edward's story about Aed sneaking out at night in the twelfth century flashed in Breanna's mind. This must have been the exit Aed used. Breanna struggled to keep up in her pregnant condition. Itsy noticed Breanna's difficulty and took the laptop from her. She tucked it under one arm while holding the briefcase in her other hand.

At the end of the tunnel was a staircase leading up to a wooden door. Taking the stairs two at a time, Edward put a hand up, and they both stopped. He opened the door a crack and peeked out. Satisfied the coast was clear, he told them to stay close. He led the way into the garage. There waiting was the limo with Mr. Maxwell in the driver's seat.

As the two women ran toward the car, a recognizable voice yelled, "Itsy!"

Itsy grabbed Breanna's hand to stop her flight. "Michael?"

Shots rang out, and Edward ducked behind the limo door.

Meanwhile, Itsy dragged her friend towards her husband on the other side of the massive building. Breanna wasn't resisting, but she was frightened and found it hard to move fast.

Michael closed the distance, and both women noticed a semiautomatic in his hand. They didn't have time to make contact before Edward was on them. He grabbed the gun from Michael, twisting it from his hand. Edward's nanos gave him superhuman strength, and Michael didn't stand a chance. The strong man began pounding his opponent. Itsy dropped Breanna's hand and shoved the briefcase and laptop into her friend's arms. She jumped in to help her husband. Itsy gave Edward one of her roundhouse kicks to the head. The kidnapper staggered but recovered quickly. He swung at Itsy, who was able to duck under his right hook to give him an upper jab to his nose. He backhanded her, and she flew about ten feet away.

The cracking sound was proof that Itsy had broken the bone. Still, it barely caused Edward to flinch. The nose began instantly healing itself. Michael was up off the cement and used his whole body as a battering ram. Edward reeled backwards but grabbed Michael's arm as he did. Edward twisted and used his two hands to pull Michael's right shoulder out of the socket and break the forearm at the same time.

Breanna fought the urge to throw up at the sound of snapping bones. She watched in amazement as Michael's body rapidly healed itself. *Nanotechnology? How?* Edward picked Michael up off the ground as if he were Itsy's weight. He was about to deliver a blow when the tiny woman raced at Edward again. Itsy was fast. She had been training every evening to keep up her fighting skills. She grabbed Edward's arm, set to punch her husband, and used her entire body to wrap around Edward. It would have brought down most men, but Edward's muscle mass and strength were excessive. He dropped Michael like a puppet onto the floor and flipped Itsy beside her husband. Edward brought his foot up to stomp on her head, but she rolled out of the way. He kicked her, and Itsy's ribs made a terrible sound as they cracked.

Breanna backed up against the wall behind her. She wanted to stay away from the fighting and away from the limo.

Edward turned to Michael and kicked him twice in rapid succession. Then Breanna saw Edward look towards the gun. As he took a step in that direction, a shot rang out and hit Edward in the middle of his stomach before he fell. Joshua came running in to help his friends with a handgun. No sooner did he reach Michael than Edward stood up and grabbed Joshua by the arm. He flung Breanna's husband into the wall next to her, and she heard the thud as his head hit the bricks. Blood smeared as he slid down to the ground. He didn't move. *No healing nanos?*

Breanna glanced at Edward, who was facing Itsy and Michael. She saw Mr. Maxwell get out of the car with a gun. Without thinking, she knelt and pulled Joshua's from his hand. The nanos in her eyes zoomed into her prey, and she shot him in the heart. Mr. Maxwell fell dead.

43

WHEN HE WITNESSED his butler's death, Edward became enraged. His assault on his two remaining assailants increased in speed and savagery. Each injury resulted in their programmed nanobots rapidly healing their bodies, but Breanna didn't like the looks of the situation. Her friends would eventually lose the fight once there were too many injuries for the nanos to heal. The utter chaos inside the garage matched the noise of gunfire and yelling outside the building.

Refusing to focus on the man she had killed, she wanted to care for the living. She checked Joshua's pulse. It was faint, but he was still alive. He obviously didn't have the same nanos as Itsy and Michael. Breanna acted quickly. She removed a syringe from the case and opened the laptop. Giving Joshua the shot in the arm, Breanna quickly typed in the activation code.

Joshua's body began a rapid growth process. The healing program kept up with the muscle development, and within a minute, he woke up, transformed before her. He was Joshua, but much more. Dark eyes stared at her as realization filled them.

"Edward's going to kill them, and you were dying. I had no choice." Inwardly, she was thanking God that it worked. There had been no way to test the program.

Joshua jumped to his feet and engaged Edward. The two men were locked in an equal match of supersoldier to supersoldier.

Breanna crawled over to Itsy, who appeared to be barely holding on to life. Her nanos were stretched thin, trying to heal all the bones Edward had broken. Using another syringe, she injected her friend and activated the program. This time, she didn't wait for the process to finish because Michael looked like he might have been killed. When she felt for a pulse, she didn't find it, but decided it was within the time for successful CPR, so she could try the nanos on him instead. It worked instantly, and he began to breathe again.

When her two friends and husband were all healed and on an even footing with Edward, Breanna crawled back toward the wall. She passed the semiautomatic weapon Michael had carried, and she dragged it with her along with the laptop and briefcase.

The fighting went on for a long time. Edward refused to surrender. Joshua spotted the two guns beside Breanna. Without acknowledging her, he grabbed the semiauto and shot into the air. Only then did Edward capitulate. None of them knew if they would survive multiple bullets to the head or heart.

"Lock him in the room he kept us in," Itsy offered. Her voice was deeper but recognizable.

Michael asked Joshua for the semiautomatic gun.

When Breanna dared to meet Edward's eyes, he was glaring murderously at her. She threw her arms protectively around her stomach and made herself as small as possible, refusing to look up again. She heard the shuffling of feet and the door to the tunnel opening and closing.

The gunfire outside had stopped sometime during the battle in the garage. Breanna remained on the cold cement floor, unmoving, wondering if this was another dream. A large hand appeared in front of her face. She raised her eyes to see Joshua in front of her. Insecurities plagued her mind. All the questions about his true motives for marrying her made her drop her gaze to his hand. Thinking he only wanted the soldier program, Breanna lifted the case and laptop toward him. Joshua tucked the two objects under one arm, then held out the other hand for her.

She stole a glance at Joshua's face. The rugged man before her didn't look the same as the man she married. Maybe she could pretend he was someone else to get through the emotional turmoil he was creating in her heart. Breanna took the hand, and he lifted her nearly eight-month pregnant body like it was a rag doll. Averting her eyes from him, she remained silent.

"Come this way." Joshua's voice betrayed no emotion, but he didn't release her hand. They went outside, and she looked around at the estate, which was crawling with mercenaries on both sides. She had no idea who Joshua had enlisted to help rescue her and Itsy, but there appeared to be many soldiers. It looked like a war zone with the bodies of the dead and injured.

When they reached one of the parked Hummers, Joshua opened the door for her. She crawled inside, and he closed the door without getting in. Joshua peered into the driver's window. "Take her to the plane. We'll be there in a couple of minutes." He hit the roof but didn't turn back in her direction.

Breanna's heart was numb. No longer sure how to feel or what to believe, she stared straight ahead as she had learned to do with Edward. It wasn't safe to feel or to show her emotions. *Do what you're told, and you won't get hurt.* On the plane, she sat where directed with her hands folded on her lap. Someone would tell her what to do soon enough. Several men boarded the transport plane, none of whom she recognized. It felt like an eternity before the superhuman trio entered through the door.

Itsy ran to Breanna and threw her arms around her. "You saved us. I didn't know you had completed the project until I saw you filling the vials and downloading the program." Itsy fastened her seatbelt in the seat beside Breanna and pulled Breanna's across for her. "It was incredibly brave of you to defy Edward."

The taller and bulkier Michael stood behind his wife, who now looked to be Breanna's height. He kissed Breanna on the cheek. "Thanks, Bree. It's sure good to see you." He looked over at Itsy. "Both of you. We knew you were alive, Bree, thanks to the paparazzi photos, but we knew nothing about Itsy."

He plopped down next to his wife and fastened his seatbelt.

Feeling overwhelmed, Breanna couldn't speak. She noticed from the corner of her eye Joshua sitting further down with some of the soldiers. *He doesn't want to be near me. I guess he got what he wanted, so I'm of no further use. I'm not going to give him the satisfaction of seeing me cry.*

44

THEY MANAGED TO fly out of Ireland without a problem. Breanna didn't know how it was arranged, but it didn't matter. She was free. *Why don't I feel free?* She closed her eyes to shut out the world.

When she opened them later, they were still in the air. Itsy and Michael were gone. Joshua looked like he was helping the wounded. Breanna unfastened her seatbelt and asked the closest man where the bathrooms were on the plane. He pointed to a sign near the front. It meant walking past Joshua. *Put on your big girl pants, Breanna. You've got to go.*

Even though she pretended to be brave, inside, her stomach was rolling. As she passed Joshua, Breanna noticed he was administering her nanobots to the men who were in critical condition. When he glanced at her, she spun her head away. The bathroom was small and not a welcome place to spend any more time than necessary. As she exited, the plane hit an air pocket, and there was a sudden drop. Breanna's legs gave out, and she fell. Joshua was beside her in a flash. He put an arm around her and gently lifted her into his arms. Without a word, he carried her back to her seat. She felt the heat in her cheeks, and her heart was racing.

When Joshua placed her in her seat, he grabbed her seatbelt. "You should keep this on. These are not like commercial airliners." She nodded, then lowered her head. "Bree. Look at me, please." Her head snapped up. *Follow orders, it's always safer.* His eyes narrowed, but his voice was gentle, "You don't have to be afraid of me. I'm not Edward." She blinked but couldn't speak. "I forgive you. I know you did what you had to for Itsy and yourself to survive." The lump in her throat made it impossible to speak. Her heart physically hurt, and to keep from crying, she pressed her lips together tightly. Joshua let out an audible sigh. He fastened her seatbelt and went back to triage with the injured.

Breanna sat still and silent. She squeezed her hands in her lap. Hearing Itsy's deeper but recognizable laugh from the back of the plane, Breanna twisted her head to see her friend on Michael's lap. Itsy was animated with arms waving and a broad smile. *Thank you, Abba, for my friend. For her happy ending. She went through a lot over these crazy eight months. Thank you for Michael's life.* Breanna didn't realize she had a smile on her face as she watched her friends.

"It's nice to see them together." The sound of Joshua's husky voice beside her caused her to jolt. "Sorry, I didn't mean to startle you."

"Did you use my program on Michael?"

"Yes. When Bobby told me what happened, I went back to the lab and began frantically working out the missing pieces to your program. It took me a while, but I got it. I was able to use it on Michael to bring him out of the induced coma."

"I'm glad. I had the memory stick from your briefcase and found it there. I had to get it working to heal Itsy."

"What happened to her?"

"Edward had her badly beaten as a warning to both of us. She had a brain injury as a result, and she was getting worse. It really scared me." Breanna glanced back at her friend, remembering the fear of losing her.

His hand covered hers. She stared at the large, muscular appendage as if it belonged to an alien. This man was a stranger to her. Breanna wondered if she had ever known him at all. "I'm sorry you went through all of that," he said. "It must have been awful."

Not taking her eyes off his hand, she asked, "How did you copy some of Lucinda's and my programs? I was with you in China at the mainframe. Why wouldn't you copy it all?"

"I didn't copy it. One of the Mossad agents who came with me to China located your and Lucinda's rooms and took your tablets. He hoped they'd be overlooked. When we returned to Israel, the tablets were given to me to figure out the programs. We didn't know they wouldn't be complete, but it made sense since the finished program was on the computers with larger memories."

"So why did you need me to complete them. You could figure them out. Obviously, you did for Michael."

"You're right, I didn't need you to complete them. I loved you and wanted to be with you for the rest of my life." Placing a finger under her chin, he lifted her face. "I never lied about any of that, Bree."

"But you lied about everything else. How can I trust you're not lying now?"

Joshua released her chin. "You're right. I should have told you everything before we got married. So many times I tried, but I was afraid of losing you."

The tears were at the corners of her eyes, and she stared at the ceiling, willing them to run back where they came from.

"Seems like it happened anyway. If you want, I'll sign the divorce papers."

Breanna unfastened the seatbelt and moved as fast as she could to the bathroom. Safely behind the locked door, she let the tears flow freely.

ITSY AND BREANNA were back in Canada, hidden in one of the Montreal safe houses. It had taken two days to get there with many people working to cover their tracks. They were smuggled in on cargo planes so no trail would be left for Edward.

Itsy came to the room assigned to Breanna to check on her and find out what was happening with Joshua. "You're an idiot. I'm sorry to call you a name, but really, Bree. Don't let him sign the divorce papers. You love him, and he loves you. You need to talk this out … yell it out … whatever it takes."

Breanna rested her hands on her belly. "I don't know how to talk to him or what to say. The way he looks at me. It's not the same as it used to be. I can't explain it, but I don't know if he loves me anymore."

"Did you talk about Bella?"

"He didn't mention the baby at all. Joshua didn't even look at my stomach. It was as if he was trying to avoid it." She made circular motions over the mound. "And Bella's not moving as much. I hope she's okay. On the Internet, they say that when the baby gets really large, they don't have as much room to move. And she might be slowly moving into position to be born."

Itsy bent over to speak to the bulging tummy. "Soon, baby Bella. Soon I'm going to hold you. Aunt Isabella can't wait."

"What if Joshua doesn't want me or the baby? What if he only wants the baby? What if he tries to take her?" Itsy was the one person in the world she could confide in. Breanna was still worried about her dream. Could it have been prophetic?

Itsy said, "I don't believe it for a minute. He would never take your baby from you. The whole situation is such a shock to him. Remember, he didn't know you were pregnant when you left. And Edward went around telling the world it was his baby. That's got to mess with the guy's mind a little."

"He probably does think it's Edward's baby. Then he won't want to kidnap my child."

"Bree, you've got to tell him. You can't have the baby without telling the real father."

Breanna folded her arms over her stomach. "I can do whatever I want. Joshua hasn't asked me. He just assumed. Why do I have to share her?"

Itsy waved her two hands in the air in exasperation. "It's wrong. That's why you have to tell him."

"Well, he's not here. He didn't come with us. Joshua said he had to turn the program over to Mossad. It's what he wanted all along." Breanna let out a huff. "If he shows up, I will tell him. Deal?"

"No deal. This isn't a game. Maybe you should call him. You know, offer the olive branch."

Pouting, she said, "Why are you on his side? You're my friend."

Now it was Itsy's turn to fold her arms. "I am your friend, and I am saying this for you." She softened her voice. "I will always be on your side."

Placing a hand on her forehead, Breanna said, "I don't know how to do this anymore. Edward robbed me of my sense of self. I'm confused, and I swing between fear and anger. Edward eroded my trust in Joshua and men in general. What do I do?"

"You need some therapy. Unfortunately, with Edward looking for us, you'll just have to give yourself time to heal." Itsy stared off into space. "I know sometimes I wake up terrified that I'm back in the cell, afraid to say the wrong thing."

"Post-traumatic stress disorder. We both have it."

"I wouldn't doubt if you had a little Stockholm syndrome, too. Edward sure played mind games with you. And I can say it now that we aren't constantly being monitored … I saw the bruises he left on your body. He hurt you." Breanna put her hands over her eyes, trying to hide the shame of being abused. "It wasn't your fault. None of this was your fault."

Lowering her hands, Breanna said, "At first, I only thought about keeping you and Bella safe. When he said I could keep Bella after she was born, it added another layer of control. Later, it became about avoiding being punished every time I said or did something wrong. I never knew what to expect. Sometimes he was so nice. Other times, he'd snap at me. He was careful in his punishments, inflicting pain, leaving bruises, but never causing serious injury. However, it was always there, simmering under the surface, the possibility that he would go too far. I was starting to believe my happiness depended on his demands being met. If I had stayed there after Bella was born and he forced me to marry him, I would have succumbed completely. It would be the only way to survive psychologically."

"Praise God, we were rescued."

"Absolutely. God came through for us, Itsy."

Breanna placed a hand around her back and arched her aching body. "This baby is huge. She still doesn't want me to sleep."

Itsy began to rub her friend's back. "It won't be much longer now."

"Where will they send us? We've got to stay hidden from Edward. The thought of him finding us is terrifying." A shudder ran up Breanna's back.

Itsy said, "One of the people in the Montreal cell told me we are going to be transferred to northern Ontario to a camp they have off the grid."

"Not too far off, I hope. I want medical care if I need it … for Bella."

"Ha-ha! I said the same thing, not about medical care, but electricity and some comforts." Itsy went on, "I was told there were generators, so there is electricity. I'm sure they'll have medical care too."

Breanna was relieved to hear it. She placed a hand on Itsy's larger, muscular one. The scientist found it fascinating to see the changes the Nanos had made to her friend's body. Breanna looked up. "I'm glad Michael came for you. He really loves you."

"And Joshua came for you."

Breanna let out a dismissive noise. "Joshua probably came for you or the enhanced soldier program."

"For you most of all."

Placing her hands on either side of her head, Breanna rubbed her temples. "I don't know if I believe it. I want to, but I'm afraid he'll lie to me and hurt me again. Will he have an underlying motive I'm unaware of right now?"

Itsy waved a finger in the air. "That's Edward's nattering. Don't let him stay in your head. If you do, then you're still his prisoner without locked doors and armed guards."

WITHIN A WEEK, Itsy, Michael, and Breanna were in a camp deep in the forest of Ontario, north of Thunder Bay. It was freezing, and the snow drifts formed smooth, flowing hills around trees and beside the lake. The thick layer of ice over the water provided sure footing for anyone wanting to snow-mobile or ice fish.

On December 20, Breanna stared out the window at a group of bundled-up men, drinking beer and pop, as they dangled their lines into the hole drilled into the frozen lake. She was too warm with the blazing fire crackling in the hearth. The cabin was insulated, and it had electricity as promised. When she saw the number of scattered cabins and house trailers spread over the hundred or so acres, she was impressed and thankful it wasn't as far off the grid as she feared.

"Here is some herbal tea." Itsy handed her a large mug.

Taking it, she said, "Thanks, Itsy. It's pretty good when you get used to it. When I breastfeed, I probably shouldn't drink coffee either. Who knows if I'd get the baby as addicted to caffeine as I was before getting pregnant. Just to be safe, I might as well swear off the stuff."

"Perish the thought." Her friend sipped her cup of hot java.

"Let me sniff it. I can get my fix that way."

Itsy waved her cup under Breanna's nose, and they both snickered. "I talked to Bobby and my parents last night on a burner phone."

"I used the same one to contact Jean. I told her to say hi to Saul."

Using her mug, Itsy pointed to the chairs near the fireplace.

"It's so hot over there. Did they have to throw on every piece of cut wood onto the fire?"

Itsy rolled her eyes. "Take the chair the farthest away. Besides, it's not that hot in here."

Breanna waddled over to the chair and sat.

"Wow! Look at your ankles, Bree. They're so swollen." Itsy put her coffee down and got on her knees beside her friend. She pulled off Breanna's slippers. "Where are your socks?"

"I can't reach to put them on. The baby is in the way. I can't see my ankles, but the only shoes I can wear are these slip-ons." Breanna said, "Your hands feel nice. My feet feel like they're stretching against the skin."

Itsy grabbed another lower chair and pulled it closer. She put her friend's feet on it like a stool. "You've got to keep them elevated. I'm going to call Bobby, because this doesn't look good." She waved at Breanna. "Stay put until I get back."

When Itsy returned about thirty minutes later, she found Breanna sleeping in the chair. The pregnant woman's eyes fluttered open when she heard footsteps.

"Hi. I didn't reach Bobby. I think he's in class. But I called the health line. They said edema, which is the swelling in your feet and ankles, is normal, and you should put your feet up and drink water. There are a couple of things that are a little more concerning, but they are rare. The nurse read a list. I don't think you have any of those symptoms. Pre-eclampsia is one I flagged as possible, but I've got to find a clinic near here to take in your urine sample. Your protein levels would be elevated, and your blood pressure would also be higher than normal if you have that problem. There is some equipment in the old nurse's station, so I should be able to do an old-fashioned reading. Have you had frequent headaches? More than normal?"

Breanna reached out a hand towards her. "Look at you, nurse Itsy. I figured the headaches were because of our imprisonment and the stress of dealing with Edward. So, the answer is yes—more headaches than normal. The obstetrician did note that my blood pressure was slightly higher than she would like to see. It was one of the reasons she agreed with Edward about me getting more bed rest."

"Not like he let you rest." There was no attempt on Itsy's part to hide her disdain for their kidnapper. "Slave-driver was more like it. Always wanting the program to be completed as soon as possible."

Closing her eyes, Breanna tried unsuccessfully to blot out the memory of Edward.

"I'm sorry, Bree." Her friend's voice decreased in volume. "We're here now and safe. I'll try to find a blood pressure monitor. It needs to be taken a couple of times every day. There seem to be mixed feelings about complete bed rest since it can lead to blood clots, but you definitely need to rest more and keep your feet up."

"What's this I hear about bed rest?" Michael entered the room like a whirlwind. There was nothing calm about the new and improved Michael. He had reported to Breanna that he felt better than he ever had in his life. Picking up his wife, he planted a kiss on her lips. Itsy had grown in proportion to her husband, and her robustness at the nano program in her body had the same effect on her that Michael's had on him. Itsy was energetic and healthy. Breanna tried to keep mental notes for scientific purposes.

Depositing Itsy beside her friend. Michael smiled at Breanna. "Hi, Bree."

She smiled up at the giant man. "Hey, Michael."

Itsy twirled the blond ponytail that hung over her shoulder. "Breanna needs to rest more. She's got maybe three and a half more weeks until she's due, but we have to make sure she lasts that long."

Michael's eyebrows raised. "Three and a half weeks? I thought she was due somewhere at the end of January."

"Why would you think that?" Breanna asked.

He frowned. "On the television. Edward told the reporters that you got pregnant at the end of April or the beginning of May. Forty weeks would take you to the end of January."

Itsy made a clicking noise with her tongue. "Edward lied. Breanna was forced to go along with everything he said. Otherwise, he would've made her have an abortion or beat me or her. He was unpredictable."

Kneeling beside his friend's chair, Michael rested his hand gently on her arm. "I'm sorry. I didn't know he hurt you, too, Bree. Itsy told me about her beating and seizures and how you saved her with your program. But to do that to a pregnant woman."

Breanna inhaled sharply. "Not ever like Itsy. He didn't use his goons to hurt me. It was something he enjoyed doing himself. Subtle injuries." She shook her head, trying to rid herself of Edward. "It's not something I want to remember."

"He won't ever hurt you again, not if I have anything to do with it," Michael said.

"Me too," Itsy chimed in.

There was silence between the three friends as they stared warmly at each other. The light bulb went on for Michael, and his eyes went wide. "You've got to tell Joshua. He thinks it's Edward's baby." Taking the seat opposite Breanna, he said, "He thinks you want a divorce because it's Edward's baby and you wanted to marry that man. Joshua was as crazy to get you back as I was about Itsy. Even after he saw you on television and in photos kissing Edward, he believed you were coerced. But it never dawned on him that your baby was his. The guy was tortured, but he still wanted to rescue you."

The emotions that flooded Breanna were overwhelming, and she broke out into a cold sweat. Intending to run away to her bedroom, Breanna jumped up, and the world went dark.

BREANNA WOKE IN her bed. Itsy and Michael sat in two chairs beside her.

"Hey, Bree." Itsy grabbed her hand. "You gave us a scare."

Michael nodded.

"Is there anything you need? Michael carried you in here, and I ran for the blood pressure machine. Your pressure is high. There is a doctor in town, so Nancy, our neighbour here, will bring him a urine sample when you're able to give one." Itsy flipped the compress on her head. "Bobby said to have you rest as much as possible."

"I'm sorry to be such a bother."

Her friend waved a hand. "I'm happy to help. Bella needs nurse Itsy."

"Bella?" Michael glanced at his wife.

"Keep up," his wife joked. "Breanna was told she was probably having a girl. I called her Bella after me. Breanna agrees, don't you?"

Breanna smirked. "Yes, your wife named my baby. But I do like the name Bella." She closed her eyes. "I'm tired. How long was I out? That was a long fainting spell."

The concern in her friends' eyes told her everything.

"It was just fainting, right?"

"We don't think so." Itsy shrugged, "I think it was your blood pressure. I told Bobby to come. He's in third year med right now, so he knows some things." She made a face to cheer Breanna. "He's coming during his Christmas break, which starts tomorrow."

"I'm sorry to pull him away for this." Breanna twisted a thread on the quilt.

"Oh boy." Itsy made a scoffing noise. "Don't be such a hero. You're his sister, too. And he hasn't seen me since I was kidnapped in April. You've got to accept help."

Breanna's eyes fluttered, and she yawned.

"Sleep now. You need to catch up on some zees."

Breanna closed her eyes, but she heard Michael whisper to Itsy. "Should I call Joshua? He should be here."

Itsy responded in the same quiet tone. "Let's wait. I think Bree should be the one to call him."

There was a sound of movement in her room, causing Breanna to open her eyes. Joshua sat beside her. "Hi."

"Hi." She struggled to sit up, but Joshua pushed on her shoulder. "The doctor ordered that you rest. So you've got to stay in bed, Bree."

"I don't remember seeing a doctor."

"You don't remember the doctor in Cork?"

She gave her head a little rocking. "No. I remember her. I mean here." Breanna looked around the room, and it wasn't familiar. "Where am I exactly?"

Joshua smiled. "You're in a safe house."

"With you?"

"With me."

Breanna knit her brows together and tried to remember. "How? When?"

He picked up her hand and kissed her knuckles slowly, never taking his eyes off hers. The hairs on Breanna's arms stood on end, and her breathing became laboured. Blinking repeatedly, she tried to wake up. *What kind of game is Edward playing now? Is everything a dream? Maybe I haven't been rescued after all.* Too afraid to move, Breanna returned the stare. She waited for a flinch, a flash, or any kind of indication of what kind of mood he was in and what would be required of her. He would hurt her if she guessed wrong.

Joshua's face began to change. His dark hair and eyes became lighter. The strong jawline and brawny physique remained the same. *I knew it was Edward.* She pretended to be delighted. "I knew it was you. I knew you'd find me and rescue me."

He bit her knuckles, and she cried out. Pulling back his head, he scowled at her. "Liar. Breanna, you are a liar."

"N ... no!"

"If you didn't want to get away with Joshua and your friends, you wouldn't have used the soldier program on them."

She rubbed her bleeding hand. "I thought they were going to die. I had to help them."

"You didn't get in the car to get away with me. You ran toward Michael. And the program. You didn't tell me you completed it."

Her words came out rapidly. "I just finished it. I was getting the nanos ready to show you."

His eyes narrowed. "Are you sure you weren't ready? Like China."

"I didn't know they were coming. There was no contact—you know that, right?"

He grabbed her bleeding hand and began massaging it, then squeezed it hard. "You shot Mr. Maxwell."

Her screaming woke her up.

Michael burst through the door with Itsy on his heels. The light flicked on. When they saw only Breanna in the room, Itsy sat beside her friend. She spoke softly. "Bree, it's okay. We're in the cabin in Canada. You're safe."

Her breathing gradually returned to normal. She wiped her face, but found her hand was numb. It was the same one that Edward bit in the dream. *Did I roll onto it and hurt it? Is that why the dream was triggered?*

"Edward's not here. He doesn't know where we are. Lots of people worked hard to ensure we were out of his reach."

"I'm sorry I disturbed you. It doesn't feel like we will ever be safe from him. I only need some time." She rubbed her hand. "How are you going to get a good night's sleep with a maniac screaming in the next room? I don't know how to stop the nightmares."

Michael leaned over her bed. "Don't worry about us. These nanos make us resilient, and a little disturbed sleep is no big deal. We're together again, and that's all that matters." Winking, he said, "Think, you have two supersoldiers as bodyguards." He paused, then couldn't resist adding, "If Joshua were here, you'd have three bodyguards."

Breanna bit her lower lip as she thought about seeing Joshua again. *Lord Jesus, what should I do?*

"**YOUR PROTEIN LEVELS** were elevated," Bobby told Breanna. "We've got to monitor you closely now. Any sign you're in trouble … or the baby is in distress, and you might need to have a C-section. I had a doctor prescribe some medicine to help."

Breanna nodded that she understood. "The baby is the most important thing, Bobby. You promise me if anything happens, you'll look after her first."

"Bree, I'm not a doctor yet, only a med student. But apparently, there is someone who just arrived in camp who has some experience as a midwife." He tipped his head. "And the best thing is, she's someone you already know."

Breanna tried to wiggle into a better position, sitting in her bed. "Who?"

A wide smile broke across his face. "I think it will be better if she surprises you."

"I hate surprises."

"You'll like this one." He rose from the chair. "I'm going to grab some coffee. Can I get you anything?"

She rolled her eyes. "A new body. One that's not sick and stuck in this bed. I've read every book and magazine they brought in. I read the Bible the most, and that gives me a lot of comfort. Plus, everyone comes in to visit to keep me company. But I would love to get out of here. Do you think I can sit in the living room with my feet up?"

He shook his head no. "Not today, but certainly after you get some rest. If you go out there now, you won't relax, you'll visit with everyone. They need to give you more time to sleep, which is what you should do right now. I'll be back to check on you in a little bit."

Once he left the room, Breanna squirmed down into a lying position. She was to try to stay on her left side, but Bella, the beach ball, didn't seem to like that position much. Breanna ended up on her back like always, with pillows surrounding her. She rubbed her stomach. "You wait, Bella. I'm going to teach you about Jesus. There are so many great stories in the Bible. The best one is about Jesus. I bet you already know him, don't you? The Bible says God knit you together in my womb, and you are fearfully and wonderfully made. You are, you know. You're my little miracle. You're the silver lining in everything I went through in the past nine months. I can't wait to meet you face to face. My little Bella."

Breanna closed her eyes and hummed a love song to her baby. Absently, she twirled her fingers over her belly. Where had she heard the song? *Joshua's grandmother. She told Breanna it was a song her husband would sing to her.*

A week before their wedding, Joshua took Breanna to meet the family's paternal matriarch. Anne was a marvel at the age of ninety-nine. She was able to walk with the aid of only a cane. Her apartment was clean and beautifully decorated. There were large paintings and small tapestries on the walls. Anne owned a glass curio cabinet with a collection of Royal Doulton figurines. Beautiful ladies in long gowns and flowing dresses were lovingly placed on each shelf. And there were flowers everywhere—bouquets in glass vases and silver canisters. The place smelled like a garden, like a little bit of heaven on earth.

Anne was willowy, like Breanna's height. She wondered if Anne had been tall in her youth. The white-haired woman looped her arm through Breanna's and led her into the apartment. She was strong for her age. She had Breanna sit in the chair facing her, and Joshua sat beside his grandmother on the sofa. Anne asked Breanna questions about herself and her family. When Breanna told her she was an only child and had been orphaned in her first year of university, Anne clutched her chest.

"I know how that feels, dear. I'm so sorry for your loss." Joshua reached for his grandmother's hand. "I was born in 1930 in Warsaw, Poland. My childhood was a happy one until the Germans came. I was only nine, but I remember." Her eyes stared off at nothing.

"I'm sorry." Breanna knew some of the stories about the Warsaw ghetto and how the Jews were treated.

"I was twelve when the ZOB, the initials of the Jewish combat organization, began the resistance in the ghetto. We all heard the rumours that the Jewish people deported to Treblinka were murdered. Mordecai Anielewicz was only twenty-three, but he began going through the ghetto telling everyone to resist getting onto the cattle cars. I remember when he came to our small flat. Mordecai knew my oldest brother, Benjamin. They had been in school together when the war started. My parents were afraid, but Benjamin and Mordecai were brave. My second-oldest brother, Adam, was only two years younger than Benjamin at twenty-one. He was eager to fight, too. They resisted the Germans as best they could, but in the end, Adam and Benjamin died in the fighting. It only delayed the inevitable. By the time I was thirteen, I was shipped off to a work camp because I was healthy and strong. The rest of my family was sent to Treblinka. I never saw them again."

Joshua softly said, "Savta." He had told Breanna that's what his family called their grandmother. The elderly woman smiled sweetly at him, and Breanna marvelled at how few wrinkles were on her face despite all her hardships.

Anne continued, "After the war, I was lost. I ended up here in Israel at the age of sixteen. We were a nation of orphans surrounded by a hostile world. I met Joshua's grandfather at the first home I was placed in. He was so mature at eighteen. I was impressed at how dark and handsome he was in comparison to my blond hair and cream-coloured skin. Joseph was what I imagined a true Middle Eastern Jew should look like, even though he came from Paris. He had lost all his family in the camps. But he escaped and fought with the Resistance even though he was very young."

Anne rose and went into her bedroom. When she returned, she had a framed eight-by-ten photo in her hands. She handed it to Breanna. "That was my Joseph and me at our wedding in 1948. We celebrated Israel becoming a nation. And Joseph celebrated me becoming eighteen." She laughed. Then she sang a short Yiddish song in her quivery voice. "This was the love song Joseph would sing to me. It's a simple song, but it meant the world to us."

Breanna stared at the picture. She thought she was looking at Joshua, and the resemblance between the two men was remarkable. Beside Joseph stood a model-pretty, tall, thin woman with long blond hair parted at the side, looking like a Hollywood pin-up. "You made quite the dapper couple."

"We thought so." Anne stared at the floor as she remembered the past. Then she came back to the present. "I have one piece of advice for both of you. Marriage is not easy. Oh, sometimes it will be wonderful and carefree, but other times it will be work. Hard work. And you never know how much time you have on this earth. Your loved ones can be taken at any moment. Therefore, my advice is, fight for love, for your marriage, and each other. Never give up. If you do that, your love will become stronger than you can imagine."

"Thank you." Breanna smiled at Anne.

"Call me Savta." Patting Joshua's hand, Anne said, "I like your fiancée."

49

THE FOLLOWING DAY, Breanna had surprise visitors. When the young family came into her room, Breanna squealed, "Taddy, Fred, Daisy!" Taddy came over to the bed and hugged Breanna. Fred smiled at her while he wrestled with a twenty-two-month-old toddler who did not want to be held. Taddy sat on the chair and dug into a large bag to pull out homemade coloured blocks and cloth books. Fred sat Daisy on the floor surrounded by her toys. Not wanting anything to do with what was given, the dark-haired girl began searching her mother's diaper bag. Breanna was charmed by the child.

Fred chuckled. "You see what you've got to look forward to?"

Taddy made a face. "He sounds like it's a hardship. Daisy has her daddy wrapped around her little finger. He spoils her."

"Just like I spoil her mother." He gazed lovingly at his wife.

Taddy's eyes sparkled. "Yes, you do."

Breanna asked the couple, "What are you doing up here at the cabins?"

The lady covered in tattoos and earrings became serious. "It's getting a little scary out there in the world for Christians."

"And it's only going to get worse," Fred said. "It made sense to move our family here. I wasn't sure how much longer we'd be safe in Toronto."

Breanna's heart sank. "Is it getting that bad?"

Taddy placed a hand on the side of the bed. "Bree, it's hard to explain, but some groups call us haters, and they think we should be killed or rounded up into prisons. It's mostly the fringe that thinks that way right now, but it's becoming more and more popular."

Fred bent down to play with Daisy but glanced up at Breanna. "We sold the store and basically everything we had; then the cell helped us disappear up here."

Breanna frowned. She knew how much the store meant to her friends, but she decided to stay upbeat and try to cheer them up. "It's really nice to see some familiar faces. I missed you two … three."

"I talked to Bobby and Itsy," Taddy said. "They think you might need my services soon." She pointed to Breanna's pregnant belly.

"When did you become a doula? I had no idea you dabbled in it."

Taddy answered Breanna. "More than dabble. I'm not just a doula; I'm a midwife now. I started studying before I was pregnant with Daisy, and I began practicing this year. Fred was able to cover running the bookstore, and he brought Daisy to work with him when I had to race off to help deliver a baby."

"That's great!" Breanna wondered if a midwife would be all she needed with this health problem. "Have you heard of pre-eclampsia?"

Taddy patted Breanna's hand. "Yes. Bobby told me. You've got to be careful, and we'll watch you closely. I told Bobby that you could probably use a little time out of bed, so long as you keep your feet raised. Also, there are a few things you should be practicing in preparation for the birth. It's a little late to start, but better late than never. I'll get you up to speed."

"I appreciate that, Taddy. If I weren't stuck in this predicament, I'd offer to help you get settled in a cabin." Breanna softly added, "I'm glad you've come for friendship and my baby. It gives me peace of mind that someone here is qualified and knows what they're doing."

Taddy said, "Bobby could do it."

Breanna shook her head, "But he returns home after Christmas, and my baby is due the first or second week of January."

"I still like to consult with Bobby and have medical services available if they are necessary," Taddy noted.

Fred asked innocently, "What about Joshua? Where is he?"

50

CHRISTMAS WEEK AT the camp was a lot of fun. It was particularly special because everyone was a Christian and celebrated the birth of Jesus. Breanna was permitted to leave the bed for Bible readings, prayers, carols, and lots of food and conversation every night. Pine boughs lined the large stone fireplace with candles that were lit for the evening celebration. The "cabin" she shared with Itsy and Michael was a three-bedroom, two-bathroom home. They were given one of the larger structures because of Breanna's condition and Itsy's refusal to leave her alone. Now that Breanna couldn't go outside, all the other camp dwellers came to the larger residence.

Twenty-three people, including three children, lived in eight cabins of various sizes and several trailers. Discussions were held about the need to add buildings given the hostility in the world toward Christians. They expected an influx of escapees when Christians became the hunted. Some of the residents were against making the camp too large because of the risks of drawing attention to themselves. Other camps already existed across Canada, the US, and the world. Breanna listened to the discussions but never added an opinion one way or another. She felt blessed to be in this place.

The night before Christmas, Bobby read the story of Jesus's birth from the Gospels of Matthew and Luke. Breanna empathized with Mary more than she ever had. Comparing herself to Jesus's mother, Breanna mused. She knew what it was like to be pregnant in a perilous situation, as Mary experienced—unmarried in a time when women could be stoned to death. Breanna had experienced the constant threat of Edward deciding to force her to have an abortion, right up to the time of birth. God arranged for Joseph to accept a baby that wasn't his. Breanna carried Joshua's baby, but he didn't know it, and he didn't acknowledge the baby he thought was Edward's. Mary gave birth outside of a hospital with no one to help but Joseph. At least Breanna had a midwife and her best friend. Then the holy family had to flee to Egypt to protect the baby Jesus, and Breanna had to escape from Edward and maybe stay in hiding for the remainder of her life. She knew her baby was not going to be the saviour of the world, but Bella was precious to her.

The carols came after the Bible reading. Fred and another lady, Nancy, played guitars. Michael clapped the spoons, and another couple of people pounded on makeshift drums. They didn't sound great, but Breanna thought she had never heard better. Joy filled her being, and she felt the peace of Christ permeate the room.

Then came the potluck. Breanna felt sheepish about being waited on, but Itsy, Taddy, Michael, and Bobby policed her every move. They even questioned her when she rose to use the bathroom. The food was always delicious, and Breanna ate what she could fit into her stomach with the large obstruction preventing her from overeating.

Daisy crawled up beside Breanna and squirmed her way to fit between the adult's body and the arm of the chair. The little cherub came to love visiting Breanna during the day with her mother. Another person spoiled her with treats and toys. Some of the residents bought toys from second-hand shops in the closest town, anticipating more children in the future. Taddy brought some to Breanna's room to keep Daisy occupied.

Cozy beside Breanna, Daisy chatted in her baby babble with her hands waving. Breanna pretended to understand her and answered, "Really? I can't believe that happened." To which Daisy laughed and continued her story. Breanna raised her eyebrows and waved her hand. "No way. Oh, Daisy, that is wonderful. Did you learn anything new today?" The tiny hands twisted and turned, and the dark curls swayed as Daisy nodded her head. Out came more babbling. Breanna couldn't hold back any longer. She began to giggle, and as she did, Daisy joined her. Taddy put her hand to her mouth and started also. It wasn't long before most of the gang were laughing. Some didn't even know what started it, but the atmosphere was charged with celebration.

At the end of the evening, Itsy began to sing "O Holy Night". Breanna listened. Her friend's voice was deeper than in the past, but Itsy could still carry a tune. Breanna closed her eyes and relaxed. It was a perfect end to the best Christmas Eve she could remember.

51

SEVEN DAYS PASSED, and the following day was the end of 2030. Breanna had been exceptionally tired and slept most of the day away. It was dark when Breanna opened her eyes again. Slithering slowly, she was able to get her legs over the edge of the bed and pull herself up. She waddled to the bathroom. It was not until she returned to her room that the shadow of someone slouching in her chair near the window made her jump. The body frame was large. *Did Edward find me?* She didn't want to turn on the light or move. Squinting, Breanna tried to focus with the moonlight that came through the thin curtain. *Dark hair. Joshua.* There was a light snoring sound and rhythmic breathing. *Asleep. Lord, am I dreaming again?* She was too tired to do anything but return to her bed. *I'll deal with it when I wake up.*

When her eyes fluttered open in the morning, she remembered the figure in the chair, and she twisted her head to find it empty. *A dream. At least not a nightmare.* After she had lounged as long as she could, the necessity of the bathroom forced her to move. Breanna grabbed her towel, a clean dress Taddy lent her, and all the necessities for a shower. The water came out warm without waiting, so Breanna knew someone was awake and had used it. She showered in a hurry so as not to waste their precious commodity.

Breanna waddled back into her bedroom, feeling clean and less tired than the day before. Dark eyes met hers, and she froze.

"Hi, Bree." Joshua's voice was deeper but sounded tired.

His hair was still wet. He had used the water before her. Not that it mattered, but her mind flitted to all kinds of useless information in her panic. Her throat was dry, and she couldn't think of anything to say.

He got up from the chair, took the things from her hands, and put them on top of her dresser. Joshua returned to her and led her back to the bed. "You look like you've seen a ghost." He gave a nervous chuckle and moved his hand through his thick black hair. "I guess I have been a bit of one."

She stared at him as if she were dreaming. Breanna waited to see if he would morph into Edward.

"Itsy says you have to keep your feet up." He began fluffing her pillows so she could sit in the bed. Reaching to help her, Joshua said, "Here."

Breanna complied with his direction. *Just focus on breathing.* While she did that, the smell of soap and spicy aftershave caused her to be hyperaware of the man before her.

She wiggled into position and made herself as comfortable as she could be. Joshua stared at her face. She lowered her eyes, not able to maintain his scrutiny. *Why do I feel guilty? I ran away like a coward. That was wrong. I went to Edward's home willingly. That was wrong. I killed a man ... two men, now. That was wrong.* Tears began to burn tracks down her face. Breanna's hands flew to cover her eyes.

Joshua's voice was gentle. "You did what you had to so that you and Itsy would survive. I know that." He handed her some tissues. "Breanna, I'm as much at fault as you are. If I had told you the truth, maybe I wouldn't have driven you away."

She sniffled as she wiped her tears. *Itsy must have told him everything. I guess Michael called him.*

He stood up and went over to a backpack she hadn't noticed leaning up against a corner of the room. Inside, he fished out a stack of crumpled papers that looked like a legal document. When Joshua returned, he placed them on her lap. Breanna glanced down and recognized the divorce papers. "I'm not signing them. I refuse to give you a divorce. Even if you want one. I refuse. You'll have to fight me for it."

She stared at the papers. *What do I want? Not a divorce? My marriage?*

"Say something, Bree. Savta said to fight for our marriage, and that's what I intend to do. I'll try to make it up to you, all the lies. I'll try to be a good father. My father was a great example for me to follow. Give me a chance. Give us a chance."

"I'm so confused. My brain is screaming at you, but my heart is saying I don't want a divorce." She threw the papers on the floor and then turned back to him. "I'm a mess. I don't know what Edward's voice is and what my thoughts are." She put her arms around her belly and rocked. "The one thing I know for sure is, I want my baby. I won't give her up. She's innocent in all this."

Joshua's eyes dropped to where her arms lay. It was the first time Breanna had seen him look at her pregnant stomach. "God created her. Of course she's innocent." He reached out tentatively and placed one large hand on top of Breanna's stomach, and she watched all his expressions change with each emotion he was experiencing. "It never entered my mind that you would give up your baby." Then he reiterated, "But I want a chance to try to be a good father. Give me that chance, Bree."

"Oh boy," Breanna winced.

"What's that?" His eyes went wide. "I felt something inside you."

She began to take shallow breaths.

"Breanna, are you all right?" Joshua took his hand away from the baby as if he had caused her pain.

The contraction gradually subsided. "I'm okay." She chuckled. "I think it was only a false labour pain."

"It's too early."

"Yes. It's too early."

ONCE THE CONTRACTION disappeared. Breanna shyly took Joshua's hand and placed it on her stomach. "I called her Bella. Well, in reality, Itsy named her after her full name of Isabella."

"She's a she?"

"It looked like it on the ultrasound. I only had one, early on." Breanna kept her hand on top of Joshua's. His hand was so much larger than it had been. Her hand looked tiny and dainty in comparison. "Edward let me have some prenatal care."

"He let you?" Joshua sounded like there was a bitter taste in his mouth. "Let you." His eyes turned stormy. "Maybe we shouldn't talk about him."

The hair on the back of her neck prickled. Her eyes widened as she watched for signs of anger towards her.

When Joshua saw her fear, he softened his voice. "You don't have to be afraid of me, ever."

She nodded. "Umm! Okay." It came out sounding weak.

His hand moved from her belly to her face so quickly that she flinched away. Joshua laid his hand on her cheek and gently guided her back. "I don't know what he did to make you so scared. But I won't hurt you." His jaw twitched as he visibly fought the rage he felt for Edward. "My anger is toward him, not you."

Taking a deep breath, Breanna found the clean scent of her husband brought back happy memories. His soft strokes on her cheek were soothing. Then Joshua began to sing his grandparents' song in Yiddish like he had many times before. He said he wanted it to become theirs. Breanna closed her eyes and absorbed the calm. She started to hum along.

"Yow!" Breanna arched her back and her knees bent up. She held her inhale and when the pain eased slightly, she exhaled. *Focus on breathing.* Taddy had shown her what to do. Breanna tried to put what she learned into practice.

With eyes like saucers, Joshua asked, "What can I do? Should I get help?" Breanna nodded.

"Itsy," Joshua yelled. "Come quick. Breanna's in trouble."

Her blond friend flew into the room as the contraction subsided. Breanna said, "Something's wrong. My water broke." Breanna was glad they had put a waterproof mattress cover on the bed in case this very thing happened.

Itsy turned to Michael, who had come running behind her when Joshua shouted. "Get Taddy. It's too bad that Bobby left a couple of days ago." Michael didn't lose a second in cutting out of the room.

Then she turned to Breanna, not wanting to panic her friend. "It's okay. You have Taddy and me and a couple of other helpers here." She pulled back the covers to reveal a large wet spot on the bed. "Joshua ..." Itsy twisted her head and found him standing against the wall like a scared rabbit. "Joshua, snap out of it. In the kitchen, you'll find big pots. Fill them with water and get them on the stove. We'll need warm water." He didn't budge. "Get moving, soldier." That got him scurrying out of the room with one backward glance at Breanna.

In her head, Itsy was reviewing what Taddy had been teaching her about childbirth when Breanna had another contraction. Itsy did the breathing exercise with her friend. When that contraction was finished, Itsy checked to see if the baby's head was visible. *Taddy, you'd better come quick. I can't do this.*

On cue, the dark-haired midwife raced in with her bag. They began a hurried cleanup of the room. Michael came in carrying the bassinet he had built for Breanna and Bella. It had a small mattress covered with flannel. He placed it in the corner by the door but backed out to help Joshua.

The labour wasn't too long, but it was intense. Breanna dilated quickly. Taddy worked briskly, speaking gently all the while, to encourage Breanna. Itsy did whatever Taddy directed, but she also encouraged Breanna to breathe. Joshua was by the bedroom door. Michael stayed in the living room.

"Get her some cold water ... or better yet, some ice chips," Taddy ordered Joshua. "She needs some hydration." He whisked out of the room.

Breanna wished she could order him back. She wanted him with her. Then she felt Joshua slide a piece of ice into her mouth. As it melted, she realized it was exactly what she needed. Breanna reached for his hand. He held it.

Taddy snapped, "No, let her go."

No sooner did she say that than Breanna had another contraction. Joshua was surprised at the strength of Breanna's grip and thought she might break a few bones in his hand. He was thankful for the soldier nanos in his body. As the pain subsided, so did Breanna's grasp. Prying his hand from hers, he gave it a shake.

"Don't say I didn't try to warn you," Taddy said. She raised her head to Breanna. "Now comes the hard part. The baby's head is crowning, so when I tell you, you've got to push with all you've got. Only when I tell you."

Breanna's voice came out weakly, "Okay."

53

"IT'S A BOY!" Itsy exclaimed, a little surprised.

The baby began crying. "Cry, little guy. Clear out those lungs," Taddy said as she handed the newborn to Itsy to clean him gently with warm water.

Breanna was lying back on the pillow, drenched in sweat, but watching Itsy with her baby. Itsy cooed at the dark-haired, darker-skinned baby.

While she was packing up, Taddy said, "Congratulations, Breanna and Joshua." She removed the baby from Itsy's arms and examined him to ensure he was healthy. "He looks great, especially for being a week or two early. No issues." As she placed him into Breanna's arms, she said, "I'll be back in a bit to help you start breastfeeding." Taddy placed her midwife bag in the hall, then took the clothes, towels, and sheets to be washed out into the laundry area.

Itsy helped with the cleanup, but she returned without Taddy and said, "I think you're going to have to pick another name." Peering over to Joshua, who was standing against the wall out of the way of the cleanup, she added, "Congratulations, Daddy." Then she pushed him forward to allow him to see his son.

Joshua stared at the newborn with eyebrows knitted together. Then he glanced at Breanna before returning to the baby. "He's dark."

The new mother said, "Like you. He looks exactly like you." Breanna's eyes didn't leave her son. She examined his face, his little fists rolled into balls. She wanted to check out his whole body, but that would wait because, as far as she was concerned, he was perfect.

"Great, he gets the Mini-Me instead of me," Itsy joked.

Joshua sounded incredulous. "He looks like me?"

Breanna glanced up with a frown. "Why shouldn't he look like you?"

"I thought he'd be blond, like Edward or a redhead like you. I thought he was Edward's baby." He shook his head, clearly confused.

Breanna snorted. "Didn't Itsy or Michael tell you?"

Joshua shook his head. "No. No one told me anything."

She looked at her friend. "When you called him to come here, you didn't tell him?"

Itsy held up her hands as a sign of surrender. "We didn't call him. It was up to you."

"No one called me. I came on my own. I couldn't stay away from you any longer," Joshua said.

"Oh." Breanna brushed the baby's head with her lips. She was letting what Joshua said sink in. *Joshua came on his own.* "He's got a whole lot of hair. Like his dad." She lifted her head towards Joshua. "He's yours. I didn't know I was pregnant when I ran away. I found out after Edward took me prisoner."

"Edward said the baby was his." Joshua was in shock. "I thought that I could still be a father to the baby even if he weren't mine. When I saw the magazine with your picture, smiling, pregnant, with Edward's arm around you, I was so mad at you, I destroyed a punching bag at the gym. Once I settled down, I realized he must have forced you. Then I examined the magazine photo closer. Your eyes betrayed you. In some photos, you looked numb, like you were drugged. Others, there was an underlying sadness. But when I got the divorce papers and saw your signature, I guessed I was wrong and saw only what I wanted to see. I was confused."

He moved to sit beside Breanna on the bed. He reached out his hands. "May I hold him?"

Ice gripped her heart. "You can't take him. He's mine." She held the baby tightly.

"Bree, don't hurt the baby," Itsy said sharply when she saw the fear in Breanna's eyes. Then she softened her voice. "Let Joshua hold him. No one will take him away from you. We're all safe people here. Edward won't get the baby." Breanna's grip loosened. She'd never hurt her child.

Joshua's head moved from Breanna to Itsy. He realized what was happening. So he joined in and, in a loving voice, said to his wife, "Bree, we are one. Married before God. This baby is a miracle, confirming our covenant. I'm his father, and you are his mother. That will always be. No one will ever take this baby from you, ever."

Tears pricked her eyes as the realization of her behaviour hit her. Breanna offered the baby to Joshua. He leaned over the baby and kissed her gently on the cheek. Then held his son, sitting beside her to reassure her. He stared at the infant in amazement. "Thank you, Jesus, thank you for this precious gift." Joy shone on his face, and Breanna breathed a little easier. Joshua turned his head and smiled at Itsy. He mouthed the words, *Thank you.*

54

WHEN ITSY BROUGHT Michael into the bedroom, Joshua asked Breanna if he could show the baby to their friend. Breanna nodded. Even that movement had her fighting down an irrational terror of losing her baby. Itsy went over to Breanna and acknowledged how hard it was for her. "It's going to take time to get rid of the fear you've carried for eight months."

"What are you talking about?" Michael asked while admiring the baby.

"Edward's constant threat to Breanna of aborting the baby, or killing him once he was born, or giving him away to someone else."

The anger that flashed in Joshua's and Michael's eyes was understandable. It was the first time they had heard about Edward's psychological abuse of Breanna. Neither spoke, not wanting to upset the baby or Breanna.

Itsy continued talking because she wanted her husband and Breanna's husband to understand why Breanna was traumatized. "Edward was a monster. Hurting Breanna physically, emotionally, and playing games with her mind. When I tried to warn her, Edward had me severely beaten by several men. Bree had no choice; she had to put up with all the abuse for me and the baby."

Joshua wanted to kill the man with his bare hands. He had never felt like murdering someone in cold blood, but he did right then. His emotions threatened to surge into a blind rage, but he looked at the angel sleeping in his arms, and he prayed for strength to forgive. Joshua forced a smile and brought his newborn back to Breanna, placing him in her arms. She looked exhausted, but he knew she wouldn't sleep right now.

Joshua decided to change the subject for all their sakes. He said, "We need to pick a name."

Michael snickered. "What's wrong with Bella?" Itsy came over to him and he folded her in his arms, kissing her forehead. "I like that name."

"Sorry. I think Bella's not going to do," Breanna said. "I guess the boy part of my dream was prophetic."

"Oh, yeah. Bree dreamed she was having a boy." Itsy didn't add that it included Joshua taking the baby away from Breanna.

"My wife is the prophet." Joshua winked.

Breanna held up a finger. "Maybe we need to name him after a prophet?"

"Okay, everyone list their favourites," Itsy suggested.

Joshua had been a Christian longer than the other three. He didn't hesitate. "I like Abraham because he believed in God."

Breanna looked horrified. "Abraham Abrams. That's awful. And didn't he almost sacrifice his firstborn son?"

"Not a good choice?" Joshua mocked.

Breanna vetoed that suggestion. "No."

Itsy smirked. "We can rule out some names like Melchizedek, Nehemiah, Obadiah."

"Ezekiel, Hosea," Michael said.

Joshua added, "Habakkuk."

"Belteshazzar," Breanna said.

Joshua waved his hand. "That's it, Bree."

Breanna asked, "What's it?"

"Belteshazzar was Daniel's Chaldean name, but what do you think of the name Daniel?" Joshua raised his brows. "I like the name Daniel. He was a great prophet of God, and he was faithful to him."

Breanna ran her finger over her infant's forehead, "Do you want the name Daniel?" He made a little smile, which was probably some gas, but she decided it was a sign. "He approves of that name."

Itsy and Michael agreed. "That is a beautiful name. Do you know what it means in Hebrew, Joshua?"

"I think it is, 'God is my judge'."

Itsy clapped her hands lightly so she wouldn't disturb baby Daniel. "And God judged him worthy, so God shut the mouths of the lions. Let's pray and prophesy over this infant that God will protect him from the lions and anyone who would come against him."

The four friends prayed for protection and health for Daniel. They each took a turn declaring great things about their lives.

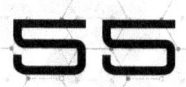

55

BREANNA WOKE UP several times through the night to check on Daniel. With the soft glow of the nightlight Taddy had given her, she was able to see well enough. Each time that he was sleeping soundly, she held a finger under his nose to ensure he was breathing. When he cried, she fed him and changed him. She marvelled at the tiny miracle.

Joshua rose with her when Daniel woke for his feedings. He stared at the two with love in his eyes. One time, Daniel stirred shortly after eating, and Breanna had already fallen back asleep. Joshua took the baby, who seemed so fragile; he was afraid of hurting him. Rubbing the infant's back, he was able to get him to burp. Joshua rocked Daniel back to sleep in the chair, humming his grandparents' love song.

Breanna opened her eyes to see Joshua in the chair holding Daniel. Her mind flashed to the nightmare of Joshua stealing her baby away. She sat straight up in bed and cried out, "Don't take him. Please, Joshua, don't take Daniel away from me."

Knowing what was happening this time, Joshua gently returned Daniel to the bassinet. He went to Breanna and took her in his arms. In a soothing whisper, he said, "I'm not taking him, Bree. He only had to burp. Daniel is yours and mine, and we will stay together." Joshua began to rock Breanna and hum their love song gently. She gradually relaxed her body and nestled her head closer to his neck. Breathing in his soap and aftershave, she felt like she was home again.

"I'm sorry; I'm a mess," she murmured.

He held her tighter. "You're not the one who needs to apologize. All of this was done to you, not by you. My grandparents got through the trauma of the Holocaust, and we'll do the same."

"How is your family? How is Savta? I miss her and I miss them." Breanna pulled back to smile at him.

Joshua's mouth dropped. "Savta passed while you were away. She was one hundred, and I think she was happy to go be with Grandpa."

She reached for his face. "I'm sorry I wasn't there for you. She was an amazing woman."

"I'm glad she and Grandpa were Messianic Jews before everyone else in my family came to believe. I'll see her again."

"Yes, you will."

"Sleep now." Joshua moved them both into a prone position, and he cradled the wife he had missed for nine months. It didn't take long until he heard her rhythmic breathing. He remained awake, thinking of everything that happened to them. Then he poured out his thanksgiving to God for his little family.

The next few days, everyone was getting into a routine of functioning. Breanna was still given a pass on doing housework, but the other three picked up the slack. Despite the lack of sleep, Joshua felt better than ever. He wasn't sure what was due to the soldier program and what was because of the joy of being reunited with Breanna and his new son.

Breanna was no longer relegated to bed rest, so she brought Daniel out to the living room so the camp dwellers could stop by and see their two newest citizens, Joshua and the newborn. A parade of friends visited, bringing a plethora of congratulations and homemade baby gifts. Daisy was her usual charming self and was able to say "baby" and kiss Daniel sweetly on the cheek.

After everyone left, Breanna threw a towel over her shoulder and fed her newborn. Joshua took over burping duty. Michael threw wood on the fire, and Itsy brought in tea and coffee. Breanna took her usual herbal blend while the rest had hot java.

Joshua savoured his. "Not too bad given we're roughing it."

"Ha, it's not at all rustic," Michael smirked.

"I was thinking last night, it's as if everything worked out the way it was meant to be," Breanna said.

Itsy began choking on her drink. "What do you mean?"

"Well, think about it. If our roles were reversed, things could have been worse. I could have been with Joshua, and Edward could have shot him and kidnapped me. Who would have been able to save Joshua? No one else would know he had the program, never mind how to figure out my nano formula to help him. And what if Edward went for Itsy after having me use her as leverage? If he shot Michael, then Joshua wouldn't have been alive to save him. As it was, Joshua was able to use it to save Michael, and I was able to save Itsy because Joshua had my incomplete part saved on that memory stick."

"I would have preferred no kidnapping," Joshua said.

"Well, me too, of course." Breanna pointed at Joshua. "If I had known that you kept the enhanced soldier project on the computer, I might have destroyed it in my anger. In the end, I was able to use it to save all three of your lives."

Itsy agreed. "I guess that part was good. Thanks, Joshua, for hiding it from Bree." She giggled.

Breanna waved a hand. "But that's not all. If I weren't pregnant, then Edward would have forced himself on me. God protected me with this baby. Also, the ultrasound technician misread the gender of the baby, so Edward began to think he could accept a girl who looked like me. Would he have thought that way if he knew I was having Joshua's son? Even though it's sexist, I think Edward is old-fashioned that way. Because of that, I had a hope of keeping my baby. Then you guys came in like the Avengers and rescued Itsy and me before the baby was born. Perfect timing, since our baby is a boy who is a replica of his dad. Edward might have killed him because of that fact. God saved our baby."

Itsy nodded. "I guess it all makes sense when you look at it that way. God took the evil done to us and turned it around. And here we thought God had deserted us. He was with us all along." She raised a hand to heaven. "Thank you, Jesus."

Breanna rubbed her chin. "I just have one question for you two: what took you so long to come get us?"

Michael answered, "First, Joshua needed to finish the formula to heal me. That took months. Then we had to plan our rescue operation. Joshua called the men from the Chinese raid to see who could help, and we needed to transport them all to one location. We had to get aerial photos of the estate, buy equipment, and figure out how to carry this out in a foreign country. The one thing we didn't know was where he was keeping you locked up. The logical place was in that tower he showed us, Bree. As luck would have it, he tried to move you. I was going to hide in the garage and use it as cover against Edward's hired guns, but there you were."

Joshua said, "I was working as fast as I could to finish your healing program. Luckily, I could build on what was on your laptop from the Chinese plant. Then I had to train Michael and some of the other men who had never fought a battle before and figure out a plan. That day at Edward's estate, I was dodging bullets and ran into the garage as cover. Imagine my surprise to find Itsy and Michael fighting Edward. I didn't see you, Bree, leaning against the wall until Edward grabbed me, but it was too late. It was fortunate that you had finished the soldier program."

"It was all orchestrated by God. There were too many coincidences to be otherwise." Breanna was amazed at God and felt a twinge of shame that she had doubted him during their captivity.

"Romans 8:28 says, 'We know that in all things God works for the good of those who love him,'" Joshua quoted.

"Where did you go after leaving us in France?" Itsy asked Joshua.

Breanna answered, "Back to Mossad with my program." Her voice had a slight edge.

Her husband glanced at her. It was obvious the question triggered Breanna's memory of his lies. Joshua said, "Yes, I did take it to Israel. Mossad locked me up for going rogue in the raid on Edward's estate. I was released after a week of interrogation. My supervisor fought for me. He argued that Edward held you two against your will to have Breanna recreate the super-soldier project. They understood why two husbands would rescue their wives, and, as a bonus, they were happy that Israel had a program for their army. When they let me out, I was officially retired. Edward was notified that Israel had nothing to do with the raid. After I went for a quick visit with my parents, I left the country before Edward could retaliate against me." He stood up and went into the bedroom.

"That was an abrupt ending," Michael noted.

Joshua walked back into the room holding a laptop and a small case. He unzipped the bag and pulled out a couple of syringes. "I went underground with the copies I held back from Mossad. The watcher cell outside of New York City, my original one at Cornell, helped me make a lot more programmed nanos and copies of the file. I was smuggled into Canada by another watcher cell and turned those who wanted into enhanced soldiers. We tried to spread the soldier program across Canada, the US, Europe, and other cells around the world. It makes sense that we should be able to defend ourselves."

Breanna said, "I saw you inject nanos and activate the program in some of the men on the plane who were seriously injured."

Joshua tapped the arm of his chair. "Did you leave any trace of the program behind for Edward?"

She held her hand palm up. "Unfortunately, I had it only on the laptop for a long time, but the final week before you rescued us, I put it on his main computer to work out the last piece of Lucinda's half. When the shooting started, I didn't have time to delete it. We only had time to grab the nanos and the laptop, where I copied the completed formula." Breanna shook her head. "Edward only needs a biomedical engineer to extract a few more of his nanos and copy the programming to others. He could add more to his body afterwards. He saw me use the program on you three, so he knows it works."

Joshua grimaced. "He'll use it on his mercenaries."

"And probably his sister," Itsy added.

"What? She's dead!" Michael exclaimed.

Breanna scoffed. "Well, so was he, or so we thought. Edward showed me her burned and broken body. He had her frozen in a cryogenic chamber. He said his butler arranged for it right after the plane crash outside Montreal." She looked at her husband. "He intends to use it on Lucinda. He said he was going to raise the dead."

56

2031

THROUGHOUT APRIL AND May, the little community swelled in numbers with Christians escaping persecution. The men built more cottages. Some people were transferred out west or farther north because of the lack of space. Resources were stretched, but no one seemed to mind. They had gatherings every day, sharing food, jokes, and stories. It always ended with a Bible reading, prayer, and songs. The love of Jesus seemed to overflow out of the Christians' spirit. God's glory was poured out stronger than ever before by most of the people.

In June, a Christian broadcaster named David arrived. Almost all worldwide television stations were now under the control of one large company. Only the countries that were not part of Edward's trade deal maintained control over their content. Canada had signed the trade deal early in its inception, so when David refused to surrender control of his channel, which was dedicated to teachings on Jesus and the Bible, they shut him down and revoked his licence to broadcast.

David told the other Christians that the world was experiencing another pandemic, and vaccines became mandatory. The World Health Organization was now called the One World Health Coalition, OWHC, and it had veto powers over many individual governments when it came to public health. People were still dying from the pandemic even with the vaccine. But anyone who raised concerns was called a radical, a lunatic, or a terrorist. Often, these same people ended up dying from the pandemic or being arrested under the worldwide Antiterrorist Act that was outlined in the trade deal. Terrorism was to be crushed for the good of the world.

Only a few countries refused to sign the deal—Israel being one, but also several in Africa, and a few others around the globe. They said they would not give up their sovereignty on these issues but would consider the OWHC's recommendations. These were the same ones to maintain control over broadcasting in their countries.

David said that one name kept coming up in association with the television stations, the OWHC, vaccine production, and a worldwide trade deal. That name was Edward Connor. He was one of ten billionaires who controlled these companies, organizations, and corporations. It wasn't a surprise to the people in the camp. Itsy, Michael, and Joshua alerted them to Edward possibly being the antichrist.

One new bit of technology brought into the camp by David was a satellite television. Some of the men helped build an antenna so that news from the outside world could be piped into the camp. Depending on where the antenna was pointed, they could receive information from the one main broadcaster, but occasionally they could hear from the independent countries. The nightly world news was on the agenda many evenings. Things were looking dark on the earth, so the Christians prayed for everyone who suffered in the natural disasters, people who were dead or dying, and the families of the dead.

By the beginning of July, it was getting hot. The blackflies, mosquitoes, and no-see-ums were enjoying a buffet with the campers. The Indigenous peoples aided the refugees with natural remedies, as well as guidance in farming, fishing, and hunting. They understood from history what it was like to be an unwanted population. Most of them were also Christian, or they believed in one Creator of the world. They were not happy with another layer of control over the country. To them, it was another form of colonialism.

On July 15, Edward Connor appeared on a special broadcast around the world. It was replayed on a loop that day so everyone would have a chance to watch. David raced over to Joshua, Breanna, Itsy, and Michael, who were outside weeding the communal garden. Daniel was beside his mother, in a baby stroller with mosquito netting draped over it. The sweat was dripping off the older preacher's face from the summer humidity.

David was wringing his hands. "Quick, you need to come now. Edward is on television. It's terrible news. Terrible." He retreated the way he'd come, shaking his head the whole way. They wasted no time in following him to a new, larger log cabin. It was the community church, their communal kitchen, and now their television room. Inside, all the residents except those on sentry duty were gathered. They sat on the floor or the chairs off to the sides, and they all faced the satellite TV.

Before she looked at the screen, Breanna heard the voice, and her legs began to give out. Joshua grabbed his wife, and someone pulled a chair over for her. Breanna buried her face in her hands, not wanting to see that face ever again.

Edward's voice was strong and authoritative. "There have been several terror attacks on my property and research facilities in an effort to sabotage my nano projects, which are meant for the betterment of humankind. Christians have perpetrated these. While they preach love, they murdered my guards, my butler, and my sister, and they tried to kill me. They kidnapped my pregnant fiancée and locked me up. Before they took my beloved Breanna, she was able to salvage my sister's project that would prevent death or even raise the dead.

"My sister, Lucinda Connor, has been frozen in a cryogenics chamber since the terrorists crashed our plane. I had her body frozen while I attempted to recreate a program she created before her untimely death. The purpose of the program was to create new and improved soldiers, but it turns out it also rapidly heals injured body parts or illnesses. I've had it tested, and it even cures cancer. Lucinda had injected me with her nano program when the plane was going down. She saved my life but couldn't save her own.

"I am living proof that this nanotechnology works. But I am not the only one. I present my sister, raised from the dead."

At that, Breanna had no choice but to lift her head to the television. Walking onto the stage was Lucinda—a larger version, but whole and without apparent blemish. The woman exuded an evil energy even through the satellite image. When the camera zoomed in, Breanna noticed Lucinda's eyes. They were not the ones she remembered from China. Breanna gasped as she realized it was a demon. No part of his sister's personality or spirit was in that body. Edward was possessed, but Lucinda appeared to be a devil.

57

EDWARD ANSWERED A few questions from the reporters. It was notable to Breanna that Lucinda said nothing. Then Edward continued his monologue: "With the world experiencing one crisis after another, the board of directors of the One World Health Coalition decided it needs insightful leadership. One person to take the helm, so to speak. By unanimous vote, I have been chosen to lead. The board will discuss matters and come to conclusions. My role will be to give my yea or nay to break any ties."

Joshua snapped his fingers in the air loud enough that everyone could hear. "That won't last. He's used to running the show. Power is not shared with Edward; he must be in charge."

Edward put his elbows on the news table and clasped his hands together. He looked directly into the camera. "Given the terrorism practiced by these Christians, and their continual opposition to progressive laws … well, all of you know the Christian interference is rampant … countries involved in the trade deal have issued worldwide blanket arrest warrants for any known association with this terrorist group. Since the attack on my compound and kidnapping of my fiancée in December, many countries around the world have been building special camps and prisons to hold these fanatics. Your leaders are urging anyone who knows of Christian activity to call law enforcement to deal with them. Remember to keep yourselves safe. Many of them are armed and dangerous, as my dead associates prove. They are not permitted to spread their philosophy of hate; their brainwashing will no longer be tolerated. The Christians who surrender peacefully will be processed to the work camps. They will be given plenty of opportunity to give up their practices. Once we are sure they're freed from the ideology, they will be released back into society. I have been advised that any Christians found to be terrorists will be tried as such. Several countries have the death penalty in these circumstances. For the ones that do not have capital punishment, there could be extradition to the countries that do. Truly, it's a sad day when the world must resort to these draconian measures for the betterment of humankind."

After Edward finished his address, he fielded questions from the reporters. They were all favourable, preplanned, and scripted to place Edward in a good light. His appearance ended, and a new program had three television hosts discussing the need to crush the terrorism of Christians. They told stories of Christians who opposed societal issues that were contrary to the Bible, twisting the facts to vilify the individuals or groups. In the end, they concluded by espousing the benefits of arresting Christians. These journalists worked for the One World Television Company, so they completely supported the OWHC and Edward Connor. The two female and one male hosts seemed particularly enamoured with the two Connors. It was obvious to Breanna that they were under the demonic influence of the Irish siblings. She knew it too well since she'd experienced the spell Edward had on her before she became a Christian.

Once the journalists had finished their discussion period, the interview with Edward was played again. It was on a loop, as David had said. This time, Breanna, Joshua, Itsy, and Michael heard the beginning of the program.

"Hello. My name is Edward Connor. I realize that many of you have heard my name or seen me in the news regarding the trade agreement that was ratified by most countries earlier this year. My name also came up with news of my fiancée's kidnapping and subsequent brainwashing by a group of militant Christians. I had appealed for any news of her safety and that of our baby. I remain hopeful that she is alive and that she can be helped to overcome the Stockholm syndrome she's experiencing."

Itsy yelled at the television. "Liar." Then catching herself, she said to those present, "Sorry."

Edward did the voice-over as a video of him and Breanna coming out of the obstetrician's played for the audience. It looked innocuous, but Breanna remembered everything about that day. He was squeezing her hand hard enough to serve as a warning, so she flashed him the smile he required. Lifting her hand to his mouth for a kiss, Edward showed off the engagement ring on her hand. Edward finished by drawing her to him, and he kissed her passionately for the cameras. That day, Breanna tried to blank out all emotions, which was probably why Joshua thought she looked drugged.

As she watched the television, Breanna's chest physically hurt. Her body began to vibrate. She dropped her head, feeling the heat rising to her cheeks. All her friends, and most importantly, her husband, were watching her kissing Edward. She wanted to crawl into a hole and never come out.

She heard Edward's voice but didn't look up. "Breanna, if they allow you to hear this, please come home." He sounded sincere, but Breanna knew the evil in the man's heart. He continued, "I'm making every effort to find you. Don't worry, it will only be a matter of time. To anyone who has any information, there is a number at the bottom of the screen. It's a hotline dedicated to that one goal. There's a substantial reward for anyone who finds my Breanna."

Breanna searched for Joshua's hand, and he grabbed hers. Her voice was strangled, "It will never be over. He will never stop looking for me."

"That's enough of that psychopath," Michael snapped, and he turned off the television.

David said, "Maybe, but the Lord will protect you. He's coming back soon now."

Michael twirled toward David, "Yes, but only after seven years of the tribulation. And as bleak as it seems, we don't know if it's started yet. Edward has not become the supreme dictator of the world and revealed himself as the antichrist."

"That won't happen until the Holy Spirit is removed from the earth," said Nancy. "When the rapture happens.

Breanna looked at her. "What's that?"

Joshua said, "Remember from our wedding. The snatching away of the bride once the groom's father says it's time for the celebration."

Thankful for a happy memory, she responded, "I remember being carried by the groomsmen."

Joshua told Breanna and the others present, "I explained that it was a picture of the rapture. Jesus will come to take his bride to heaven." Her husband reminded her of the ceremony. Breanna looked into Joshua's eyes and saw loving compassion.

David said, "We don't know the day or hour. It could be in five minutes or five years. We don't know if it's pre-trib, mid-trib, or post-tribulation."

"My thought is that it's pre-trib," Nancy stated with conviction. "The antichrist will be revealed once we are removed from the earth."

Itsy put her two cents in. "I think it will be pan-trib."

David shifted his gaze toward the blonde. "What's that?"

Itsy shrugged her shoulders. "It'll all pan out in the end." Everyone laughed. Then she quoted scripture. "Do not be anxious about anything, but in everything by prayer and supplication with thanksgiving let your requests be made known to God."

David said, "Philippians 4:6. One of my favourites."

"I'm glad I got it right." She raised her brows, then she said, "Don't worry, Bree; we're going to protect you. So is God."

58

"DANIEL IS ALWAYS ravenous. I can't seem to feed him enough," Breanna complained to Taddy the following day.

"He's six months old now," Taddy replied, "so that he can be supplemented with solid food. I'll show you how to make homemade purées." She cuddled the infant in her arms. His arms were moving constantly, and he cooed. He put the teething ring into his drooling mouth. Daisy played with the toys Breanna offered her while they all sat on the living room floor. "Introduce one food at a time. See if he likes it and how he tolerates it."

"I think that would be helpful. Plus, he's got six teeth already, and he bites me hard."

Taddy began laughing. "Oh, I remember that well."

"If all goes well with solid food, I think I'll start weaning him."

Taddy's head snapped up. "Why? It's not my place, but it's a little early, isn't it?"

Breanna stared at her son with pain in her eyes. "I've got to, Taddy. Just in case ... Edward."

Her friend shook her head. "You can't think like that, Bree."

"Yeah, I do. In case ... for Daniel. If anything happens to me, Joshua, and Itsy, I'd like you and Fred to take Daniel. He looks dark like you and Daisy because of your Indigenous heritage. He could pass for your son, and you could keep him safe from Edward." Tears pooled in the corner of her eye.

"We're all in danger with this new law."

"But they don't have your picture plastered on the television. David said that the news frequently posts my photo from before I was pregnant. It could be that I will have to leave here to keep all of you safe. I know you would care for Daniel as your own. Daisy already thinks she has a little brother." Breanna placed a hand on Taddy's arm. "Please consider it. I won't leave him unless I have to, you know that."

Taddy kissed the top of Daniel's head. She said, "Only if it's necessary. Fred and I adore him, so it's a no-brainer that we would take him as our own. Did you know I can't have any more children?"

"Oh, Taddy. I didn't know. I'm sorry."

She explained, "I had complications when I had Daisy. We tried to conceive again, but we had no luck. After many tests, the conclusion was that I can't have another. We would take Daniel in a heartbeat. He would be ours until you're in a position to take him back."

Dipping her head, Breanna said, "That must be so hard for you and Fred. I'm so sorry."

"Maybe it's for the best with Christians being hunted."

"Can you do me another favour?"

"Sure."

"Don't say anything to anyone yet, except Fred, but tell him to keep it a secret. I want to talk to Joshua about it and then to Itsy."

Taddy bobbed her head in agreement. "I wonder what Joshua will say … and Itsy. She's a firecracker."

Breanna clicked her tongue. "She is a bit of a pistol. It's so nice to see her back. When Edward held us prisoner, she couldn't say anything out of fear that he might kill her."

"It sounds horrible. I was sorry to hear what you ladies went through. He's a piece of work. Do you really think he's the antichrist?"

"I don't know for sure. I was basing it on that prophetic dream I had a couple of years ago." Daisy started to pile the toys on Breanna's lap. She toddled around the room picking up other things and bringing them to her auntie. "But look at his behaviour and now his rise to power."

"Yeah! And the world loves him. That's one of the clues." Taddy reached out as Daisy went by to check her underwear. "Here." She handed Daniel back to his mom. Then she began a verbal wrestling match with Daisy to get her daughter to use the potty. It was comical to see the mother arguing with the two-and-a-half-year-old about using the plastic toilet. Taddy would say, "Potty," and Daisy would answer, "Diaper." Taddy sighed, "It's so much easier to take off her underwear outside and cover her with a little dress. Then she crouches near the bushes."

"Well, she has some idea because she knows how to ask for a diaper when she has to relieve herself." Breanna said to the toddler, "Daisy, do you want to use Auntie's potty?"

"Auntie's potty." Daisy ambled over to Breanna with her arms raised.

"I can try this," Breanna said as she picked up Daisy and took her into the bathroom with Taddy carrying Daniel, coming in from behind. The redhead held the child on the toilet, and Daisy successfully used it. "Yippee! You're a big girl now."

"Yippee!" Daisy clapped her hands.

Taddy was proud of her daughter. "Thank you, Bree. You're good with children."

"So are you." Breanna smiled at Daisy, then Taddy. "That's why I asked you to take Daniel if I have no choice."

59

"NO, ABSOLUTELY NOT," Joshua's jaw twitch. "We're not giving our baby away."

Breanna bit her lower lip. "Of course not. But I want a backup plan if Edward kidnaps me and you've got to launch a rescue again."

"Is that why you've been giving Daniel some solid foods and using a bottle once a day?" He glared at Breanna, who was feeding their son in the bedroom chair.

She stared back at him. "No and yes."

"Which one?"

"You must have noticed that Daniel is not satisfied with only breast milk anymore. Look at the size of this guy. He needs some solid food, and Taddy said that infants can be started at three or four months with baby cereal. We didn't have any, so I held off, but he needs something to fill his tummy." Breanna handed the baby to Joshua, and he sat down on the edge of the bed to burp him. "Using a bottle is to help Daniel if I disappear suddenly. It won't be such a hardship on him."

Joshua tilted his head. "We should trust God that we're safe here. I don't want anyone but us raising our son."

"You think I want that to happen? The thought of losing Daniel makes me crazy. I could give up breathing before giving him up. But I love him too much not to plan to protect him with everything I've got, even if I have to die." She tried not to dwell on the idea of never seeing her son again. Imagining it made her heart drop into her stomach, and she gasped for air to fill her lungs.

Clearing her head, Breanna said, "Edward can never get his hands on our baby, no matter what we have to do."

Daniel let out a burp and fell asleep on his father's shoulder. Joshua kissed the top of his head and breathed in the scent of his son. "I'd kill the man before he gets his hands on Daniel."

"I say I'd die; you say you'd kill. The point is that we both would do anything for our son. That's why we need an emergency plan."

"What about Itsy?"

"She would be first to care for him, but now that she's part of the soldier program and with her MMA training, I think she'd end up fighting with you."

"And Michael would not leave her. He picked up the training I gave him quickly enough when we came to rescue you at Edward's estate. Since then, the classes Itsy and I teach have improved his skills. Add the supersoldier nanos, and we make a fearsome trio. But you and the others who are practicing with us are doing well also." Many of the camp residents decided to learn self-defence. More joined after hearing Edward's television address to the world. Some were ardent pacifists, and they abstained. There was no condemnation or requirement either way. Joshua explained to everyone that in Hebrew, the commandment that says "thou shalt not kill" actually translates to "thou shalt not murder." That was why the Jews could fight the pagan tribes in the Promised Land. Being a soldier or defending yourself was not murder. It eased Breanna's conscience about killing Edward's butler. She was defending herself and her friends. Even when she wasn't training with Joshua, she practiced around the house. It could come in handy someday.

After Joshua's reaction to her backup plans for Daniel, she decided she might as well broach another idea she'd been kicking around. "I've been thinking that I should use the nanos on me. I could dye my hair, change the style, and the muscle and bone structure difference might throw off anyone hunting me."

Joshua grimaced. "I like you like this." He placed Daniel into the crib he had built for their baby. Lifting Breanna out of the chair, he kissed her on the forehead. "I like your hair." He kissed her nose. "I like your freckles." He kissed her mouth. "I like your lips."

She enjoyed his attention and was grateful that God had put them back together.

Later that night, as they cuddled in bed, she said, "I'm serious about the nano program. I'm considering it once Daniel is weaned. You know how terrified I am of Edward. I don't care if they kill me for being a Christian; I don't want to be in that man's grasp again. With the training I'm getting from you and the soldier program, I could defend myself against him."

Joshua held her close. "I know. I want to tell you he will never get his hands on you again, but I don't want to lie to you either. Life holds no guarantees, and bad things do happen to good people … and Christians. I want you to know, I will support you and love you no matter what you decide to do. We are one."

"We are one," she repeated.

60

DURING THE LAST two weeks of July, a staggering number of Christians made their way to the camp. Another camp was hastily built north of Algonquin Park and another north of Pembroke. The network of cells that built and ran the camps had connections to others throughout Canada, mainly in the north, where the populated areas were sparse, and trees were plentiful. Word was that Christians were in hiding around the globe. The ones not in hiding were being rounded up and shipped to camps. It was beyond comprehension how the non-Christians would go along with this, given the history of the Holocaust and the Japanese internment camps less than a hundred years before.

Joshua was concerned for his family, but he couldn't risk calling them in case Edward had their phones bugged. When he thought of them, he would become frustrated and go work out. Breanna knew better than to disturb him when he was in one of those moods. She understood because she would have loved to talk to Jean and introduce her to Daniel. Instead, she busied herself with weaning Daniel and switching him over to solid food in a slightly hurried but methodical manner. By the end of July, he was drinking whole milk from bottles and eating some puréed foods, so she reduced his breast-feeding to once a day.

The last week of July, a new group of nine refugees arrived at the camp. Joshua went to help welcome the group and find space for them. The communal cabin became a makeshift home for the nine. That evening, most of the citizens gathered around a campfire outside and sang praises to God.

Breanna was in her kitchen, puréeing and canning baby food for the next few weeks, when Itsy came running in. "You are not going to believe who's here. You need to come see."

Breanna flipped her head towards her friend and said, "I'll be there as soon as I finish here."

"What can I do to help?" Itsy came over to stand beside Breanna at the stove.

"You'll miss the fun. I'll come shortly."

"Let me help you." Itsy washed her hands and put on oven gloves to remove the canning jars from the boiling water.

Breanna made a sound of exasperation. "You're bossy."

They both laughed.

"You know, you could just tell me."

"What would be the fun of that? We can let these cool now, so the seals set. Come on."

No sooner did Breanna remove her gloves than Itsy began dragging her toward the door. "Okay, I'm coming."

The two girlfriends walked briskly to join the crowd around the bonfire. Joshua held Daniel downwind of the smoke, and Michael was standing beside him. Both were engaged in conversation with another man who had his back to Breanna. When the women arrived to join their husbands, Breanna peered at the newcomer.

"Hakeem! What are you doing here? I mean … you know what I mean." She gave him a friendly hug.

Dr. Sahal twisted his hands, palms up. "My ophthalmology office was closed because I am a Christian. The receptionist turned me in, but my nurse called and warned that the police were at the clinic looking for me. My wife and I fled and came north."

"That's terrible. I'm sorry for the loss of your business."

"It could have been worse if I hadn't been warned." Hakeem looked old. His hair was now completely gray, and the lines on his face outlined his worry. "Breanna, I must tell you. I must tell all of you some horrible news."

Breanna's pulse increased. "What?"

"Jean Steinberg was arrested."

"What? Oh no … no." Breanna was in shock. Once back in Canada, except for one brief call, Breanna purposely did not contact Jean again to protect her. Joshua placed one arm around his wife.

"I don't know all the particulars. But Agent Parker was going to look into it and see how she could help. We suspect they interrogated Jean to find out where you are because they knew your connection to her." Hakeem shook his head. "The next thing I heard, Jean died of a heart attack. I don't know if they purposely killed her like John, but I would think it would have made more sense to use her as bait to catch you."

Breanna sat down on the closest log bench. She placed her head in her hands and began to sob. When she could speak, she cried, "It's my fault."

Joshua sat on one side of her, and Itsy on the other. Joshua said, "It's not your doing."

"It's Edward," Itsy hissed. "Forgive me, Lord, but I am thinking very bad things about that man."

Michael stood in front of them. "None of this is your fault."

"Yes, it is," said another newcomer. A man in his early twenties with long sandy-coloured hair stared at Breanna. "I saw your picture on the news on a loop. They said you were kidnapped and that a Christian terrorist group was responsible for these laws against Christians. Now people all over the world are being arrested and killed because of you."

Joshua's eyes flashed, and his jaws clenched. He handed Daniel to Itsy and was about to confront the man when Michael beat him to it.

Michael said to Breanna's accuser, "You don't have a clue what you're talking about. If you're a Christian, then you should know better than to believe what they say on television." Michael placed his hands on his hips, trying to control himself so he would not take the refugee and shake the daylights out of him. "It was the other way around. Edward Connor kidnapped Breanna. She was forced to work on nanotechnology for him so he could take over control of the world. Breanna destroyed one of his projects to put nanobots into food and medicine to kill anyone who opposed him. It turns out it only delayed the process, as he had more to make. Breanna was forced to help program the project that made supersoldiers for Edward to sell around the world. He used it on himself and his sister. But Breanna was able to smuggle it out of Edward's compound when we rescued her. As you can see, Joshua, Itsy, and I are recipients. The program went to Israel because that country would not sign Edward's trade deal, which allowed him global control through OWHC and other companies he owns. Joshua made sure it also went to Christian resistance fighters around the globe.

"I once believed in Edward Connor and helped draft some aspects of the trade deal. He's a genius because his power does not come from this world. When I became a Christian, my eyes were opened to his evil intent." Michael was calmer now. "Edward always intended to kill off Christians because they cannot be as easily seduced by the demons possessing him. This situation gave him the license to do it. If Edward is the antichrist, then the persecution of Christians was going to happen with or without Breanna. It's in the Bible."

Itsy added, "All that aside, Edward is a liar. I was there. You didn't see what Edward did to Breanna when she was pregnant by her husband, Joshua, not Edward. I saw the bruises. I saw the emotional abuse. You need to be careful what you believe."

Hakeem nodded. "Breanna saved the world, and if Edward had died in the plane crash, caused by his sister shooting the hydraulics and not by the Christians as he claims, we wouldn't have to face his reign of terror now. I was there at the beginning." Twisting back to Joshua, Hakeem said, "There's more bad news. Esther Parker has been arrested as a terrorist and is to be sent to the US to be executed, since Canada doesn't have the death penalty yet."

61

"I HAVE TO go, Bree," Joshua told her. "I've known Esther for two years from the watcher cell. We're colleagues and friends. We owe her a debt of gratitude because she saved your life by lying to Edward so he wouldn't have you killed."

Breanna held onto her husband's arm. "I don't want to be separated from you. We were apart for nine months."

He stared at her. "What would you have me do, allow Esther to be possibly tortured and killed?"

She wrapped her arms around his chest. "No, of course not. But can't someone else go? Aren't there other cell members who would be willing to help?"

Joshua gently lifted her chin, and his dark eyes held her in an emotional embrace. "I'll get help, but I've got to go. A soldier never leaves another one behind. Plus, I have dual citizenship, so I can legally be in the US if it's required."

"Edward will be waiting for you. He'll know you were associated with Esther too."

"Michael is coming with me, and there are other Christian men that I have injected with the nano soldier program who would join up. Itsy will stay with you to protect you and Daniel."

She pulled away from him and stood by Daniel's crib. Even though they were arguing, they kept their voices hushed for their sleeping baby. Breanna stared at their son. Would he grow up without a father? She couldn't think that way. "Itsy won't be happy to be apart from Michael again."

Joshua put his arm around Breanna. He stared at his son, already missing the two people who meant the most to him in the world. "I have to go."

She whispered, "I know."

"There's something else."

Breanna sighed. "Isn't there always?"

He gave a sardonic snort. "Yes, I suppose there is." Joshua pulled her into his arms. "You can't stay here. It's not safe anymore. That young guy's attitude tonight made me realize that others believe the same as he does. They don't know the truth." He kissed her forehead. "Taddy and Fred are going to bring you up to Nunavut to her family. The community will protect you from the new colonialists in the global takeover. They will keep you safe from Edward. She told me where they live, and I will come find you when Esther is free."

"Nunavut?"

"Apparently that's where she was born and grew up."

"I didn't know."

"Me neither. The good thing is that it is so sparsely populated and far north, Edward will never find you. You need to keep our son safe, Bree."

She squeezed him as tightly as she could, and given his muscles, it didn't hurt. "Come back to us, Joshua. I love you. Daniel loves you. We need you."

The following day, Itsy was in a grumpy mood most of the morning. Breanna realized Michael must have told her about his and Joshua's plans to rescue Agent Parker. Once Itsy had a couple of cups of coffee after her work-out, she settled down.

"Feeling better?" Breanna asked.

"Not really, but what choice do I have. What choice do any of us have? I need to do some serious repenting about Edward Connor. I wish I had killed him when we had the chance on his estate. He would have killed us. But he gave himself up, and we decided to be merciful. How many will die because we decided to be kind?" Itsy vented.

Breanna said, "Killing someone is not an easy thing to live with unless it's self-defence."

"How do you feel about going to Nunavut? I always wanted to visit, but I'm not sure about living there."

"We will do what we have to do to survive like we did before. And we'll pray like crazy for our husbands to come back soon."

"Amen to that," Itsy said. She pulled her long blond hair into a ponytail and fastened it.

"I can't get over the transformation you went through with the soldier nanos. You're still you, but you are so much more. Your hair is whitish blond with no darkness underneath now, and it has waves instead of the straight locks you had in the past. Your face is flawless, and you are now five feet six inches tall. We can't call you Itsy-bitsy anymore." Breanna chortled at the memory of the name she had teased her friend with in her first year of university.

Then she added, "How that program can change bone, muscle, and hair is beyond me, even though I helped write the last of it. You look like a movie star, Itsy. I told Joshua I should use the program to change my looks, too. Everyone is looking for me thanks to Edward's constant publishing of my photo. They wouldn't suspect a muscle-bound person, and maybe the change in bone size and my hair will help with a disguise." Breanna watched for Itsy's reaction.

"I think that's a great idea. You've stopped breast-feeding, so it wouldn't hurt Daniel. We could certainly travel more easily if no one recognized you."

"Joshua wasn't as sure about me changing my looks. Maybe he likes his wife weak."

Itsy scoffed. "I think Joshua would love you no matter what. We still don't know all the possible long-term effects of these nanos in our systems, though."

"No, but Edward has had them in his system the longest, and he doesn't look like he's worse off than he was before. In fact, he looks better than ever, except for the evil lunatic thing. The three of you have been good since the beginning of December. It heals your injuries instantly, and none of you has been sick even one day. It looks promising so far."

"Well, if you want to do it, I say go for it."

"It's a shame to waste the limited programmed nanos we have unless it's necessary, but it might come to that."

"Hey, look on the bright side. If you do use it, you might get rid of those freckles you hate." Itsy made a face. "Your one true beauty."

Both women laughed.

62

IT DIDN'T TAKE the three couples long to pack. By the early morning of the second day after Hakeem and his wife had arrived, they were ready with camping gear and food. Breanna was glad she had made a good supply of baby food for Daniel. Joshua and Michael decided to accompany the others to a rendezvous point five kilometres west, where they would meet up with Indigenous friends of Taddy's who would serve as guides for the journey north.

It was difficult to say goodbye to the people who had been part of their community for the past eight months. They had been through so much in a short period. Nancy said, "We'll miss you guys. Are you sure you've got to go?"

Breanna said, "The longer I stay here, the more danger all of you will be in. You heard the announcement on the television. All municipal and rural police services, RCMP, and CSIS have been amalgamated with the World United Nations Security Services troops policing the globe. The main objective of WUNSS is to maintain peace and a balance of power. But all of us know it is to capture Christians, especially me."

David was panting as he arrived late to the farewell gathering. "It's true, what Breanna said." He continued, "What's worse is that there was a formal announcement this morning at five from the World United Nations headquarters in Dublin that all the nations that signed the international trade deal will be looking to amend their laws to allow the death penalty for terrorists under the Antiterrorism Act. It's to expedite sentences rather than going to neighbouring countries to carry out executions. Like in Esther's case, trials will be rushed through a kangaroo court.

"Also, beginning today, the WUN will provide a reward of groceries for a month to anyone who turns in a Christian. With the food shortages in North American cities and some other countries, our brothers and sisters in Christ are in even more danger. We must pray earnestly for us all." He put his hands together in a sign of prayer. "But remember, there is hope; we must keep our eyes to the sky, the Lord Jesus will return soon." Then he looked at the departing people and shook his head. "Still, I'm sorry to see you leave. I've only known you for a short time, but I feel close to all of you. Where will you go?"

Michael shrugged. "West. Maybe we can lose the WUNSS in the Rocky Mountains. But it is a long way for us to go, so we need to say our goodbyes now." He lied to protect his friends. No one could betray them by accident or by torture if they didn't know their true destination.

The community expressed lots of hugs, goodbyes, and "I'll miss you"s. Finally, the group was off. The first part of the journey was by car. Nancy drove them three kilometres west down a dirt road until it ended, then she headed back to the camp.

Fred carried a backpack, and on his chest was a carrier he had made so Daisy could face forward. Joshua was laden with the same items, and he carried Daniel in a similar carrier made by Fred. Breanna, Itsy, and Taddy carried the remaining supplies and food. Breanna also carried the laptop with the supersoldier program and the remainder of the associated nanobots.

The next two kilometres consisted of a hike through a heavily forested area. The bugs were insatiable, even with the homemade repellent worn by the group. Breanna quipped, "I'm not going to miss these bloodsuckers." It took longer than expected with the heavy packs and children in tow. Joshua, Michael, and Itsy were the only ones not covered in sweat or showing signs of tiring. They didn't even notice the bugs.

There was a high-pitched bird whistle. Taddy said, "Stop. Do you hear that?" Another whistle sounded. Fred responded with a similar whistle twice.

Four men emerged from hiding in the trees. All had black hair in various lengths, painted faces, and camo gear, as if they were hunting. They held rifles, and knives and axes were tucked into their belts. Taddy and Fred greeted two of the men, who looked similar enough to be twins or brothers, close in age.

Taddy introduced them: "This is Samuel and his brother Saul. This is Itsy, Michael, Bree, and Joshua. These are our two babies."

Breanna noticed Taddy refrained from saying the children were from different families.

Samuel pointed to his other two friends. He said, "This is Joseph." The man dipped his head. "And Matthew." Matthew raised his hand. "They're great trackers. We should be able to weave through the bush undetected. We can get you to Nunavut."

63

THE GROUP CONTINUED west for several more kilometres, where they came upon an old logging road. Matthew pointed south. "Follow this for about three clicks," he said, referring to kilometres, "and you'll see an old red Dodge Caravan. Here are the keys." He tossed them to Michael. Then he pulled some papers from his pocket and handed them to Joshua. "Notes that will serve as introductions to other Indigenous tribes. We are united and won't be divided this time. That's how the Europeans conquered us. Now we fight together. And since Christians are also their enemies, we fight alongside Christians."

Joshua unhitched Daniel's carrier and handed him to Taddy. "I want to say goodbye to Bree." Taddy held the baby and kissed his cheek.

He set his backpack on the ground, and Breanna, Itsy, and Michael followed suit. Itsy and Michael embraced and spoke quietly to each other. Joshua put his arms around his wife and kissed her.

"Get Esther and come back to us right afterwards," Breanna said, blinking back the tears.

Joshua placed a hand on her cheek. "Not a minute longer than necessary." He kissed her. "The Lord bless you and keep you. May his face shine upon you and give you shalom."

"Jesus, protect my husband and Michael and all of us. Bring us together again soon. Take care of Esther until Joshua can rescue her. Amen." Breanna took a step backward. If she didn't let him go now, she never would.

There was a noise of engines suddenly gunning it along the road towards them. Joshua waved at Taddy and called to her. "Run. Take him and go."

With a nod, Taddy turned and headed west into the woods, still carrying Daniel and with Fred right behind her carrying Daisy. Joshua waved again, and their four Indigenous friends followed behind the couple and the babies.

Headlights crested the hill. Joshua turned to Breanna, who looked between her husband and son. Her mind flashed to her husband taking her baby away in her dream, and in a twisted kind of way, it happened here in front of her. She hesitated as she realized this was not the same thing. Joshua yelled at her, "Run. Catch them." She grabbed the backpack with the laptop and nanos and headed into the woods behind the first group, who were already out of sight.

Itsy stayed behind with Michael and Joshua to fight. The army jeeps stopped in front of them, and about a dozen soldiers hopped out, guns raised. Itsy was the first to jump. The bullets flew, and while they stung, they didn't stop the three. The nanos instantly healed their wounds.

Breanna glanced back when she heard the gunfire, and she was grabbed from behind by a soldier who had spotted her fleeing. She used the defensive moves she had practiced and was able to get out of his grasp. Another soldier grabbed her, and the first put handcuffs on her. They carried her to a nearby Hummer and threw her and her pack into the back seat. There were no door handles she could use, and a heavy wire screen separated the front and back, like a police car. Without hesitation, she opened her bag and silently booted up the laptop. She took a vial of nanos and jabbed it into her leg. Tapping the keys, she was able to activate the programmed microcomputers.

The soldier in the front passenger seat heard the clicking and turned in time to see a transformed prisoner snap the handcuffs and rip out the metal screen. He fumbled for his sidearm, and she snapped his neck. Even she was surprised by her strength. Everything happened so fast, the driver was caught off guard. He pulled his gun, and Breanna disarmed him. In the scuffle, the gun went off and hit him in the throat. He slumped over the steering wheel, and the Hummer careened out of control, crashing into a tree. Breanna grabbed the two guns, tucked one into her belt, and shoved the other into her backpack. She ran to the road and backtracked to her husband. The gunshots fell silent, and Breanna feared the worse. As she rounded a curve, she saw all three of her loved ones with torn clothing from the bullets, but they were standing.

"Bree?" Joshua's mouth fell open.

64

"OH, WOW! BREE." Itsy stared at her friend.

"What? What do I look like? Is it horrible?"

"Your freckles are gone," Joshua said.

"Well, that's a good thing. What about the rest of me?"

Michael reached into his bag and brought her a mirror. Breanna dropped her backpack and took it. Her eyes looked the same. But the other changes were significant. Her hair was now straight, not wavy, and the colour was a lighter strawberry blond rather than red. Her freckles were gone completely, and her skin was blemish-free, including the small scar on her forehead from the stitches she received as a toddler. Her nose was straighter, her lips fuller, her jaw slightly more pronounced. She looked like a model. Glancing down at her body, she saw tightness and muscle. The baby fat she had carried after having Daniel had disappeared. She lifted her torn shirt to see that the stretch marks from the pregnancy were gone. When she glanced up at Michael, who stood beside her, she realized she was taller by another three inches at least.

Joshua walked up to her, examining the changes.

"Wow," she exclaimed. "I feel great." She flexed her muscles and laughed. "What do you think, Joshua?"

"Ah—you're different."

"Like all of you."

Joshua's mouth twitched. "I didn't think you would do it."

Breanna shook her head. "I was undecided, but then I had no choice. Two soldiers captured me and were taking me away as a prisoner. I couldn't go back to Edward." She frowned. "I didn't realize how strong I would be, and I snapped one man's neck. The other, I shot with his gun during a scuffle."

Her husband said, "You did the right thing." He put his arms around her.

"We'd better go, Itsy, if we're going to catch up to Taddy and Fred." Breanna inclined her head in the direction the other group had taken.

Joshua held Breanna close. "It's safer for them if you don't go."

Her eyebrows furrowed. "What do you mean? I have to be with my son."

"Looking like you do with the enhanced soldier program will only bring attention to them. Right now, it's a group of natives with one white husband travelling with two infants. Add you and Itsy to the group, and it'll raise red flags everywhere. I worried about sending Itsy before, but I knew you'd need her for protection, but now ...." Joshua shook his head.

Breanna felt the heat rise to her face and tried to shake off Joshua's hold. "No. It was only an emergency plan if Edward caught me. They can't take my baby."

"Bree—"

Joshua was cut off as Breanna punched him in the jaw in a blind rage. When she ran towards the woods, Joshua followed and grabbed her from behind. She tried to use the fighting moves she had learned, but he successfully blocked her. She dropped and spun her legs in a sweeping motion to throw him to the ground. When he fell, Breanna attempted to jump to her feet, only to have Joshua grab her legs and bring her down. Breanna kicked him in the thigh. Joshua grabbed her leg, so she twisted her body in an attempt to release herself. Instead, she ended up in a worse position. Joshua took a dominant posture, sitting on her hips while she lay on the ground. Her arms were flaying at his face and chest. He grabbed one, then the other, and using gravity, his weight, and muscles to hold her, he pinned her to the ground.

She screamed at him, "You promised you wouldn't take Daniel. You promised you wouldn't take my baby." Tears streamed down her face. "You're a liar. I should have known not to trust you again. You do nothing but lie."

Joshua's jaw twitched as he forced down his hurt. "Daniel is my son, too. Do you think I want him away from either of us?"

When Breanna recognized the pain in Joshua's eyes, she stopped struggling and sobbed. Joshua wrapped his arms around her, and the two of them held each other.

Meanwhile, Michael hugged Itsy, who was weeping.

When Breanna could speak, she said to Joshua, "I'm sorry for what I said. I didn't mean it. No matter what I do, I lose my baby, and Edward wins."

"No, he doesn't," Michael quipped. "We won't let him win. We'll rescue Esther, then we'll get Daniel. Now there are four of us to protect him. Edward Connor doesn't get to win."

Itsy dried her eyes. "That's right. We will make him regret starting a war with us and with Christians. Until the Lord comes or we die, we fight."

Joshua helped Breanna to her feet and said, "We fight."

Breanna nodded. "We fight."

65

BREANNA CHANNELLED ALL her hurt and rage towards Edward, who had started the whole thing. It strengthened her resolve to do battle. She felt bad for the soldiers who might have been deceived into fighting for Edward, but she wasn't going to let them capture her and her friends because of it. She resolved to witness when she could but to attack when she couldn't. *If they are to be redeemed, God will have to do it before we have contact with them.*

Wearing the uniforms and sunglasses they had taken off the dead soldiers, the four drove a Hummer south toward Thunder Bay. Michael drove while Joshua used their laptop to contact different members of the cells using encrypted messages in code. Meanwhile, Itsy sat beside her husband in the front seat and used the vehicle's computer, which someone had signed into, and was able to access the information about Esther's extradition to the US.

Itsy paraphrased: "She's slated to be flown to Cuyahoga County, Ohio, for execution. The head of the WUNSS signed the order under the Antiterrorism Act. It says here that in two days, she's being flown out of the Canadian Forces Base in Trenton, Ontario. They have a convoy picking her up at the CSIS headquarters in Toronto for the transfer."

"We've got to get there fast. How in the world do we prepare for this in two days?" Breanna asked.

"Once we get to the airport in Thunder Bay, we fly to Toronto," Joshua said.

Breanna tipped her head to the side. "Just like that. No questions asked. We waltz in and fly out?"

Joshua reached over and gave her hand a light squeeze. "No, not just like that. I've contacted a guy from one of the Christian cells in Thunder Bay. He has a small plane, and he'll fly us to the private hangars at Pearson International in Toronto. It's within Ontario, so there shouldn't be a problem. We don't need passports. Wearing these WUNSS uniforms will give us carte blanche to be unhindered. People are too afraid to rock the boat—at least that's what my buddy says."

"What's the plan then?" Itsy asked. "We grab Esther on route to the base?"

Joshua explained, "I've contacted a cell group outside of Toronto, and they agreed to help. We plan to have the escort stop for coffee or a bathroom break at a service station. The one outside Port Hope will be our target."

"How are we going to make them stop?" Michael asked.

"I think I can program some nanos to give them diarrhea. We will have to slip it into their coffee or food." Breanna said, "Oh, but I have to slip into a lab somewhere to access some nanos and equipment."

Joshua said, "I think I can cover that part. I still have the code to get into the lab where I used to work. If they haven't changed it, we can tie up the guard if he's awake, and get in and out quickly."

"And like that"—Itsy snapped her fingers—"we have a plan."

"Now, carry it out without a hitch," Breanna said. She added a prayer: "Lord God, if it is your will, please help us rescue Esther. She's your daughter, and you love her. Let all go well without any more deaths. Amen."

When they reached the address given to Joshua by his friend with the plane, they pulled into a ranch outside of Thunder Bay. In the yard were five men with cowboy hats and boots, looking like ranch hands, but Joshua knew better. One was barely visible on the porch with a rifle leaning up against the post. The others were most likely armed or had weapons close by. Another had a gun tucked into his belt under his denim jacket. A large man, over six feet and maybe two hundred and fifty pounds, ambled over to the Hummer as they stopped. Joshua told the others to remain in the car. He stepped out with his arms raised to show he would not be aggressive.

Joshua asked, "Jimmy?"

With a brief nod, Jimmy responded, "Joshua?"

Joshua said, "Yup! And I have three other supersoldiers with me."

"Nice uniforms."

"The former owners won't be needing them anymore."

Jimmy nodded again. And held up a hand to let his cohorts know his guests were cleared.

Joshua waved for the three to come out of the Hummer. As they exited, he said, "Hands up so they can see them."

Itsy, Michael, and Breanna got out slowly and raised their hands.

"I thought you had the girl with you?" Jimmy asked.

"Which girl?" Joshua played dumb.

Jimmy smirked. "The one all over the news."

Joshua chuckled. "We've been holed up for months, but we saw her once on a satellite television. Pretty girl, too many freckles for me though."

Breanna knew he was putting it on, but she wanted to slap his arm about the freckles comment. Instead, she gave her unemotional stare—the one Joshua called her drugged look when she was with Edward.

"Come with me." Jimmy led them towards a barn, but he turned to the right, and Breanna saw the small plane on a private runway. "I've filled the tank for the trip. My story will be that you commandeered my plane for official WUNSS business that you told me nothing about. I didn't ask for ID, and none was offered. I was being a good citizen." He climbed into the pilot's seat, and the two women and Michael sat in the back. Joshua took the copilot's seat. Glancing at Joshua, Jimmy said, "Have you ever flown?"

Joshua raised his brows. "A couple of times out of need. I hope it's not needed this time."

Jimmy broke out into a full laugh and even snorted. "Me too, brother."

When he reached for the controls, Breanna noticed the cross tattoo on his wrist and the number 2000. "What does the tattoo of the two thousand mean?" She couldn't resist asking.

"That's the year I was saved by the grace of Jesus," Jimmy answered.

She couldn't hide the awe in her voice. "Thirty-one years?"

"Yes. I was a hard drinkin', womanizin', cussin' sinner, and God brought me out of all that mess. I was miserable and was too drunk to realize it. But he's a good God." Jimmy started the engine.

"He's a great God," Michael agreed.

"Amen," said Itsy.

Breanna stared out the window, thinking about her baby and wondering how he was doing without her. She gulped down the lump in her throat and forced herself not to cry. *I know you're a good God. Daniel, the prophet, predicted the antichrist, and Daniel, my son, is a thorn in the antichrist's side. Rescue my Daniel from the roaring lion that is Satan, the way you rescued the prophet, Daniel.*

66

EVERYTHING WENT ACCORDING to plan. They were able to sneak into Joshua's old place of employment and program some nanobots to cause diarrhea for the soldiers transporting Esther the following day. Since the old guard on duty was snoring at his workstation, she also copied more nanos for the soldier program. Joshua kept watch in the lab as she completed the task. They put some of the nanos in syringes, and others they stored in sealed jars for later. Michael sat in a car the Christian cell had left for them at the airport, all prearranged by Joshua on the laptop and a burner phone supplied by Jimmy. The facility was quiet on the dead-end industrial street, and nothing was moving in the vicinity. Itsy kept an eye on the sleeping security guard. He was snoring louder than a jet engine.

Within two hours, the four were on their way to a rendezvous with one of the unsuspecting transporting WUNSS officers. Itsy was able to find out the driver's name and home address from the computer she removed from the Hummer and reconnected through a satellite link.

They followed him as he left his house, and when he stopped at a Tim Horton's, Breanna jumped out of the car with the nanos in a syringe. Before she entered the building, she unbuttoned the top of her uniform to show off some cleavage. *Sorry, Lord.* In her spirit, she felt God say not to sin but to rely on him. She refastened the buttons. *I trust you, Lord.* Standing in line behind the officer, she accidentally bumped him and dropped the debit card that had been inside the pocket of the uniform's original owner, Sam Helton. He picked it up at the same time she bent down. The man saw her face and gave a toothy grin.

"Thank you," Breanna said. She noticed that her deeper voice came out sounding sultry. She held out her hand for the card. *Please don't let him know this Sam from work.*

The officer didn't give the card a second glance because he couldn't take his eyes off her face. "You're welcome." She was trying to think of what else to say when he asked, "You're with WUNSS, I see."

"Samantha, but everyone calls me Sam." She flirted with her eyes. "And you are?"

"Calvin." He held out his hand to shake hers.

Breanna purposely made her hand shake weak. "Oh look, Calvin. You're up." She pointed to the young man at the register waiting for the next customer. "Can I buy you something?"

"Coffee." Breanna suddenly had a craving for the drink she hadn't had for a year and a half. It was the smell in the coffee shop. "Large, double cream, one sugar."

Calvin turned to the man at the register. He said, "Same, but make mine a large, double, double."

Turning back to Breanna, Calvin flirted. "I don't have time to sit with you this morning, but maybe I can get your number ,and we can do it another time."

It was easy to look disappointed because she was, as she needed him to stay longer to get the nanos into his coffee.

When the coffees were placed on the counter, she grabbed the wrong one purposely and said, "I'll write my number on your cup. Do you have a pen?"

He turned to the man at the counter to ask for one, and Breanna squirted the contents from the syringe she had hidden in her palm into his cup. When he turned back, she wrote fake contact information on his cup. "Thank you again," she said.

Calvin held up a hand. "Have a great day, Sam."

"You too, Calvin. Talk soon."

"You bet."

Probably not.

After he left the building, Breanna bought three more coffees and four breakfast sandwiches on Sam's bank card, then ran back out to the waiting car. "Success and coffee for everyone."

"Bree." Joshua's eyes narrowed. "I saw you unbutton your top, then redo it. Was something wrong?"

"Oh dear." Breanna crinkled her nose. "No, I was going to try to attract the guy with some cleavage, but the Holy Spirit convicted me. It's not right to cause a man to sin with lust. It would have been on me."

"I'm glad God set you straight." Her husband shook his head.

Breanna raised her shoulders in apology. She was feeling guilty even though she hadn't followed through with her plan. The growl of her stomach reminded her of her hunger, and she took a bite of her sandwich. "We'd better go to CSIS headquarters and follow this transporter for Esther."

Itsy and Michael remained silent during Breanna and Joshua's conversation. They were busy enjoying breakfast. "Thanks for the food and coffee, Bree," said Itsy.

"Uh-huh!" she said with her mouth full. "Hey, we should call me Sam during the operation. I don't want Edward to hear of Breanna being involved in this, or living in Canada, for that matter. Later, I'll go by the name Bree in case anyone slips up." They all signalled their agreement.

Then Michael shoved the rest of his sandwich into his mouth and took a large gulp of his drink. He drove the car to the government building. Using the burner phone, Joshua spoke to another carload of enhanced Christian soldiers who were waiting for them. Within the hour, an armoured transport truck left the underground parking. Joshua used the nanotechnology in his eyes to zero in on the driver. He verified that Calvin was in the driver's seat.

Joshua told his friends and wife, "It's showtime."

MICHAEL'S RACE CAR driving skills were not required in this instance. He managed to control himself and drove behind the transport truck on the 401 highway, following different cars and changing lanes to blend in. The other car of Christians did the same and traded places with Michael occasionally. Once they were outside Toronto and the suburban cities beside it, Michael moved directly behind the armoured truck, and Breanna began typing the computer program on the laptop for the nanobots Calvin consumed. When they passed the sign with the appropriate distance to the service centre, she hit the enter key.

"Done," she said.

Michael dropped back and let a couple of cars pass him. The four Christians were silently praying for success, and they were sure the other carload was doing the same. As predicted, the truck turned off at the Enroute highway food and gas station. They followed cautiously behind.

Calvin hopped out of the truck, leaving his partner behind in the passenger seat. Breanna typed in another code. Wearing a helmet with a dark visor that came with his outfit, Joshua followed Calvin into the washroom. He heard the poor man groaning in the toilet stall, when suddenly Calvin fell onto the floor, pants around his ankles.

Joshua knocked on the stall door, "Hey man, are you all right?" There was no answer.

Joshua busted the locked door and gagged. He placed the man back on the toilet and leaned him up against the wall. Joshua checked Calvin's pants and found the keys.

When he came out of the station, he motioned with a thumbs-up. The other three put on their matching WUNSS helmets with visors down. The Christians in the other car wore sunglasses, bulletproof vests, and police helmets. Joshua came up to the truck in a direction so the passenger guard would not see him. Using the keys to unlock the door, the other soldier said, "You okay? Huh?" He saw it was not Calvin, but before he uttered another word, Joshua gave him a punch to the head and knocked him out.

Sliding out again, they went to the back of the truck. Joshua used the key while the Christians trained their handguns on the back. Jerking the back door open, they were surprised to see a truckload of soldiers with weapons drawn. Five of them were products of the enhanced soldier program. Gunfire ensued. The four friends were surprised to find the uniforms were bullet-resistant, similar to a vest but with new technology. The Christians disarmed the regular soldiers and knocked them unconscious. All the people who had nanos in their systems self-healed after every bullet that managed to connect.

Hand-to-hand combat broke out between the eight Christian supersoldiers and four of their WUNSS equivalents. People at the station stayed out of the way. Some shot videos, but no one thought to call the WUNSS because so many of those fighting wore those uniforms.

The rapid healing of all of them made the fighting difficult. Breanna jack-hammered one guy, hitting him on the head repeatedly. After pounding him to the ground, Joshua used a heavy chain from a tow truck parked next to the armoured vehicle to chain up that soldier and the one he was fighting. Michael used a crowbar as a set of handcuffs on another. One of the Christian men lost his weapon in the fight and pulled a large hunting knife out of its sheath. The man continually healed from every cut until the Christian slit the WUNSS man's throat. It brought the officer to a halt for a few seconds. The Christian swung the knife like a samurai sword and took the man's head off. It was a shake-up for all the soldiers who saw it. He was the only fatality that day. But all of them realized they were not invincible.

While this was going on, Itsy jumped into the back of the prison truck to fight the last officer, who had stayed behind to watch Esther Parker. When Itsy entered, he purposely shot Esther point-blank. Itsy used her MMA fighting skills to try to demolish the man. After several blows between them, Itsy was able to give one of her roundhouse kicks, causing him to tumble out of the cab, and several Christian men descended on him. Itsy carried the critically wounded woman past everyone and called to Breanna using the name Sam. Breanna ran over to the car as Itsy placed Esther in the backseat.

"Tr ... trap," the middle-aged woman coughed out.

"We see that, Esther. I have the soldier program here. Do you want me to use it to heal you?" Breanna was already getting the program keyed in, and Itsy grabbed the syringe with the nanos.

Esther's eyes widened as she recognized the two women.

Breanna nodded. "We used it on us."

"Yes." It was barely a whisper.

Itsy emptied the syringe into Esther's arm while Breanna activated the nanos. Within a few seconds, Agent Parker's appearance changed, and she healed from the bullet wound.

"Let's get the guys out of here," Itsy said.

Sirens sounded down the highway. The Christian men chained the fifth enhanced soldier and hopped into their vehicles. Their two cars were speeding off as the flashing lights pulled into the parking lot.

Michael's racing skills kicked in. "I love this baby. It looks like a beater, but the engine is pure power." He sped around traffic, cruising at over 160 kilometres an hour. The other Christians' car had been fitted with a similar engine, and it was matching his speed. They passed Michael. That vehicle got off the highway at the first exit after the service centre, and the five friends took the one after it. Michael raced through the country while the others in the vehicle watched the road and skies for signs they were being followed. Joshua knew where they were going, and he directed Michael from the front passenger seat.

About thirty minutes later, Joshua said, "Slow down now."

"Here? We're in the middle of nowhere." Michael followed Joshua's instructions.

Joshua pointed. "There it is. Turn right there."

"Where?"

"Here. Back up a bit."

Michael backed up slowly and found the driveway obscured from the road by overgrown trees. There were no visible markers, so it was only by knowing the place existed that someone could find it.

68

MICHAEL DROVE SLOWLY down an overgrown dirt road snaking through the forest. It looked like a road to nowhere until he pulled into a large open expanse. It was a farm complex with three wood barns, a couple of work cabins, and an old house with several extensions that looked like it was twenty years late for a new paint job. Initially, the place looked deserted, but as the friends scanned the area, they could see armed men and women. Michael stopped the car, and the five of them exited slowly. They opened the trunk and removed the backpacks they had brought with them from the other camp. A large, muscular woman walked out of the house, took the keys from Michael without a word, and drove the car into a barn to hide it from view.

Joshua explained to his friends, "This was one of the places I came after I left Israel. I knew of this camp and rightly guessed the people would gladly take the nano enhancement." He turned and checked out Agent Parker's new look. Smiling at her, Joshua said, "Hi, Esther. Nice to see you."

She gave him a quick hug. "Thanks for the rescue ... and this." Esther held out her arms, waving them around. Because of her new size, her clothes were torn and stretched to the limit. "I feel great, but I think I need a new outfit."

Itsy said, "We all had the same problem. We were too busy fighting Edward to do much about it at first. Joshua, Michael, and I had to supersize our wardrobe. Bree here, hasn't had any chance of that yet. This suit is all she has in this size."

"Someone inside will have clothes for Bree and Esther," Joshua told them. "We need to all change out of these uniforms, and the bullet-hole damage has to be mended." He grabbed Breanna's hand and led the way into the house.

The number of people inside intimidated Breanna. She drew herself closer to his arm. Joshua sensed her nervousness and gripped her hand tighter.

"Joshua, welcome back." A black man in his early thirties stood up and held out his hand to shake.

"Hey, man." Joshua released Breanna to grab his friend and placed his other arm around his shoulder. "This is my wife, Bree. Bree, this is Brice."

It surprised Breanna when Brice gave her a huge hug. "So wonderful to meet you."

Joshua introduced the rest of his little group to Brice. After that, he moved around the large kitchen, then into the living room, and shook some hands or nodded to others.

Itsy whispered to Breanna, "Where do all these people sleep?"

Another woman sitting near the two female visitors said, "We sleep in the house or the outbuildings. We rotate guard duty, and all other jobs like cooking, cleaning, gardening, and hunting."

"Oh!" Itsy was surprised. It was more of a soldier camp than the lay one they had lived in north of Thunder Bay. Hence, the members were all willing to use the soldier program. "Itsy." She held out her hand.

"Lyndsay." The other woman had a firm grip as she shook Itsy's.

"My friends here need some clothes. They had to change to save their lives." Itsy pointed to Esther Parker, whose eyes darted around the room, taking everything in. "Esther. She's the woman we rescued today." Then Itsy reached over to Breanna and drew her closer. "And this is Bree."

Lyndsay gave them the once-over and said, "We've got a box of donations. Everything is oversized for us here. Maybe you both can find something."

"Thank you." Esther's voice was deeper but still professional-sounding, like the day Breanna met her.

Breanna said, "Thanks."

Lyndsay stood up. "Sure. Suppose you could leave the uniforms. We could probably use them for other jobs."

"Sounds good to me," Breanna said.

Itsy smirked. "Can't wait to get out of this thing."

"You might not say that when you see what we have." Lyndsay laughed.

Itsy held up her bag. "Lucky for me, I have a change of clothes, but Bree and Esther will need some."

Lyndsay began to lead the women out of the living room when Joshua called out, "Esther." He waved when she twisted her head. "Here are the other guys that helped rescue you today." Joshua introduced the group from the other car.

She bowed her head and said, "Thank you so much. You're all my heroes."

69

ONCE THE FIVE visitors showered and changed clothes, lunch was served for them and the other four men who were involved in Esther's liberation. Brice came and joined them. Breanna guessed he was considered a leader in the group, the way he spoke and the deference the others gave him.

"Welcome, everyone," Brice asked. "Esther, we're happy today was a success. Why did the WUNSS decide you'd be the first Canadian to be executed in the US under the trade deal? Were you going to be an example or a warning?"

Esther answered, "Thank you for helping with my rescue. I think I was to be an example, a warning, and a trap. I worked for CSIS, and I was also part of the Toronto Nano Organization, the watchers. As you know, CSIS was amalgamated under the WUNSS. When they arrested Jean Steinberg, a widow of a former Toronto cell member, I tried to have her released. That raised suspicion, but I think I was already red-flagged by Edward Connor for lying about Breanna when he wanted her investigated. He gave the WUNSS information about me. Edward has a lot of pull with them, although he's not formally the director. With his help, they arrested me as a terrorist and traitor. They interrogated me for days and used some drugs to get me to talk. I repeated the name of Jesus in my head to resist, but it was powerful stuff.

"I was asked a lot about Breanna." From the glare Joshua gave her, Esther caught on that no one was to know Bree was Breanna. "Breanna was Edward's pregnant fiancée. From what I heard, she was kidnapped. Everything is taped in those rooms, so I have no doubt Edward would have access to them. Anyway, I could honestly say I hadn't seen or heard from Breanna for a few years. I said nothing about our watcher cell."

For the first time, it dawned on Breanna that Joshua's and her conversation at Mossad had been recorded. He couldn't answer her questions, not because he was spying on the cells, but because he wasn't, and he was supposed to be doing that for Mossad. She questioned his loyalty to her and their friends, but he had been faithful. Breanna had forgiven him for something he didn't do. *I have to apologize to him later.*

Esther continued, "The trial was rushed through without any defence. I thought I was dead. When I was put in the prisoner transport, I was surprised at the number of guards, including those terminators in the back with me. Then I realized I was going to be used as bait to catch other Christians." Esther clicked her tongue. "Now I'm a supersoldier too. I'm impressed by how much younger I look and feel. All of you guys look great."

Brice said, "Billy reported that he cut off the head of one of these enhanced soldiers, or as you called them, terminators ... I like that name. We knew that if someone had too many injuries at once, such as with a grenade, the nanos could be overwhelmed, and then they couldn't heal. But it makes sense that losing our heads would be instant death."

"We should start training with swords," Michael said.

Joshua added, "It would be the best way to defend ourselves against the WUNSS terminators." He glanced at the older woman. "Esther, that name for them might stick." Switching his attention back to Brice. "With their success compared to regular soldiers, I suspect there'll be a push on buying more of Edward Connor's program."

"I agree. We need to get the message out to cells around the world." Brice slapped his hands on the table and pushed himself up. "Follow me to the communications room."

"Itsy is great with computers." Michael offered his wife's assistance, knowing she'd be interested in what they had set up at the farm. "She has one taken from the WUNSS, which was how we knew when and where Esther was to be moved. Maybe Itsy can help while we're here."

"Sure. Why don't you all come with me?" Brice led the way, and the five followed him up the slanted wooden stairs, which had seen better days.

A large room was set up with computers, printers, satellite dishes, and a variety of other technologies. "This is Luke. He's our computer wiz, along with Cindy, hacker extraordinaire." Brice introduced the five visitors to the two computer geeks.

Cindy said, "We link up with satellites but bounce off different servers around the world. We have the system rigged to change every few minutes randomly so that we are untraceable."

Luke folded his arms in front of his chest. "But they've got some serious talent working for them, so we always have to stay one step ahead."

Joshua asked Brice, "Could I send a quick message to my colleagues at Mossad and tell them to train with swords before we send them to the cells? Israel is one of the few holdouts on signing the trade deal."

"Eventually they will, according to Bible prophecy," said Luke.

"We should be raptured by then." Cindy gave a sideways smirk.

Breanna noticed that Christians were talking more often of the rapture. *I hope we are taken out of here soon, Jesus. It's getting bad.*

Brice returned to sending the messages. "I think it's a good idea, Joshua. We want Israel to stay away from the peace treaty and the antichrist as long as possible. I know prophecy says it's going to happen eventually, but I wish that God's chosen people would stay a million miles away from that man. Thankfully, Edward hasn't made his move to be dictator of the world yet, but he's moving into position. Waiting for the rapture, maybe. Whatever the reason for his delay, soon it will be checkmate." Brice moved around the computer desks to stand behind Luke. "Itsy's going to help you during her stay."

Itsy sat down in the chair Brice held out. Itsy said, "I hope you can teach me some new tricks." She pulled out the laptop taken out of the Hummer.

Cindy's eyes went wide at the appreciated addition of Itsy and the WUNSS computer. "I hope we can learn some things from you and from that."

Breanna, Michael, and Esther left the room with Brice. Joshua stayed behind to contact his buddy in Israel and his contacts in various cells. The other three were taken to a private bedroom that had an adjoining closet-sized room, maybe a former nursery. Brice said, "You can rest up for a little while."

"What do you plan to do now?" Esther asked Breanna.

Not wanting to mention her son, she said, "We planned to head west. Now I'm not sure. Joshua will decide if we stay here and fight or leave."

"I got the signal from Joshua not to tell anyone you are the Breanna that Edward is looking for so desperately. That's why I acted like you were not the same one." Esther thought she should explain her omissions.

Breanna flattened her lips. "Thanks. I appreciate it. It's safer for everyone."

With a little hesitation, Esther asked, "I saw you were pregnant on television. Where is your baby?"

Tears instantly fell from Breanna's eyes. She missed Daniel so much that it hurt her heart. But she needed to keep him safe. When she was able to speak, it was barely audible. "She died during an ambush by the WUN soldiers up north." It was best if everyone believed Daniel was killed.

"I'm sorry, Bree." Esther hugged her from the side.

Michael realized what Breanna was doing and said nothing. He went into the nursery room, stretched out on the single bed and fell asleep immediately. It had been a long couple of days.

Esther lay down on a cot in the main bedroom and closed her eyes.

Breanna left and returned to Joshua and Itsy. She wrote on a notepad and slipped it under their noses, telling them to say her baby "girl" was killed during their fight with the soldiers in the woods. Both understood why. The paper was shoved into her pocket to be destroyed later.

70

A FEW HOURS passed before the last three visitors returned to the room to get some rest. Itsy crawled in beside Michael on the small bed. Joshua and Breanna took a double bed against the wall. It didn't take long for all of them to fall asleep. Esther remained sleeping in the single bed across the room.

Michael woke up a short time later and held his wife for a little while. Eventually, he moved to the small armchair beside the bed. He sat staring at Itsy as she slept. He prayed for her and thanked God for the blessing she was in his life. *I hope she knows how much I love her. Lord, she is the best gift you have ever given me. The thought of anything happening to her makes me feel sick. I'll have a hard time not killing the person who hurts her. You'll have to step in. But I trust you, Jesus. Take control of our lives.*

It was early the next morning before any of them stirred. Michael realized he had fallen asleep in the chair. He still felt as strong as ever, but he was hungry. When he stood to stretch, the others woke up.

The activity downstairs was busy. Breanna thought of it as a cooperative chaos, with people of different races in their twenties to fifties. All were Christian, and all were enhanced soldiers. They went to cook breakfast and make coffee, but Brice a woman with him shooed them away. "I'm on KP duty this morning. This is Alison, my wife."

Alison brought over a tray with coffee mugs, sugar, and cream. She placed it on the table in front of the guests. Pointing to a large industrial carafe, she said, "Help yourselves to the coffee. Brice will have your bacon and eggs done in a minute. Don't expect fine cuisine, but it's edible."

When they had filled their mugs and returned to their seats, Alison said, "Joshua, I wanted to ask you about this soldier program. One thing many of us here are noticing, and maybe it's on purpose or maybe it's an accident, but none of the married couples are conceiving. Two couples actively tried, but they were unable to get pregnant. I've forgotten to take my pill many times, but nothing. In some ways, it's not a bad thing given the state of the world and it being the end times, but not one pregnancy."

Itsy almost dropped her mug and clumsily placed it down on the table. Breanna's hand flew up to her mouth, and their two husbands looked just as shocked.

"I didn't know that was an effect of the nanos in the body." The scientist in Breanna kicked in.

Joshua said, "If it is causing sterility, I didn't know. I don't think anyone knew."

Michael placed a hand on his wife's shoulder in an attempt to comfort her. Itsy had told him she wanted a few children. He said, "With Christians being targeted for arrests and death, maybe it's not such a bad thing. Children can be used as weapons against their parents." He caught himself as he said this, realizing it was a sore topic for Joshua and Breanna.

Brice said, "We always wanted a large family. Now all this has happened. I'm glad I don't have to worry about my children."

Breanna left the table and ran upstairs. In the bedroom they were all sharing, she allowed herself to cry. Joshua came in behind her and hugged her. "I told them you lost a baby before becoming an enhanced soldier. They said to apologize to you. They didn't mean to be insensitive."

"Daniel is probably better off without us, but I miss him so much."

"So do I."

Joshua pushed her away from his embrace but kept his hands on her shoulders. He raised his brows and said, "Let's go be with him. Let's go up north. Other people can fight this battle."

Her heart leapt with joy. "Can we go? Are we deserting our friends in their hour of need?"

"We did what we came here to do. I'm sure Taddy and Fred will help us hide." Joshua looked as happy as she felt.

"Can we ask if Itsy and Michael want to come with us?"

"Absolutely. It's hard to imagine being without them now. Besides, more of us need to love and protect Daniel." Joshua said, "I'm going to see if Brice can help us plan some of the trip. But I'm going to say we're going out west. Maybe we can get some supplies, money, and a car."

Breanna kissed her husband. "I love you."

"I love you, too. I hope you know that now, don't you?"

She winced, "I'm sorry I ever doubted you. When Esther reminded me that everything was taped in the interrogation rooms, I realized why you wouldn't answer my questions at Mossad headquarters. It wasn't because you were guilty of spying on the cells and marrying me only to have me work on the soldier program. It was because it was the opposite, but you couldn't say it for them to hear."

He nodded. "Then you ran off afterwards before I could explain. I thought for sure you would remember Esther telling you about it when you found out she was a watcher for our Christian cell."

He brushed a strand of hair off her face and tucked it behind her ear. "I made mistakes, you made mistakes. None of that matters now. Let's agree to forgive each other and move forward."

"And go get our son." Breanna tilted her head and kissed Joshua.

71

ON THE MORNING of the third day at the camp, the two couples were packed and ready to leave. Itsy and Michael decided to go with their friends. They invited Esther to travel with them to the camp north of Thunder Bay, but she decided to stay with the group on the farm. None of the options was safer than the other, given the current state of the world. Given her enhanced abilities, she thought she could do the most good where she was.

Brice and the group of soldiers were given most of the nanobots programmed at Joshua's former employer's lab. They already had a copy of the program that Joshua brought with him the first time. This way, if anyone else came to the compound fleeing persecution, they could be given the option of enhancement. Breanna and Joshua wanted to keep some nanobots for themselves if the need arose in the future to help someone else. They could tell the person about the likely side effect of sterility. It seemed that after the initial shock, everyone at the farm accepted the prognosis. Many commented that it was for the best. Itsy remained unconvinced, but she kept it to herself.

As they loaded up the car the cell had given them, Luke came running out of the house. He stopped and faced skyward as if he were dodging bullets, then ran back to the doorway. Luke yelled, "Itsy, Joshua, all of you, come to the computer room right now. Hurry." He ran back into the house. The alarm in his voice made all of them follow him at the same pace.

Cindy had the show running on all the computer screens in the room. Brice stood with his arms wrapped around his chest. Alison was beside him, looking like a deer in headlights.

Breanna ran into the back of Joshua, who stopped suddenly a couple of feet past the doorway to the right. She moved to the side of her husband. Itsy and Michael were directly behind them, and they shuffled into the room to the left. Esther, who had been outside saying goodbye, came in last. She stood beside Breanna.

On the screen, they saw a video of the fighting that took place at the Enroute service centre to free Esther. It was obviously from someone's phone. Then it switched to another point of view taken by another witness. Then another. The beheading of the soldier was recorded and played for the world to see.

The scene switched to a reporter interviewing the director of the World United Nations. The reporter asked, "These are obviously videos taken by eyewitnesses from the general public. What exactly are we witnessing on these videos?"

The director said, "As you know, the terrorist and traitor, Esther Parker, was arrested in Canada for her part in aiding and abetting Christians while she was working for the Canadian secret police. She was the first person in the world to be sentenced to death under the Antiterrorism Act, covered under the world trade deal. Canada has no death penalty yet, although this incident will expedite it now. The terrorist was being transported to Ohio, where it is lawful to carry out lethal injection. Suspecting there could be trouble, the guard detail was beefed up to ensure we'd be ready if attacked. However, we were greatly surprised."

"As you can see by the videos, the Christians sent in supersoldiers boosted with nanotechnology. The WUNSS had a few enhanced soldiers on board, but they were outnumbered. This technology was stolen by the Christians when Edward Connor's estate was attacked. The videos show the extent to which the Christian terrorists will go, including beheading an officer. They managed to free Esther Parker and get away before backup could arrive.

"This has moved up the threat level by Christians. Their claims of peace cannot fool the world. They will not rest until all people bow to their ideology. It is necessary to clamp down hard on this menace. All countries involved in the world trade deal have agreed to declare a state of emergency on a global scale. As such, they unilaterally declared that the WUNSS may use the death penalty in their countries without transporting prisoners elsewhere. Firing squads will be used for unenhanced terrorists, but beheading will be used on the nano-boosted terrorists."

The screen cut to the reporter. "We have asked that Edward Connor join us for this emergency broadcast." Edward walked out on stage looking humble and serious. Behind him was Lucinda, appearing as scary to Breanna as she had the previous time. Edward took a seat at the table with the director and the reporter. Lucinda remained standing off to the side in the background.

"Mr. Connor, my understanding is that you agreed to work with the WUN to address this new threat level."

"Yes. I was quite alarmed when the director contacted me. He sent me over copies of the deeply disturbing videos. Of course, I have offered my full cooperation to the WUN. I have my labs running day and night to produce enough of the supersoldier program to enhance all officers. This will also include every country's military and security personnel."

Luke froze the screen.

"Oh, dear Lord," Alison exclaimed. "They will overwhelm us with sheer numbers. What chance do we have?"

Esther said, "I'm sorry to have caused this mess."

Joshua shook his head. "It wasn't you, Esther. It was Edward's plan all along. He wants to kill anyone who would oppose him ruling the world. Breanna tried to shut down the program originally because of this very reason."

"We need to trust the Lord. He had Gideon whittle down his army to three hundred men so the Lord could prove the victory was his. David slew Goliath, and God shut the lions' mouths. Then there were the men in the fire. God is able," Brice said in a strong, confident voice.

"Amen," said Joshua. "Remember the amount of damage the resistance fighters did to the German army during the Second World War. A small band hitting and disappearing can do lots of destruction. Pick and choose your fights. Rescue the innocent. Keep them off guard."

Michael added, "You'll definitely want training to include sword fighting."

Brice nodded to Michael. "Turn it back on, Luke. We need to finish it."

Edward continued his interview. "I have my experts examining the footage frame by frame. Facial recognition programs will not work on four of them, as they wore helmets. However, we will try with the other four. Also, previously gathered intel may provide us with the names of these terrorists. Perhaps they can lead to my finding my fiancée."

The reporter appeared sympathetic to Edward. "The whole world is sending you best wishes for finding her. The picture of her is in every corner of the globe. She will be found."

"Breanna might be suffering from Stockholm syndrome from the terrorists' brainwashing." Edward furrowed his brow and shook his head. "She may be unwilling to leave her captors, but when she is home safely, I will get the best doctors to help her overcome the trauma." Edward stared into the camera. "Breanna, if you're watching this, don't worry. I will never give up looking for you."

Breanna felt nauseous at hearing Edward's refusal to give up.

Edward concluded his part of the interview by saying, "These terrorists will suffer the consequences for their actions. I will say this to them for the whole world: Your head will be cut off from your body. Yes, that's a saying you should get used to; heads up."

Joshua wrapped his arms around Breanna, and Michael did the same with Itsy.

Breanna spoke first. "We can't leave. We've got to stay and fight."

"Are you sure?" Joshua asked.

"No one will be safe near us. The director of the WUN and Edward Connor put targets on our backs." Staring into Joshua's eyes, she pleaded for him to see she was referring to Daniel. He would never be safe near them.

Joshua understood and closed his eyes as he kissed her forehead. Tears formed at the corners of Breanna's eyes, but she didn't allow them to fall.

Michael's cheeks were flushed. "I wish we had killed that man when we had the chance. We were too kind." He began waving his hands in the air. "Heads up. Heads up."

Itsy placed a hand on his arm. "Let's turn that around on Edward. We can say it as a signal for all Christians. Heads up, our redemption is coming."

"Jesus is coming on the clouds," Esther agreed. "Heads up."

Everyone in the room felt the Holy Spirit pour his glory into the room. They raised their hands to the Lord and shouted as one, "Heads up!"

FROM THE

HERO

ARCHIVES

ANDREA SELLEN KELL

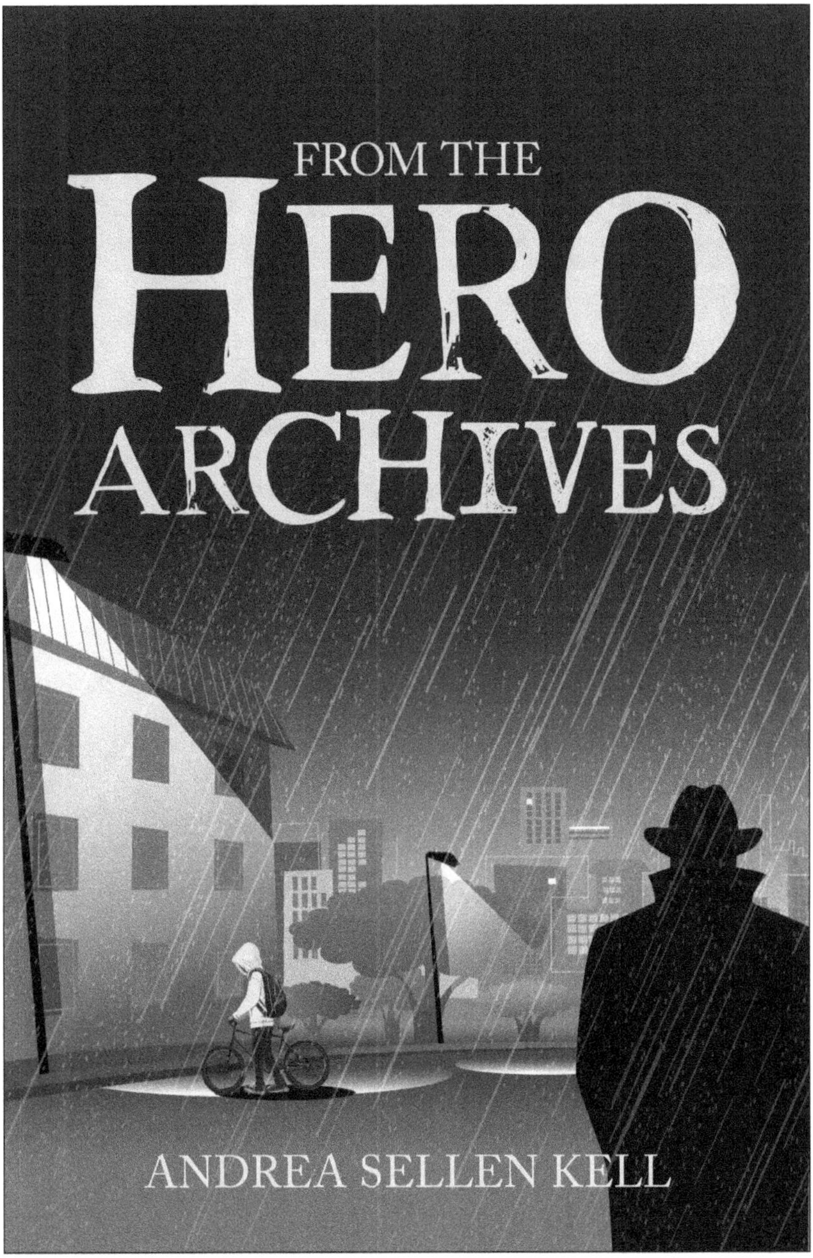

CASTLE QUAY BOOKS

IF YOU LIKED THIS BOOK, YOU'LL LIKE

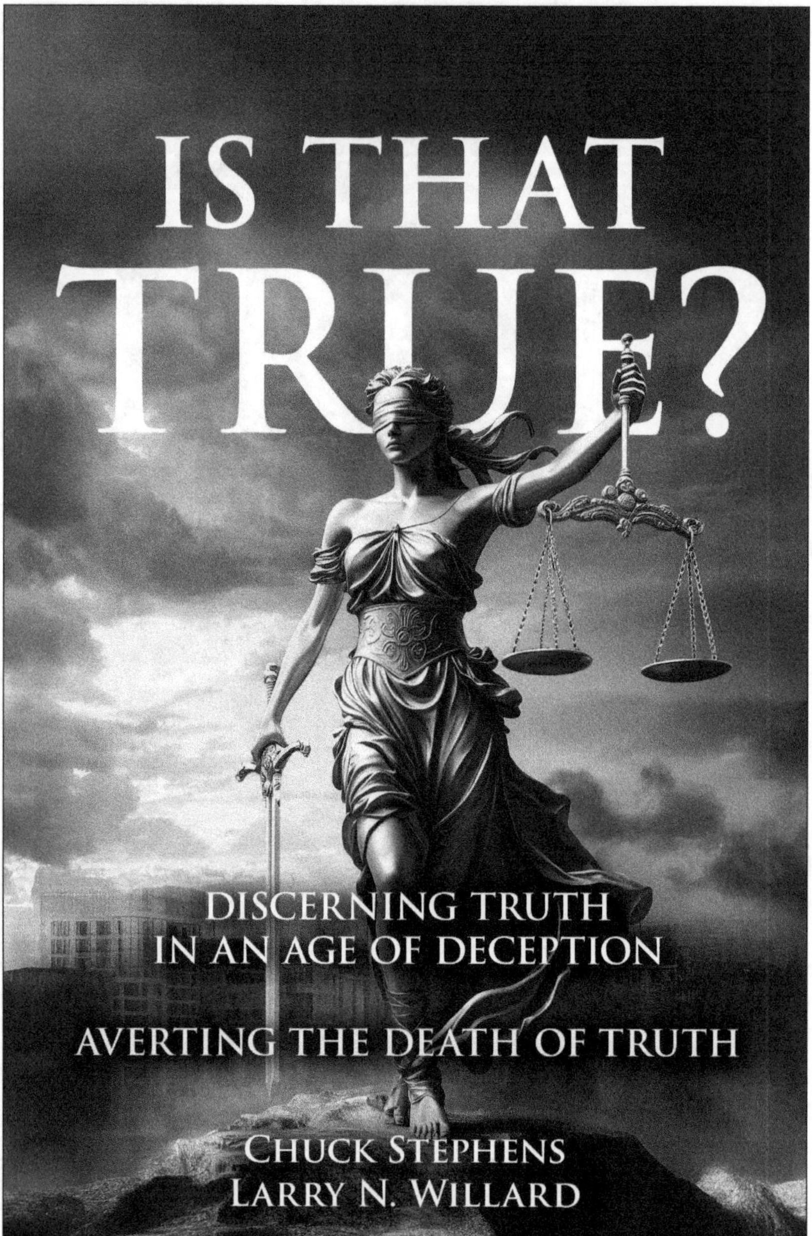

IS THAT TRUE?

DISCERNING TRUTH
IN AN AGE OF DECEPTION

AVERTING THE DEATH OF TRUTH

CHUCK STEPHENS
LARRY N. WILLARD

CASTLE QUAY BOOKS

ALL ENEMIES FOREIGN AND DOMESTIC

— MATT ROBBINS —

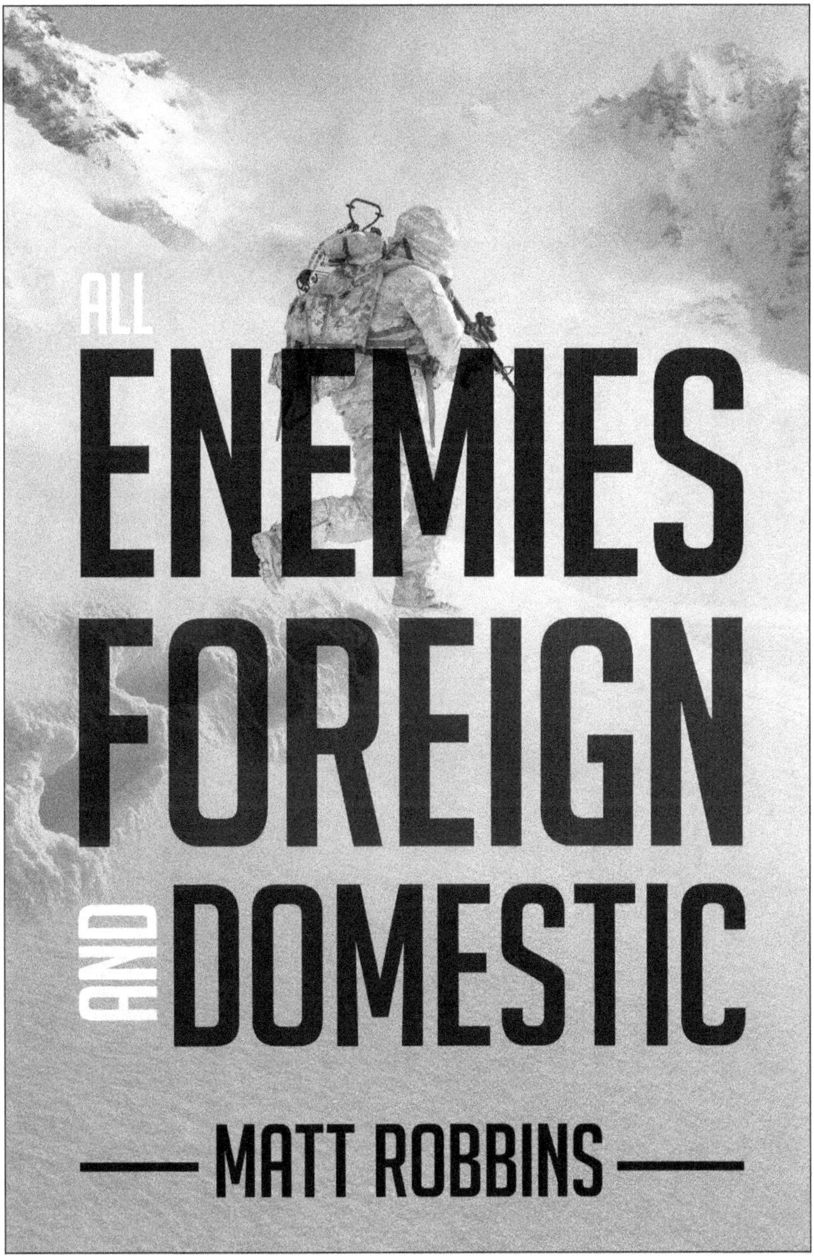

CASTLE QUAY BOOKS

LOVE

Personified

KIND
ENDURES
BELIEVES
BEARS
HOPES
PATIENT

Is loving tacos the same
as loving my enemies and loving God?

Exploring Biblical models of REAL love

TIM WHITEHEAD

CASTLE QUAY BOOKS

IF YOU LIKED THIS BOOK, YOU'LL LIKE

WINNER OF THE WORD GUILD
BEST NEW MANUSCRIPT AWARD

UNIVERSITY OF
LOST
CAUSES

LARRY J. M^cCLOSKEY

CASTLE QUAY BOOKS

IF YOU LIKED THIS BOOK, YOU'LL LIKE

FINDING COURAGE

A Four-Week Devotional Journey

Steve A. Brown

Author of best sellers
Jesus Centered and *Leading Me*

CASTLE QUAY BOOKS

www.ingramcontent.com/pod-product-compliance
Lightning Source LLC
Chambersburg PA
CBHW071838020726
47502CB00004B/1413